A Salem Awakening

Jeff Tomberg

D1714921

Chapter 1

They all ran in quickly and pushed hard on the heavy door behind them, trying to close it as fast as possible. It moved too slowly for their liking. "Hurry, slide the crossbar," yelled James. Thomas pushed the large wood crossbar through the metal latches on either side. The door was now tightly secured. Nobody from the outside was going to get in - there was no way they could. The five men of the Salem Town Council found their places around an old, large wooden table. Four of them were breathing heavily from a combination of excitement and fear. The fifth, their leader Tobias, calmly sat at the head of the table and crossed his legs with a feeling of ease, just as he always did.

The other four men were discussing what just happened. They were trying to figure it out, attempting to find words to describe what they saw in a way that made sense. They were debating against each other, but were somehow all in agreement – all except for William. Tobias enjoyed watching them argue. But rather than stopping the discussion, he wanted to see where it would lead. Tobias considered himself a keen observer of others and he liked to collect information about people based on how they reacted under different circumstances. This was the perfect case study for him - four frightened men trying their best to exude bravery, while trying to understand the incomprehensible event they just witnessed. Well, incomprehensible to them – Tobias certainly understood what happened. He would learn much about these men today – information he would stow away in his memory for a later date when it would benefit him.

James stood and stepped away from the table, a tactic intended to focus the attention of the others on him. He paced around the room looking down at the floor and then up at the ceiling, talking as if he knew the answers but was only able to speak in questions.

"Did that actually *prove* she was a witch? Did we have to burn her at the stake so quickly? Why couldn't we have taken some time to discuss this? What will this do to the women and children of the village?"

James found his way back to the table, but instead of sitting down, he leaned on it with both hands. He thought better while standing. The other three men quickly stood at their spots around the table and leaned against it as well. All four men were now standing on opposite sides, leaning in toward each other, repeating the same futile questions over and over hoping someone would have the answers.

The old wooden table could barely hold the weight of everyone leaning against it. Only Tobias was still seated, the one who always remained stoic and calm during town council meetings. He saw no reason for the agitation, though he certainly understood the fear the other men felt.

"We can't allow this to happen again. The women and children are already fearful – now they see that a true witch lived among us," Matthew yelled. He banged his fist on the table so hard that even he was surprised it didn't collapse.

Thomas spoke next, "How many others are there? We need to speed up the trials to make sure we find each and every witch - and kill them all."

The other men roared in agreement, mostly because they were afraid of what would happen if they didn't. Each man wanted the tribunal to make sure it eradicated all witches from Salem and the

3

Massachusetts Territory. On this point they could all agree with no debate.

After about thirty minutes, the men had nothing left to say. They quieted and settled back down around the table. Still not having said anything, Tobias sat rubbing his chin, appearing to be deep in thought.

Finally Matthew spoke as the silence was too uncomfortable for him to bear. "Tobias, you've been very quiet. Have you nothing to contribute?"

Tobias slowly drew in a deep breath and held it for a couple of seconds, rubbing his chin throughout. He exhaled loudly, though it was more of a sigh than a deep breath. He lowered his hand away from his chin and after a moment, he stood and turned around, facing his back to the others with his hands clasped together behind his back. At first he was looking down, but still with his back turned, he raised his head. This captured the attention of the other four men who all leaned in to listen to his words, inching closer assuming he was about to whisper his thoughts. Tobias stepped forward slowly, moving away from the table, still with his back facing them.

Finally he spoke calmly and intently, annunciating each word quite distinctly, "There are two competing issues you are discussing."

He stopped walking and turned half way around so the men could now see his profile, his head leaning back as if he were speaking to the ceiling.

"First, you all rightfully understand the need to rid our village of witches. On that we all agree - there is no need for debate." He leered at William, but his comment seemed incomplete, as if everyone knew the missing words implied they should not have been debating in the first place.

He turned fully toward the others and walked forward, slowly. When he finally arrived, he placed both hands down onto the wood slab, extending out past his shoulders quite a bit. The result was him leaning against the table, but his head was at almost the same level as the others who were all seated. He looked at each person for what seemed like minutes as he continued to speak.

"Second, you all seem to believe we should be worried about how the women and children will *feel* learning we have witches in our town. It is this point with which I take issue."

He stood upright and smiled, and with a welcoming gesture of outstretched arms continued, "My friends, we are the leaders of this town. They expect us to make the difficult decisions and to deal with the difficult situations. We must show no fear in the face of evil, and these witches are most certainly evil. Instead of worrying that our women and children will be frightened, we should determine how to frighten those wretched witches. We should realize that witches *are* women and children, and we need to show them that *they* should be afraid of us - not the other way around. I came here into the Town Hall after the burning so that we could discuss our next steps. But you four put down the crossbar in fear that the villagers would riot. Why?" He paused for a moment that felt longer than reasonable. "Are you afraid yourselves?" He paused for even longer this time. "Listen outside - do you hear anything? There are no villagers banging at the door. They have all gone home. Our God-fearing residents now know we will do whatever it takes to defend them, and the witches in town now know we will do everything we can to eradicate them. We are doing exactly what the town wants and expects. There is no riot, there is no mob trying to enter this building, and there is no reason for the crossbar."

Three of the four sat back in their seats, satisfied with that explanation. Tobias had appeased them – they now realized they were doing exactly what they should be. They felt good, even though the stench of Jane's burning flesh still filled their nostrils.

But the fourth man was puzzled and spoke in objection, "Tobias, let us pause for a moment and reflect on what happened out there. You admit we are targeting women and children."

Tobias blithely interjected, "Well the witches *are* women and children. That's a simple fact."

William ignored Tobias' interruption and continued, "Even though the concept of witches is not founded in any scientific basis, we put an accused witch on trial by trying to drown her. Her hands were not constrained, and after she was dropped into the ocean, she used her hands to untie the ropes from her legs and ankles. It wasn't some kind of spell. When she emerged from the water, that was not an indication that she was a witch. Rather, it was an indication that she was human and found a way to survive."

Tobias had no use for William's brand of ungodly science and responded, "By definition, if a person survives the witch's test of water then they are a witch. And once we know someone to be a witch, our laws stipulate, in no uncertain terms, that they must be put to death immediately. Today we did everything we were supposed to do, and we did it completely by our laws. We did our jobs and if any of you don't have the stomach for that, you should immediately resign from the council."

William responded slowly and softly while unconsciously shaking his head back and forth, looking at Tobias with an incredulous stare. "I knew Jane to be a good woman, and a good mother. She did not deserve this. Nobody does."

6

Tobias stood and replied with finality, "Her death removed one witch from our town but has also resulted in another positive outcome. From now on, any accused witch performing the test of water will have her hands bound to her body."

Tobias removed the crossbar from the door, opened it while looking back at the other four members of the council, then turned and walked out with nothing but confidence at his side. William was left confused wondering how Tobias could view his last comment in any way positive. As the other three men stood to leave, William muttered, "He is leading us down an evil path, and we are blindly following him because that's easier than resisting." The other men heard William's warning but paid no attention.

Chapter 2

Abigail Sampson sat on the wet rocks at the shore trying to analyze how nature worked. Though she couldn't see the fish and other animals that frolicked under the ocean's surface, she often imagined what that world must be like. Abigail wondered, "How fascinating it must be to live in the sea amongst the maze of unique creatures, far away from all the insanity taking over Salem." People were dying because of the trials. She realized creatures died in the sea as well, but at least in the ocean everyone knows who is the hunter and who is the hunted. Lately in Salem, that line was blurred.

She needed to be cautious now. The last accusations and trials were weeks ago – much longer than normal. Previously, the Town Council made accusations almost weekly. Just as a long-dormant volcano rumbles back to life causing everyone to fear an imminent eruption, all of Salem was on edge, expecting a new accusation at any moment. And it could happen to almost anybody.

"I can not live in fear of an accusation," Abigail decided. "I will not. But try as I might, I can't get the fear out of my head." Every leaf that crunched under the weight of a boot, every twig breaking under a friend's foot, caused her to turn and look over her shoulder. All of Abigail's classmates felt the same unpredictable dread. And each friend had their own way of dealing with it.

Abigail played a game with herself where she would think of words and phrases that made no sense to her, and she would try to figure out their etymology - how and why the words came into existence, and by whom.

She thought to herself, "Today's phrase – 'the air is crisp'." Abigail paused for a moment to contemplate the words. "Hmph!" she concluded. "How can the air be crisp? To be crisp, the object must be solid. Air is no more crisp than water. A ripe apple fresh from the tree – now *that* is crisp."

"Father and Mother always talk about how crisp the air is, but what they really mean is that it's cold outside. I wonder how that started." Her forehead curled, and she looked to the sky over the waves as if it contained the answer. "Who was the first person to say '*crisp*' when they really meant '*cold*'? And why would they do that? Too often, people want to appear more clever than they really are. Salem is full of people pretending to be something they're not. It just seems so silly to me."

Abigail had no use for silliness. It was a waste of time – time that could be better spent reading a book or examining nature. It was time she could use to learn something. Time was an important narrative throughout Abigail's life. "I never have enough time to do all the things I must or want. I wish I made better use of it, so there was more time for learning."

None of the other children in school were as serious about education as was Abigail. In fact, she knew she was the smartest child in school. Her competitive nature liked it that way. She also knew it was impolite to brag or show off her intelligence. Abigail became skillful at blending in – being like the other girls. Mother told her she must. And because of the accusations and trials, it was now even more important she not stand out from the others. The other children needed to like her – better yet, they should not even notice her. But she mustn't be too invisible either. "That would also draw attention," Mother told her.

When the trials began, Abigail decided all the others must like her, but not so much that it would cause them to be jealous. She needed to be everybody's friend, just not their *best* friend. "I must blend in and hide in plain sight." This fit nicely with the advice Mother always provided, "There are others, you know."

During the warmer months, she sat close enough to the water so the spray from the waves would dampen her face. The water was salty, but not too salty. "That's just like me – visible, but not too visible," she nodded with a sense of satisfaction. Because of her mother's persistence, Abigail relished being one person split into two distinct parts, but never too much toward either side.

During the cooler months, she sat farther away from the water. She still enjoyed having the salty mist spray onto her face, but it was much too cold for her to get wet. "It's too *crisp* outside for that," she murmured, proud to have used the phrase she proved to be so utterly ridiculous.

Her favorite time of day at the shore was mid-afternoon. She would face east, toward the Old World of her parents, while the back of her head basked in the comforting yellow light of the sun. Its warmth even exhilarated the hairs on her arms, and together with the cool mist from the breaking waves, she felt as if Heaven had come to Earth. At this point in the day, the sun was still fairly high in the sky. Within another hour or two, it would fade beyond the tree line behind her and it would be time to return home for supper. But while the sun connected to her from high above, she felt every positive 're' word she could think of – renewed, refreshed, reborn and she even created a new 're' word that best described how she felt each day when she arrived at the shore – re-alive.

Abigail almost always had a book under her arm – she preferred non-fiction so she could learn something. She could run as fast as the boys, and at five feet six inches, she was taller than most of the others in her class. She wasn't the prettiest girl in school. Scott Peterson always teased her that she wasn't even in the top ten of the eight girls in school. "I'm surprised you know how to count to ten… or even eight, Scott," Abigail rebutted. But she was attractive in her own way and Scott only teased her because he had a secret crush on her – a secret everyone in school knew about, including Abigail.

She was at the awkward stage where she was no longer a child and not yet a true woman. Her looks were trying to keep pace with her growth, but were not always successful. Her smile was wide but amateurish, her gait was gawky to the point of being clumsy. But Abigail had the most beautiful hair – long, thick and flowing. It was the physical quality of which she was the most proud. It was dark and lush, and fell to her elbows, allowing her to cover her face completely when she wanted to hide from the world. But the thickness of her hair made it difficult to put into a ponytail or bun when she wanted the sun to shine down upon her, or have the spray from the waves soak her face.

She often wanted to cut her hair – not too short, maybe just down to her shoulders. Abigail pleaded with her parents, "That would better frame my face and highlight my natural beauty." Her mother was always silent during these discussions, which Abigail assumed meant her mother agreed with her. But there was little solace in that, as her father was vehemently against the idea. He would respond, "We need to find a suitable husband for you. Women do not have short hair. You need to make yourself as feminine and attractive to the boys as possible. They need to see you as a good potential mother for their children. I'll hear no more of this."

It made no sense to Abigail. Her father wanted her to have a husband, yet he turned away every boy who showed any interest in her as not being good enough for his daughter. And if Father wanted her to have more suitors, wouldn't he want her to change how she looked, since her current appearance produced no one suitable yet?

Abigail loved her father very much – he was a wonderful provider for the family. Though he shared little emotionally, they always had what they needed to survive and even to thrive. And yet she could never understand him. He was in every way a complete enigma to her – a stranger cloaked in a familiar veil.

Chapter 3

Samuel Sampson was a model Puritan. He worked hard, and he both loved and feared the Lord. Samuel came to the Massachusetts Territory nearly two decades prior from his childhood home in Coventry, England. He was already married at the time and, along with his wife Willa, was grieving the loss of their second child. Both of their first two children, Archibald and Ichibad, died suddenly at young ages and the Sampsons needed a change in order to put their immense sadness behind them. The New World offered a chance for a new beginning. They didn't want to forget the past nor leave it behind, but neither did they want the constant reminders of their loss. Their neighbors, friends and even their families either pitied them or thought them responsible for the deaths of their sons. Samuel understood why they thought this. Many times, he wondered if he did something that angered the Lord and caused their deaths. But he was not one to question God's will, so instead of staying in England and fighting off constant suspicion, traveling to the new settlements seemed like the right decision.

Abigail was born a year after the couple arrived in Salem. She meant everything to Samuel. But he was not able to show her how deeply he cared for her, nor what he hoped would become of her future.

Samuel lived a life of hard work and devotion to God. He endeavored to avoid others in the village, preferring to keep to himself. This was his preference even before the trials began. But the trials illustrated just how good a decision it was for the safety and security of his family.

He would wake with the sun and spend the whole day in his fields, tending to his rather large crops of corn and wheat. His only breaks were for lunch and prayer. Because of their plentiful harvests, the Sampson family would take their lot, sell what they could at a fair price from the rest of the crop, and give the rest to those less fortunate than they were. It was a good life – a godly life, he often reminded himself.

Through his hard work and sweat, Samuel could keep his family fed and provide shelter and clothing for them. Because his crops were bountiful, he sustained his family through the cold, dreary Massachusetts winters. This was no small feat. Every winter, many villagers would fall ill, and many perished, because they did not store enough during the plentiful times to eat when the weather, or their fortunes, changed for the worse. Samuel never hesitated to help when he could, and he never judged those who did not save enough – not outwardly, at least. Many villagers owed their lives, and those of their families, to Samuel, but he never asked for anything in return. "It's what the Lord commands me to do," he'd say as he declined what little the villagers offered to pay. "He provided this bounty for my family, and it's our obligation to share what we can." Samuel took his obligations seriously. In his role, he needed to.

Samuel never smiled. He never shook the hand of those he helped, leaving their outstretched arms of thanks unfulfilled. It was his obligation to help the others – his purpose. He met the challenge with the same rigidity and vigor as his other obligations in life, and showed no emotion to the others in the village, nor to his most beloved daughter.

Only one person ever saw any emotion from Samuel – his wife Willa. And that was only when they were safely alone in their bed at night. Willa never spoke of these emotional displays, not even with Samuel. They were moments of weakness in his opinion and were to be erased from memory immediately.

He smiled exactly five times in his adult life. Once on the night of their wedding, one time each on the nights their three children were born, and once back in Coventry when he defeated his arch rival, Junius Dracul, in an election to lead their club. That election was of particular embarrassment for Samuel, as he never wanted to revel in the defeat of a rival, even though it had been a rather intense competition and he was more than pleased to have come out on top. Though Protestants do not practice penance, Samuel still performs his own type of ritual 'asking-of-forgiveness' for this lapse of Puritan judgement. Yet even for all his effort, he has never forgiven himself for taking such pure delight in Junius' defeat. It was an emotional scar he would always carry within.

Samuel cried more times than he smiled, which was his preference because life was meant to be hard. Though he would never openly admit to crying at all, he cried a total of six times as an adult. He cried once each at the death of his father and of his mother, and once each at the death of his first two sons. The fifth time he cried was the night before Willa and he left for the New World. Those were not tears of sorrow, but a cleansing of his soul. It was his way of saying goodbye to the life he had known – a life that included the joy of marrying a woman he loved deeply, and the profound sadness of having to bury two children.

The sixth time he cried was for something altogether different. It was when Abigail was eleven and Samuel noticed there was something different about her. She was much too hard-headed for any man to want her as a wife. She read books, she was smart, and she was not afraid to tell others, even her elders, when she thought they were wrong. "Nobody will want her," he sobbed into Willa's shoulder late one night. "She will be a pariah, an outcast from the village. She will live alone and have nobody to take care of. I have failed her as a father."

Samuel believed it was harmful to show any outward emotion to his family. They knew of his love because he took care of them – he provided for them. That was his job and he was good at it. It was his life – his greatest obligation, and that was how he protected his family and showed his love for them.

Abigail only knew he could feel anything at all because her mother shared his secret with her. "Your father is a stern, godly man. He loves you with all his heart, but he can't spend any of his energy showing you his love because he's too busy protecting and providing for you. He has smiled because of you and he has cried because of you. We are the only reasons he wakes every morning and works so hard. That is his way of loving us both."

Chapter 4

Unlike Samuel, Willa Sampson loved to smile. When Samuel could take brief breaks from farming and praying, the two would take walks around the village. Samuel was always serious, staring at the ground with his hands by his side. Willa, conversely, would point her face directly up to the sun, trying to soak in every warm ray of sunlight. Her smile captured the sun's warmth and exuded happiness. She had experienced unimaginable heartache in her life, but she lived each day as if it held the promise of seeing all three of her children happily playing together.

They never held hands on their walks, or ever, really. But their bond was strong, and each had complementary traits to the other. Willa was personable and outgoing, qualities Samuel constantly worried would cause her to be the target of accusations. But she couldn't help it. No matter how hard she tried, she could not contort her face into a frown, a scowl, or even just a neutral gaze. Even if her lips were not smiling, her eyes were. She could not prevent it from happening and she stopped trying years earlier.

Samuel had no such affliction. A scowl was a normal and comfortable facial position for him. If he concentrated and tried very hard, he might force his scowl into a frown. But he did not enjoy trying that. A frown was too close to a smile for his liking.

The two together seemed an odd match. Samuel was tall at five feet eleven inches, very thin and his face was somewhat gaunt, as though he never quite had enough to eat. His skin was tanned and rough from working in the sun all day and his hands were calloused many times over, which to him was a positive sign of hard work. He wore black trousers and a white blouse – every day. His pants were two sizes too big, so he needed to wear straps over his shoulders which were buttoned to his pants to keep them from falling to his ankles. His beard was unkempt and somewhat wiry, and he wore a wide rimmed black farmer's hat to protect his head from the sun. But under his hat hid the most luxurious dark black hair. It was not what one would expect with the rest of him. It was as if a fifty-year-old, tired, tanned and weakened farmer stole the hair from an eighteen-year-old young, vibrant boy. When Samuel met people for the first time, they would typically stare to see if they could find the secret to how he was able to stick someone else's hair on his own head. That peculiar stare from strangers occurred so often he barely even noticed anymore. Once, a new acquaintance thought it appropriate to see if he could pull the hair off Samuel's head. It did not end well for the acquaintance. Samuel was much stronger and faster than he looked, or that anyone would imagine.

Willa was an effervescent personality. She was attractive, but not beautiful. Her radiant smile and glowing eyes more than made up for the averageness of her other features. Nobody would call her a beauty, but every man in the village had noticed her. Standing at five feet three inches, she was about the same stature as most of the other women. She was not thin, but also not overweight. "There's just enough to keep me warm in the winter but not enough to make me sweat in the summer," she would joke with Abigail.

Everyone adored Willa, partly because of her affable nature and partly because her family provided so much for so many others. While Samuel would not accept thanks, Willa enjoyed getting to know those they helped. This annoyed Samuel, but he never tried to stop her – he knew he wouldn't be able to. Willa was almost as strong-minded as Abigail, to a point. She always knew her boundaries – she and Samuel set those when they began their relationship. She could live her life as she pleased, so long as she always respected and feared God, never showed disrespect to Samuel, and always took care of the house and family as her top priority. Willa happily agreed with these terms and was adept at enjoying herself while staying within the boundaries.

She always started her days the same way. She would wake up and pray with Samuel. As he dressed and planned his day's work, she would prepare breakfast for the family. Usually they would have fresh eggs they bartered for with their neighbor, and bread she made the night prior. When Samuel left for the field, she and Abigail would begin their daily chores. They had a system of helping each other, so they would complete the chores by late morning. The two recited poetry as they worked to help pass the time, often incorrectly correcting each other along the way to ensure the other was paying attention.

"Abashed the devil stood and felt how awful goodness is and saw Virtue in her shape how lovely: and pined his loss," Willa recited.

Abigail curled her brow a bit and gave her mother a sideways glance. "Actually, it was 'pinned the moss', Mother."

Willa smirked back at Abigail with a look of feigned derision. "I don't think Milton would approve of that, dear." They both giggled at the idea.

Abigail would stop when it was time for school and Willa would conclude the chores just in time to prepare lunch for Samuel. This meant on most afternoons Willa was free to explore other interests and activities. Some days, she would meet other wives and help with their chores, and often she would assist at Abigail's school.

Chapter 5

The schoolhouse was less than a mile away from the Sampson home – about a ten-minute walk on most days. That convenience meant Willa could help at school as often as the teacher, William Putnam, wanted or needed. Some days she would help grade the assignments, other days she would help tutor students who fell behind in their studies. She was one of the few educated women in the village, and Mr. Putnam appreciated of all her help. "It's just like a Sampson to go above and beyond when helping others," he once told an assembly of parents at a school meeting. It was a compliment which deepened the scowl on Samuel's face.

Willa's favorite days volunteering at the schoolhouse were when Mr. Putnam was performing a science experiment with the children. She loved learning along with them, but she mostly enjoyed watching Abigail become thoroughly enthralled with the projects. The only experiment Abigail did not enjoy was when they dissected a frog. She didn't realize they first had to catch a frog, one large enough to dissect, and then kill it. "Had I known prior, I would have been sick that day," she told her mother. The comment was even more ridiculous because Abigail never once missed a day of school because of illness, or for any other reason.

William Putnam was the teacher at Salem Schoolhouse for six years. He moved to Salem just after graduating from Harvard College – about a day's carriage ride from Salem. He did well for himself in school and came to Salem highly recommended by Increase Mather, a leading Puritan minister in Boston, who just last year became President of Harvard College. William was childhood friends with Increase's son, Cotton Mather, who was now also a leading minister in Boston. The two remained close through the years, but recently drifted apart. Cotton published several pamphlets that claimed witchcraft was real, and his recent book, *Memorable Providences Relating to Witchcrafts and Possessions,* was the primary fuel igniting the current spate of accusations and trials in Salem. William was both surprised and dismayed an intellectual of Cotton's stature could be a proponent of both Newtonian science and witchcraft. Though the two were always cordial with each other, Cotton's book created a chasm between them comparable to the schism within the Protestant Church itself.

For the entirety of his time in Salem, William was well-respected. As a member of the Town Council, he was often called on to provide reports which needed specificity and detailed analysis. His advice, though not always followed, always found an attentive audience. Even the ministers from other nearby villages would consult William on matters which fell beyond the realm of religion. William loved Salem and its people, but he despised what they became, thanks in large part to his old friend, Cotton.

William taught all the subjects at the schoolhouse, but science was the closest to his heart. He idolized Isaac Newton, as most educated people of the time did, and hoped one day he'd be able to meet Newton in person. "Perhaps we could have tea together and I could engage him in my theories," William dreamed to himself, knowing full well Newton would never agree to such a consult.

When he was alone, William often tried an exercise to expand his brain he learned from a classmate at Harvard College. A larger brain would obviously lead to more knowledge, and he would try anything to reach that goal. He would take three large breaths, in and out in quick and full repetition. He held the last breath in his mouth and imagined forcing the pressurized air into his head to expand his brain and skull outward. His classmate told him repeating this exercise three times each day would cause an incremental, but measurable, increase in his skull's diameter, thus allowing the brain more room for growth. He tried this exercise every day for three months, and the only measurable difference he found was because of the growth of his hair. While he decided this was a failed experiment, and quite possibly a prank by his classmate, he still tried the exercise every few months... just in case.

Recess was always a suspenseful time for Abigail. Most days, Mr. Putnam would sit at a table outside and grade papers or read a book, but on some days, exciting days for Abigail, he would remove his coat and play with the children. He was fit and good looking, with deep brown eyes. The boys enjoyed racing with him and the girls enjoyed watching him race. Generally a serious man, when he was playing, he was smiling. He knew how to balance both of the great joys in his life – the pursuit of knowledge and the pursuit of fun.

He never married, but not because he didn't want a wife. He filled his home with books and papers, and against one wall was a long table filled with half-built machines and random contraptions. No woman would appreciate his life's goals, nor be able to live in a home cluttered with such a mess. Only a true seeker of knowledge would understand – only someone who revered science as much as he. So instead of wasting time looking for a woman he knew didn't exist, at least not in Salem, he more thoroughly devoted himself to his work. And between his students, the Town Council and his own curiosity, there was no time for anyone else anyway.

Chapter 6

It was a warm Wednesday. Willa was done with the chores for the day and the children had finished lunch at the schoolhouse. They were just beginning a mathematics test. Mr. Putnam always timed these, and he was walking around the classroom with his pocket watch in hand, keeping a close eye on the time. "Eight minutes," he stated loud enough for all the children to hear, but not loud enough to disrupt their thinking.

James Boylan was nervously looking at the other children. He was a nice boy, "but he won't be going to Harvard College," Mr. Putnam thought to himself. James was always the last to finish the tests, and education was clearly not a priority for him. No matter how much he tried, William could not motivate James as he could the others. "If only James was more passionate about learning," he thought, "then I could work with him. But he doesn't have enough intellectual curiosity or self-discipline."

Abigail raised her hand to ask a question. "That figures," thought James. Then they all heard it. Time seemed to pause, as if the minute hand on Mr. Putnam's pocket watch stopped. Abigail's head turned in slow motion toward the window as her arm lowered back to her desk on its own accord, in equally slow motion. Everyone in the classroom felt a rush of coldness throughout their bodies and the hairs on their necks stood erect at a full and terrified attention.

Witch!...

Witch!...

The horrible chant was coming from outside and getting louder with each utterance. The entire class ran to the window to see where the mob was headed. There was an audible gasp from each child, followed by a deafening hush across the entire class, as they realized the mob was coming straight for the schoolhouse. Any of them might be the target.

There were about twenty or thirty villagers, some carrying pitchforks bobbing up and down in the air. Others held lit torches, even though it was the middle of the day in broad daylight. Still others carried axes or other tools they grabbed as they ran to join the mob.

Leading the group was the head of the town council and the lead judge in the trials, Tobias Warnock. He was a short, stout man whose stockings always seemed too high for his stature. He was an old-fashioned man of the Old World, coming to Salem about fifteen years prior because he felt the Massachusetts Territory needed him more than did England. The truth was, nobody in the Old World ever heard of him and the adults in Salem assumed he was a lonely man who needed to find his place somewhere. They pitied and tolerated him, but he seemed pious enough and was willing to devote his time and energy to the village, so everyone allowed him to work his way up until he became the de facto leader.

Ever since Tobias read Cotton Mather's works, he became convinced witches were real and living amongst them, and that

Salem was a central node for the regional covens. He took it upon himself to rid Salem, and all of Massachusetts, of the scourge of witches, even traveling to Boston to meet and strategize with Mather himself.

This infuriated William, who frequently tried to show Tobias the reason and logic for why witches could not be real. "The physical laws of nature do not allow for it. How could a person fly? How could the incantation of certain words in a specific order inflict one's will over someone else? That's just not how nature works!"

But Tobias would shrug off each point like cattle dismissing insignificant flies with the unconscious twitch of an ear. For every reasoned argument William made, Tobias responded with a quote from Mather's book as evidence he was correct.

William responded with utter frustration, "But the writing of one man, no matter how influential or intellectual he may be, does not explain how any of this is real." No matter how irritated William became, Tobias would remain calm and collected, which only infuriated William even further.

The veins in William's neck protruded. "Mather is a man of science. He is intelligent and curious. But this 'book' of his offers no evidence, only stories of a family in Boston. Mather knows none of his allegations have any merit. He might be sincere in his intent, but he, more than anyone else, knows nothing in his book serves to *prove* anything!"

Tobias slowly turned his face to William and calmly replied, "Ah, but that is where you miss the point, young man. Ungodly men look for proof and evidence. Godly men need only to *believe* in order for something to be true. Belief itself is the blessing which makes something real. When others *believe* it to be real, it *is* real."

The statement froze William for what seemed like many minutes, but in reality was only mere seconds. He considered Tobias' words carefully and felt like he was understanding Tobias at a deeper level, as though something mystical connected them together. It was as if they could see into the soul of the other at that precise moment. "You are playing a dangerous game, old man," William finally muttered. "People will die because of Mather and you. Innocent people."

Tobias stood, with one hand planted firmly on the table as he leaned forward to look William directly in the eyes and he replied in a deep, threatening tone, "They are not innocent if I find them to be guilty." And with that, Tobias turned and left William to himself, his mouth wide with disbelief and his knees buckling with fear over what he just heard.

Chapter 7

After a few moments, the mob reached the front of the schoolhouse. From the window, Abigail could identify each person in the crowd. She saw Mr. Godwin and Mr. Jacobs, fathers of two of Abigail's best friends. Most in the crowd were the normal contingent – the villagers who always took part in mobs, loyal followers of Tobias Warnock. But this is the first time they ever approached the schoolhouse. Seeing them active in a mob yet again almost made the ordeal seem less serious... almost. "It's the same people doing the same thing over and over, as if they are happy to destroy the lives of others in order to prove their allegiance to their so-called leader," Abigail thought. Her moral superiority did not make her feel any better.

Trailing behind the mob, Abigail saw Mrs. Porter, the mother of Millie Porter – one of Abigail's classmates. Mrs. Porter was stammering and crying loudly, screaming "No, No... Don't touch her, Don't take my baby girl!" Abigail's heart sank and that rush of coldness which was still streaking through her body somehow became even colder now and the pit of her stomach ached terribly. She could feel her breath as ice, burning cold as its jagged, icy edges scratched up and down in her throat. She attempted to swallow, but struggled.

Abigail was standing next to Millie and without thought, her hand reached out and settled on Millie's shoulder. After she made contact, Abigail turned and looked at Millie. She was staring out the window, tears streaming down her face, her whole body trembling in fear. Mr. Putnam put both of his hands on Millie's other shoulder and he was whispering something into her ear. Clearly, he was trying to comfort her. Clearly, it was not working. How could it?

They all knew what would happen from this point on. Each person in the village bore witness to an official public accusation. And once made, none of the accused ever survived. Abigail stared at Millie, knowing she already had a death sentence, and dreaded the pain she knew her friend was certain to endure. Though she was feeling immeasurable fear and sadness, Abigail felt a well of anger forming deep in her soul.

"Millie Porter," bellowed Tobias Warnock as the crowd quieted to hear him. "You stand accused of performing the Devil's bidding through the use of witchcraft." There was now dead silence both outside, and inside, the schoolhouse. The void of sound was cacophonous. "You can admit your sins and face your judgement now, clearing your name in the eyes of God, or you can claim your innocence and perform the Test of Witchcraft to determine your fate. How say you?"

It struck Abigail as odd, the way Tobias pronounced the word 'God'. He used a long 'O' sound, but not quite, so it sounded like 'augh', and his 'D' nearly had the abruptness of a 'T'. It was as if he was saying the word 'Gaught'. It seemed completely contrived, as if for dramatic effect. Abigail shook her head, bringing herself back to the desperate reality of the moment.

"She admits nothing!" interrupted Mr. Putnam. "She is but a child, and she is a good person."

Tobias held his hand up toward William, directing him to stop speaking. "If the girl chooses not to claim her innocence, we consider that her admission of guilt."

Mrs. Porter howled in desperation, "Millie.... Tell them you're innocent! Don't hurt my beautiful girl!"

Millie stepped forward to the window. The other students unconsciously cleared a path for her, so by the time her hands touched the window sill, there was a ring of empty space behind her. She clutched the sill, as she was shaking too much to stand on her own. Her voice was nervous and weak. "Mr. Warnock, you are friends with my parents. You know me. You have attended my birthday celebrations. We are God-fearing people. You know in your heart I am innocent. Please." She paused, choking back a sob. "Why are you doing this to me?"

"I know nothing of your innocence nor of your guilt. That is between you and God. I only know you stand accused. It is my obligation to pursue the truth and rid our town of the Devil and his followers. How do you plead, Millie Porter?"

This was not an actual choice. Either she admitted guilt and would hang or burn at the stake within twenty-four hours, or she would claim innocence and subject herself to a 'test' to verify whether she was a witch. Calling it a test was a misnomer – it was nothing of the kind. The theory was they would subject the accused to a fate no human could survive. If she were a witch, she would use a spell to save herself – and then immediately burn at the stake for being found a witch. If she did not survive, they would exonerate her – post-mortem. No matter what happened next, Millie was going to die. It was only a matter of how and when.

Millie tried to think quickly. Everyone was waiting for her to announce her decision. She needed a moment of clarity to consider her options, such as they were. The Test of Witchcraft always involved some method of drowning. Typically, they would tie large rocks to the ankles of the accused and throw them into the ocean. They were given twenty minutes to free themselves before the villagers would enter the water to find, and retrieve, the newly corpsed.

One person survived this trial. Jane Anderson said she loosened the knots around her ankles and free her herself after being thrown into the water. But Tobias was keeping watch and claimed her escape proved she was a witch. The council members escorted her immediately to the town square and burned alive at the stake. After that incident, Tobias made sure the accused had their hands and legs securely bound for the test.

Would Millie want to die by noose, by fire, or by water? This was the question swirling around her head. Death by hanging seemed the best option to her. She supposed it would be the fastest death with the least pain. In order to be hanged, she would need to admit her guilt and then beg God, and the village, for forgiveness. But her thoughts turned quickly to her family. If she admitted to being a witch, her family would forever be marked. Life would not be easy for them no matter where they would end up – and they would most certainly need to leave Salem. Her only option was to claim innocence and die by drowning. This way, she would find exoneration and her family's reputation would remain intact. It was quite a mature conclusion for such a young girl. But an imminent, public death focuses one's thoughts around what is truly important in life. She gathered as much composure as she could muster, lifted her head to gaze back at the mob and took a deep breath as she spoke, albeit with a stammering, weak and frightened voice.

"I... am..."

"Wait!" interrupted Mr. Putnam, stepping in front of Millie as if he were a shield of protection for her. "Does she not have the right to hear from her accuser? Does she not even have the right to know exactly what you are accusing her of?"

"She does not." Tobias replied in a calm, but firm, tone. "She stands accused, and the accuser is entitled to remain anonymous for their protection, and for that of their family. I have personally reviewed the accusations, and I have found them to be credible. Miss Porter, I believe you were about to announce your decision?"

"Unbelievable!" scoffed William in a tone only audible to those immediately around him.

"It's all right, Mr. Putnam," Millie told him in a comforting tone. "There is only one way forward for me now."

In the back of the room, they heard Christina Anderson sobbing. Everyone assumed she was frightened to tears from what was unfolding in front of them. But there was much more going on than they possibly could imagine.

"I... am... innocent," proclaimed Millie, while looking down, deflated from her sadness. At the back of the mob, Mrs. Porter collapsed to the ground, completely engulfed in her own tears. The mob released a collective moan of boos and hisses, apparently having already decided on Millie's guilt and overcome with bloodlust.

"Very well," concluded Tobias. "My men will take you to the town square for holding until six o'clock tonight, at which time they will bring you to the shore for the Test of Witchcraft." Tobias' voice deepened and became even more ominous. "May God have mercy on your soul."

As Tobias turned to lead the mob away, two men, who were only vaguely familiar to Millie, entered the schoolhouse. Each grasped one of Millie's arms and they dragged her out. By this time, her body completely lost its ability to stand upright, as if her bones were decomposing in anticipation of their near future. As Millie faded from the view of the schoolhouse window, Abigail saw Mrs. Porter following the two men, still completely engulfed in tears.

Abigail took a deep breath, wiped the tears from her eyes, and went to the back of the room to comfort Christina Anderson. Abigail always controlled her emotions when necessary, almost as if she could put them into a barrel and store them away to confront at a later time. This was a skill she learned from her father, who was the master. At this moment, Christina needed a friend. Abigail locked her emotions away so she could help Christina work through hers.

Chapter 8

Christina was a short, shy, and simple girl. Some girls did not like her very much. They confused her shyness for being aloof. Abigail did not see it that way. She understood what it meant to be shy – not wanting to be part of a group. After all, Mother always told her to blend in with the others, but only to a point. Both Christina and Abigail would prefer to sit alone and read a book rather than giggle and gossip with the other girls. Abigail understood Christina – at least she thought she did.

"Christina, I know that was terrible. We all feel awful for Millie. We'll figure out some way to help her," Abigail explained, trying to comfort Christina as best she could. This was difficult because Abigail's insides were ready to explode in a raucous symphony of grief and anger.

"You don't understand, Abi." Christina explained between gulps of tears as her voice became more depressed with each word.

"What don't I understand, Christina?"

There was a pause lasting longer than either girl felt comfortable with. There was absolute silence during the pause, which made the silence that much louder. It was the kind of silence which makes your eardrums pulse as they strain to find some faint sound to interpret so they are not sitting idle waiting in the nothingness.

"It was me, Abi. I'm the one who accused Millie."

Abigail's vision changed, as if she were chasing a tunnel moving away from her too quickly in an expanse of bright and confusing colors. The air in the classroom became hot, super heated in fact, and Abigail's ears felt like they were on fire.

Abigail's tone changed from comfort to disdain. "I don't understand. She's your classmate, your friend. Why would you do that, Christina?" Abigail was fighting the sudden urge to clench her fists. The rush of coldness, which overtook her body only a few minutes earlier, was quickly heating, and she did not know how much longer she could contain herself.

"I didn't mean to, Abi – really. I didn't think it would come to this." Tears fell from her eyes again. "But he made me. He kept asking questions, insisting there must be *something* she did that was odd. I only told him a couple of little things about her. Like how she enjoyed being silly sometimes and would dance and flap her arms like a bird. He seemed very interested in that. I didn't think he would actually accuse her with it." She looked away from Abigail and sobbed, "I want to die right now!"

Often, Millie and her mother would play by pretending to be birds. Her mother would get Millie to act like she was flying – flapping her arms. Christina didn't realize it, but during the trials, many made accusations specifically because they flapped their arms in public. It was a sign of insanity, and insanity was a sign of possession. Even children pretending to fly like birds while playing could be enough to accuse one of witchcraft. And in this case, that's exactly what happened.

Abigail continued, "Wait, Christina. *Who* made you do this? Who asked you all those questions?"

"I'm sorry, Abi. I can't say. He told me if I said anything, he would accuse me and my mother in public."

"He would *accuse* you?" Abigail stared at the floor as she tried to understand the gravity of what she was hearing. She knew there was only one person in town who could publicly accuse anyone – Tobias Warnock.

Christina's sobbing became uncontrollable. Mr. Putnam was standing nearby, eavesdropping on their conversation. When Christina's crying became more intense, he interrupted them to help comfort his student. But he heard what the girls were discussing. As he held Christina's sobbing head against his shoulder, he looked at Abigail. His eyes were wide, his brow furrowed with determination.

Abigail was still sitting at her desk, completely silent, when the last of the other children left for the day. Mr. Putnam paced around the room. The two of them were trying to understand why Tobias would include Christina, of all people, in such a horrific plot. William realized they were attempting to solve the mystery together, but individually. He decided they should talk through it with each other, and besides, the silence in the room made him uncomfortable.

"Abigail…" He paused and placed his hand on her shoulder. "Abi, this is a lot to take in. Perhaps you should go home and be with your family."

She ignored his comment and looked at him. Her eyebrows were completely uneven as she curled her forehead, attempting to decipher the meaning of what they heard. "Why? I just don't understand why. What would Tobias Warnock have against Millie or her family? They are friends. This makes no sense." The faraway tone of her voice showed just how deep in thought Abigail was as she tried desperately to make sense of the situation.

William agreed – he was thinking the same thing. None of this made sense. "I don't know, Abi. There's obviously something behind this situation we simply don't understand. We need to figure it out, but right now, we need to be there for Millie. It's already after five o'clock. Come, let's head to the shore and see if we can somehow stop this insane test from taking place. I'm sure your parents will be there looking for you."

"How can we stop this?" Abigail asked. "It's already decided. It's done." She looked away, still half speaking and half in thought. "It's not right. Millie doesn't deserve this. It just makes no sense."

"You're right, it doesn't. And I don't know how we can stop it. But we must go there and try. Come, let's go."

Mr. Putnam stood and held out his hand for Abigail. She rose and grabbed it. Though still in the throes of despair, she smiled slightly and thought, "That is the first time Mr. Putnam ever called me Abi."

Chapter 9

It was just before six o'clock, and the entire village seemed to be present to witness the test. Tobias Warnock was standing on the highest outcrop of rocks he could find. It was his pulpit, and he always wriggled his way to this location for these events. Abigail and Mr. Putnam just arrived and when Abigail saw her parents, she rushed over to them. She and her mother held each other in a tight embrace. Samuel stood next to them and rested his hand on Abigail's head in a feeble attempt to console her. Mr. Putnam moved to the back of the assembled group – he wanted to bear witness to the event, but he did not want a close-up view of the gory details about to unfold.

Mrs. Porter was at the front of the group, closest to the shoreline, and near the rock formation where Tobias stood. Her crying was continuous since she left the schoolhouse over four hours earlier. But she looked as though she aged twenty years in the interim. She was still crying, though her tears stopped flowing quite some time ago.

The two vaguely familiar men appeared from the trees. Each held one of Millie's arms. She felt much heavier now than she did earlier. Her head was leaning down, with her hair, now dirty and disheveled, hanging greasily in bunches covering her face. Her legs dragged in the sand a few feet behind the two men. They were both muscular, strong men, but were clearly struggling to hold Millie's dead weight while shuffling their feet to move her forward and up the rocks. When they arrived at the outcrop, Tobias motioned them to a series of rocks which looked down directly into the water. Tobias knelt on one knee so his face was just above the heads of the two men. He whispered to them, "Tightly tie her hands to the sides of her body, not behind her back, then get three large rocks and tie them to her legs. Be sure her hands cannot reach out and touch each other. This is very important."

The two men took a thick rope Tobias brought with him and started wrapping Millie with it. Her body was limp and seemed lifeless. First, they wrapped the rope three times around her waist and pulled it taught to ensure she could not escape. Then one man forced her right arm to be straight down her right side. He wrapped the rope around her downwardly-stretched arm and between her legs, then around her right thigh three times further. They did the same with her left side. They lay Millie on the ground facing up so they could tie the rope around her legs, near her ankles, another three times. Finally, they tied a triple knot into itself to secure the rope in place. Not even a master sailor could undo this convergence of thick rope and brute strength. Millie could not move, both because of her bondage and because of her lack of will to fight.

From the back of the crowd, William stood on a rock and yelled to everyone assembled, "Good people of Salem, we cannot allow this travesty. Young Millie Porter stands accused, tried, and convicted in an opaque process. She deserves justice and fair treatment. If we don't stand up for her today, who will stand up for you tomorrow when you or your loved one is accused?"

Abigail was proud of Mr. Putnam for trying to stop this sham, but as she looked around, she could see only a few other villagers were on their side. The coldness came back to her, and she hung her head with hopelessness, both for Millie and for Salem.

Most villagers hissed or turned their backs to William. There was no convincing them. Some gazed at William with sympathetic eyes, but were too afraid to stand up to Tobias. Doing so might expose them to accusations. William immediately saw his argument would not prevail. He looked at Millie with pity and shame in his eyes, as if to apologize for not being able to do more. Tobias caught William's stare, and knowing the villagers were on his side, didn't bother to respond to William's annoying outburst.

Millie turned her head to the audience and saw her mother. Her grief consumed her, but she reached out, desperately struggling in an impossible effort to grab hold of her daughter. Two members of the original mob had their arms around her waist to hold her back, though they did so with some empathy. Joseph Porter, who just arrived as he was working in the fields and only heard what was happening a mere hour ago, pushed the two men away from his wife and hugged her tightly, with one arm around her waist and his other arm pulling her head into his shoulder. He looked at his disheveled daughter at the top of the outcrop and his eyes quickly became bloodshot and deluged with tears. He realized this would be the last time he would see her alive and he would not even have the opportunity to say goodbye to her and tell her how much he loved her.

When the two men finished tying the three rocks to Millie's legs, further immobilizing her, Tobias stood and raised his arms to silence the murmuring crowd.

"Millicent Dorothy Porter. You stand accused of being a witch. You have declared your innocence and God, through the good people of Salem, will judge you to determine the truth. We have tied the rope around your body three times, we have tied the knot three times into a triple knot and there are three stones which will lead you to your fate. These 'three threes' are symbolic of the Holy Trinity – the Father, the Son and the Holy Ghost. We offer this as protection for your soul during your trial. Millie, please rise to accept your fate."

Millie did not move, she couldn't even if she wanted to, but the two men lifted her to her feet. They continued to hold her, though she now seemed even heavier than just a few moments before. Millie forced her eyes open, despite desperate exhaustion from having accepted what was to come. She again locked eyes with her parents and weakly mouthed "I love you" through dry, cracked lips.

The spectacle made even the most spiteful people in the crowd silent. Nobody talked, nobody booed or hissed, and nobody declared Millie's guilt. The only sounds were the waves crashing below the rocky outpost, gentle sobbing by some in the crowd, and Mrs. Porter's anguish.

Tobias broke the silence somberly. "Millie, may God have mercy on your soul." He waited a moment for dramatic effect, then nodded to the two men. They each grabbed one of the large rocks tied to her legs and threw them over the ledge into the ocean. Both the third rock and Millie's limp body flew down behind them. It all happened so fast, so suddenly. With a loud splash, Millie was gone. Mrs. Porter let out a sound that was best described as an agonizing howl as Mr. Porter pulled her in closer to his body. Millie's struggle, which only began four hours earlier, would be over in a few more minutes. But the heartache was only beginning for the Porter family.

Chapter 10

The plunge into the cold water lasted less than one second, but time slowed for Millie and she had complete thoughts on the way down. Her journey comprised three distinct segments, and she noted the irony of those being the 'fourth three' to append to Mr. Warnock's first 'three threes'.

The first segment was hard, jagged and bumpy as the two large rocks thrown over the edge dragged her body across the rocky ledge, tearing and bruising her skin on the back of her legs and arms. Her head bounced off the stoney surface of the ledge at least two times before she cleared the edge and entered the second segment of her journey.

The fall was the most pleasant part of her trip and she again noted some irony, as the fall was also her favorite season of the year. "If I must die, I'd like to die in the fall," she thought, using morbid humor to bring some comfort as she prepared for the unimaginable suffering she was about to endure.

Compared to the bumpy start, the fall was silent – almost peaceful. It seemed to last for minutes. She felt the air push against her body as it flung her hair straight above her head. She wanted to rub the hairs away from her forehead, but then realized her hands were tightly bound to the side of her body. Not having the use of her hands when she needed them seemed a most cruel form of torture.

The first sound she heard after falling from the ledge was the splash of the three stones beneath her feet. They did not fall next to each other, so instead of forming a clear splash crater in which she could land, they created three smaller separate craters a few feet apart from each other. This resulted in a surge of water directly in the middle of the three stones, which is precisely where her feet entered. It was as if the water was reaching up to welcome Millie to her liquid tomb.

Each of the stones slowed significantly when they contacted the water, almost causing them to float for the briefest of moments. Her body, however, hit the water like an axe splitting wood. She swept past the stones and went straight down. The stones ended their brief pause and dropped quickly, catching up to her feet and eventually dragging her down faster.

She thought she would be ready to hit the water, but she wasn't. It was colder than she expected. Subconsciously, she took a big gulp of air on the way down. This would be her final breath. She savored the last taste of fresh air in her mouth. The stones pulled her down to the bottom of the water, which was about twenty feet deep in this location. When the stones came to rest on the silty floor, Millie continued her descent and then floated back toward the surface. When she reached the point where there was no longer any slack in the ropes, she opened her eyes and, much to her surprise, she could see. Her cheeks were bulging in an effort to keep the precious air as long as she could. She turned her head in a quick jerking motion, half attempting a miraculous escape, and half looking around to take in her last views of the home she loved. Off to her left, about fifteen feet above her, she saw a small underwater cave she played in when she was younger. It was a good size for a six or seven-year-old, but now she was much too big for it. "I suppose it doesn't matter anymore," she realized. This was the first moment she consciously acknowledged her impending death.

Her body reacted to the circumstances of its own accord, with no intentional effort on her part. She had limited control over her movements. Millie started gyrating frantically, attempting to free either her hands or feet. She needed two of her limbs to be free in order to attempt a potential escape. She squirmed as much as she could, trying to loosen the tight bonds holding her in place. But the two men did a fine job of restraining her. The more she squirmed with her legs, the tighter the rope became around her arms. And the more she struggled with her arms, the more restrictive it became around her legs. She looked down and attempted to kick her feet out of the knots around her ankles somehow, but to no avail. She looked directly up. The sun was still in the sky, and she could see a shimmering crimson glow of sunlight above the water. "It's beautiful," she thought.

Her cheeks were still bulging, but she could tell the air was nearly depleted. Still, she kept her cheeks in that position, hoping to store every last bit of air she could. The urge to take a breath was overwhelming. Without realizing, she shimmied violently back and forth, trying desperately to move her arms, all the while looking up, praying for a miracle to save her. There would be no miracle today.

Finally, her body forced her to succumb. She could not prevent the urge to take a breath, though her mind was telling her, pleading with her, not to do so. She knew what would happen if she opened her mouth or allowed anything to pass through her nose. But the agony of not breathing became more than her body would allow her to bear. And coupled with the torturous imprisonment imposed by the rope, it was now out of her control. The pressure of not breathing was building in her head. She could feel the blood vessels around her eyes strain from the lack of fresh oxygen. The pressure forming behind her eyeballs made her entire face throb with pain. Her body was begging her for air. She was still looking straight up at the beautiful view of the sunlight shimmering against the water above her. Despite her best effort, she opened her mouth and took a deep gulp. Her body reacted pleasantly at first, relieving the urge to take a breath. But the cold, salty water quickly rushed down her throat, flooding her lungs and depriving her body of any life-nurturing oxygen. If only there was some biological process to convert her environment into the elements she needed to live, like fish using their gills to harvest oxygen from the water or plants turning toward the sun to generate energy from the sunlight.

The last few moments of Millie's life were heart-wrenching. Her body was violently struggling to survive. The fight between the outside elements which bound her body versus the ocean water now taking up residence inside her body was unwinnable by either side. There was nothing left for her to do except die, which she did, while continuing her desperate struggle for air. Finally, painfully, the last particle of air escaped her tightly bound body and made its way to the surface twenty feet above, as if her soul was ascending to Heaven using the bubbles as its transportation. Her body halted all motion and floated lifelessly above the rocks to which she was prescribed. Her lips, blue from deprivation, ceased their fearful quivering as her eyes remained open, still looking straight up to the beautiful crimson glow above the surface.

Chapter 11

Tobias kept his eyes on the water, looking for the telltale signs of death by drowning. At first, he saw no air bubbles arrive at the surface. This was normal, as the accused held their breath for as long as they could. After about two minutes, there was a deluge of rising air, causing a smattering of bubbles which were seen only from directly above because of the waves crashing against the shore. This was the sign the accused gave up, and the air was escaping their body. "Sooner than I expected," he thought to himself. "But then again, she was young and petite. Not much room to hold a lot of air." He witnessed some adults undergoing the test hold their breath for three, almost four, minutes. That was more impressive. Two minutes was well below the average.

He did not announce the deluge to the assembled crowd, so nobody else knew how long Millie lasted. Instead, he stood watching the water, holding his pocket watch in his right hand. He would need to wait another eighteen minutes so the full twenty minutes could elapse and he could deem the test complete. At that point, his men could retrieve the body. "These next eighteen minutes will be torture," he thought, already bored and not sure how to pass the remaining time while continuing to appear interested.

One could feel the ebb and flow of the crowd's mood. When Millie first went into the water, there was palpable anxiety as people waited to see if she would emerge and show herself to be a witch. After three minutes under water, the anxiety gave way to the realization that perhaps she was innocent after all. There was still anxiety buzzing in the air, but it was slipping away by the second. By six minutes in, everyone knew Millie would not emerge alive. Most in the crowd hanged their heads, ashamed for having any part in the death of another innocent. But nobody moved. Out of respect for

Millie and her family, every person waited the full twenty minutes in shameful quiet, with only Mrs. Porter's anguished cries and the sound of the waves breaking through the tense silence.

When his pocket watch showed it was exactly twenty minutes, Tobias turned to the crowd. "We now conclude the test." He looked at his two men, who left their rocky posts during the test, and walked to the shoreline near the spot where the rest of the crowd gathered. Tobias motioned for them to go into the water to retrieve the body. Both men already removed their boots, stockings, and shirts. Only their trousers remained in order to keep most of their clothing dry. Each man grabbed a knife Tobias brought for this task, held it in their teeth, and entered the cold water. At first they were hesitant, with their arms in the air like a couple of orangutans walking across a plain. When the water was up to their chests, they dove in and swam to the location Millie entered the water, directly under the rocky outcrop. Each man grabbed the knife from their mouth, took a large gulp of air, and dove for Millie twenty feet below them.

When they arrived, her body was blue and in its attempt to float to the surface, seemed it was trying to lift its attached stones. They cut the ropes connecting each of the stones to her legs. The men didn't bother to remove the rest of the rope – they left it to join the stones and rope from previous tests, becoming a morose museum on the ocean floor. They simply needed to get her back to shore where they could remove the rest of her constraints. Her body was much lighter than twenty minutes earlier, and the men easily brought her back to the shore and lay her down on her back so everyone could see her face.

The crowd moved toward Millie slowly. Most wanted to see her, their morbid curiosity getting the better of them. But they all showed restraint and respect, allowing Millie's parents to get to her first and spend a few moments alone. Mrs. Porter knelt beside her daughter's lifeless body and laid her sobbing, but tearless, head on Millie's chest. Joseph Porter kissed Millie on her forehead and, with the palm of his hand, dragged her open eyes closed. He could see the horror of Millie's last few moments in her eyes, and he did not want Elizabeth to experience that. She already went through enough. Tobias climbed down from the rocks and came to stand next to the body. Elizabeth Porter looked at him, her eyes as if he stabbed her in the heart several times. "You vile, wicked man. This is your fault."

Tobias slowly and calmly responded, "Mrs. Porter, I am truly sorry for your loss. But God has commanded us to rid our town of all followers of Satan. Your daughter was a valiant soldier in this pursuit and has exonerated herself and also your family. You should be very proud of her."

Elizabeth Porter stared back at Tobias as if her eyes alone could provide vengeance. Joseph stood and crossed his arms, careful not to let his hands touch each other. His body was facing away from Tobias but he stared at him out of the corner of his eyes with a gaze that said simply, 'I hate you'. Tobias paid no attention to either of them. He turned and walked away, heading back to his home. The proceedings made him late for supper.

As Tobias passed the back of the group, William Putnam rushed to him and placed his hand firmly on Tobias' shoulder. "What have you done?" he asked accusingly.

"My job, young man. I've done my job. And I suggest you do yours." And with that, Tobias and his two men walked out of view, leaving the crowd to comfort the Porter family and dispose of the body.

Chapter 12

The crowd dispersed. The village mortician agreed to take Millie and prepare her body for a proper burial. Since the test exonerated her, it entitled her to a religious funeral. The ministers held all funerals as quickly as they could, the same day if possible. This was in order to prevent any decay and rotting bodies that could create a stench and illness throughout the entire village. Because it was already past sundown, the burial would have to wait until tomorrow's first light. But at least Millie was now with God.

The Sampsons walked over to the Porters and offered their support and condolences. Willa hugged Elizabeth. "We're here for anything you need." Then Willa gave Joseph a tight hug. It was the type of hug normally reserved for extremely emotional situations between family or close friends. Samuel only nodded to Elizabeth, but he put his hand on Joseph's shoulder for moral support. This was a man's way of saying, "I'm sorry and I'm here for you." Joseph placed his hand on top of Samuel's – a man's way of saying, "Thank you."

"There are others," Samuel quietly uttered to Joseph. "Indeed, there *are* others," Joseph responded through his tears. Abigail overheard this exchange and recognized those words her mother always said to her. "Why is Father saying that to Mr. Porter?" Abigail wondered. But there were more important mysteries for her to consider, and she hastened on to other thoughts.

The Sampsons turned to head home. Abigail did not turn around with her parents – she wanted to stay a while longer to help comfort her friends. Her parents agreed. "Don't stay too long, dear," her mother warned as they somberly headed home. Samuel was relieved Abigail was going to remain at the shore. He was becoming increasingly concerned and there was much he and Willa needed to discuss privately.

Abigail noticed Mr. Putnam sitting to the side of the remaining crowd of only about a dozen people now. He was on a tree which fell over during a recent storm – one leg in the sand, the other bent at the knee and resting on the tree. She sat down beside him.

"What are we going to do now?" Abigail asked, knowing there was no answer.

"What *can* we do?" Mr. Putnam responded slowly through a deep frown. "Tobias Warnock is up to something. We do not know what his plan is and we have absolutely no proof he's done anything wrong."

"We have *some* proof," Abigail reminded him. "Christina admitted he put her up to this."

"That's true," he agreed, "But nobody will take the word of a child over that of a respected village elder. And besides, we'd be asking Christina to take a monumental risk to which neither she, nor her family, could agree."

"We'll figure something out," Abigail said reassuringly. She paused and then took one of the biggest risks of her life. She didn't know what came over her, but it felt like the exact proper thing to do. Abigail wasn't sure whether she should do it – would he get angry with her, would he tease her, would he laugh at her? Could she even go through with it? She summoned all her courage and placed her hand on top of his, which was resting on the tree next to her. Rather than reacting with anger or scorn, he simply clutched her hand tightly. William needed comforting as much as anyone else right now, and Abigail was one of the few in their village who respected

49

reason and logic as much as he did. He was happy to have her be the one to comfort him. To Abigail, it was a daring act showing William her feelings for him. To William, it was a simple act of comfort and solace.

William looked at Abigail, grinned, and said, "Thank you, Abigail." "Actually, if it's all the same to you, I'd prefer if you called me Abi." Her brazenness shocked her, but being this brave and forward just felt... right.

"All right – Abi it is," he said.

They sat together talking on the tree for quite some time, trying to figure out any potential meaning they could find in the dealings of the day. They theorized the most preposterous conspiracies they could imagine, but nothing made sense with the facts they observed. What could Tobias possibly have against Millie, and how did Christina fit into the equation?

It became dark, so William fashioned a torch out of a thick branch and some kindling he found. He lit it, but only after many tries. "I'm not quite the outdoorsman I'd like to be," he confessed. Abi chuckled and admitted she could do no better. "I would disappoint Father with any attempt I'd make at starting a fire," she replied.

"Your father!" Will gasped. "We need to get you home. I'm sure it's later than your parents are expecting."

"I'm sure my parents will reprimand or maybe even punish me for this," she said, "but it's worth it. I enjoy spending time with you." "As do I. But come, it's late. There will be time for us to continue our discussion later."

They stood and started back for Abi's home, William lighting the way with his fabricated torch, Abi's hand firmly attached to his.

They arrived at Abi's front door and William extended the torch forward so Abi could clearly see the doorknob. "Let's both keep thinking about this, Abi. Between the two of us, I'm confident we can discover the truth."

"Yes, of course. I'll see you tomorrow at Millie's funeral and then at school." She hated how she felt – she was looking beyond the funeral to her time in school with anticipation, when she would again be under the tutelage of only one adult, the man she was certain to dream about tonight, William Putnam.

She gathered the last of her courage for the day as she looked William in the eye and said, "Good night, Will."

Abigail opened the door, turned back to give William a shy smile and a wave goodbye that was more fingers than hand, then turned back and entered her house, closing the door behind her. William turned and walked away, still racking his brain, trying to piece Tobias' actions together into a story that made sense. He paused for a moment as he realized Abigail, his student, not only referred to him by his first name, but by a nickname – Will. This was much too informal for him. "She must have assumed it would be acceptable to call me Will when she asked me to call her Abi," he realized. Under normal circumstances, he would not allow this. But these were not normal circumstances, and besides, she was already in her house for the night. He decided he would allow this one transgression to pass.

Abigail walked in expecting a lecture and a grounding. Instead, her mother welcomed her home as she was drying her hands on a towel after cleaning the day's dishes. Father was sitting in a chair in the main room, staring into his special candle. This was something he did when he had a particularly stressful day. "Today certainly counts," Abigail thought. When he spent time with the candle, it wasn't like he was just looking at it. It was more of a meditation with the candle. Abigail could not explain it, it was something she knew her entire life. It seemed rather normal to her. But none of her friends' fathers did anything of the sort, so Abigail grew to realize this was unique and maybe even a bit strange. Father always seemed calmer after these sessions, and Abigail was happy he had a way to deal with his stress.

Every house was lit at night by a series of candles. Almost all were round, with a wide circumference. This provided plenty of fuel for the wick and ensured the candle would last for some time. The Sampsons had many candles like this. But Father's special candle was different. It was tall and thin, maybe sixteen or eighteen inches tall, which was at least three times taller than most other candles. And Father's candle possessed three features which made it completely unique.

First, the wax was nearly clear. Mother refined the wax much longer than for other candles she made. The process was arduous and always made her physically tired, but it produced a truly beautiful vat of clear, pristine wax for Father's candle.

Second, the wick itself was not a thin white string like most other candles. This wick was dark brown, almost black, and wound in a twisted manner where one could see six individual strands. In fact, the wick was so interesting it was the reason Mother made the wax so clear.

The third unique quality of the candle was how extraordinarily slow it burned. Where shorter, fatter candles would burn down in a couple of days, Father's candle could sometimes take two weeks or more for the wax to become completely extinguished. And unlike any other candle Abigail ever saw, the wick always remained intact. It never burned away. When the wax was gone, Mother would create a new batch, rescue the wick from the old candle, and create it anew.

Abigail kissed both parents good night. Her mother gave her a tight hug, similar to the one she gave Mr. Porter, as if to tell Abigail everything would be all right. Samuel looked into Abigail's eyes as she kissed him on the forehead. He knew there was much to explain to her. But he didn't know how.

Abigail laid down in her bed. It was a long, emotional day. Her ability to control and restrain her emotions again came in handy. Her eyes fell shut as soon as her head touched the pillow and she immediately drifted off to sleep, with excitement over the object of her dreams.

Chapter 13

Nearly the entire town gathered for Millie's funeral. The Porter's were well-liked and because this was the first time an accusation happened in school, many more people were interested than normal. The minister performed a loving, albeit brief, service.

"We must rid the wicked from our lives. Young Millie more than played her part in helping to keep the rest of us safe. We owe her and her family a debt of gratitude we can never repay. All we can do is live pure lives to honor her memory."

The villagers all knew Millie was now officially innocent, and they could mourn her loss publicly. This provided little solace to the Porter family, who would now be without their precious daughter for reasons they could not understand.

There were two notable absences from the funeral. Christina Anderson did not attend, though her parents did, and both Abigail and Mr. Putnam understood why. They didn't expect Christina to come. It was hard to know if she could ever forgive herself, though she really did nothing wrong. Still, the guilt she was undeniably enduring must be suffocating. "I hope she'll be all right," Abigail thought.

The other notable absence was Tobias Warnock. This enraged William Putnam. "He could have at least showed up out of respect for the family, even if he did not accept any responsibility," William said to Abigail with his arms crossed tightly. "Although," his arms loosened a bit, "the Porters certainly would not want him here, and perhaps he thought it wise to allow them to grieve without his presence to upset them further. I hate how reasonable I can be sometimes," William thought to himself. He did not want to give Tobias the benefit of the doubt, but conceded he must.

After the funeral, the crowd moved outside the church to the neighboring graveyard for the burial. There was a short stone and mud mortar wall around the graveyard, about two feet tall. It wasn't meant to be any type of security from animals or other invaders, but more of a marker telling passersby the area within the walls is sacred. The grave was dug during the night and the mortician prepared Millie's body and placed her in the casket before the funeral started. The crowd stood in silence with their heads bowed in respect and hats over their hearts as the minister said the last prayer before they lowered Millie's casket into the earth.

"God our Father, by raising Christ Your son, You destroyed the power of death and opened for us the way to eternal life. As we remember before You, our sister Millicent, we ask Your help for all who shall gather in her memory. Grant us the assurance of Your presence and grace by the spirit You have given us; through Jesus Christ our Lord. Amen." Everyone responded in a murmured unison, "Amen."

After the ground accepted the casket, the men returned their hats to their heads, and the crowd dispersed. Most stopped to say words of comfort and give their respect to the Porters, who looked more composed today but were still clearly coming to terms with how different life was just twenty-four hours earlier. The minister also remained to thank those who attended and to provide comfort as best he could to the Porters. It was in these moments of sorrow where the residents of Salem came together to take care of one another.

Because of the funeral, school began about thirty minutes later than normal, which meant it would also end thirty minutes later. The children all arrived in their funeral clothing, which was just more formal versions of the black-and-white clothing they normally wore. When the full class assembled, all but Christina, Mr. Putnam sat at his desk and spoke in a serious, somber and highly personal tone.

"I am still trying to understand everything that happened yesterday. I'm sure you are as well." He paused and looked up. "We will all miss Millie terribly. The best way to honor her memory is to continue with life as normal." He paused once again to think for a moment. His facial expression changed as he realized he no longer agreed with the words he just spoke. "No, I take that back. Not life as normal, but life better than normal. It will do no good for anyone if we fail to move forward or if we don't continue to grow. Let Millie's memory be motivation for each of you to do better with the time we have here. Make the most of your education so you can make the most of your life. We can all do this together – for ourselves, and for Millie."

Most of the students still looked stunned from the past day's events. But a few students seemed to have a renewed spark in their eye now, as if Mr. Putnam's words opened a new chapter in their book of life. In the past, Mr. Putnam tried to inspire the class, with usually only Abigail showing any interest. But today, he was excited to see a new look of determination in the eyes of James Boylan. He seemed truly to understand and agree with what Mr. Putnam was saying. Perhaps coming to grips with how Millie's life ended so abruptly forced James to confront the path he was on for his own life. Perhaps something positive *would* come from this after all.

At lunch, Mr. Putnam realized Mrs. Sampson had not yet arrived. Usually on Thursdays, she arrived by noon to help grade papers during the children's lunch break. Not usually, but always, in fact. Even on the few days where Mrs. Sampson was ill, she still made the ten-minute walk to help Mr. Putnam. It was one of the pleasures of her life, she'd say. So where was she today?

Still in the mindset of searching for conspiracy theories to understand Tobias Warnock's motivations, Mr. Putnam tried to determine why she was not there. He wrote out a list of the workable options he could think of:

1. She was coming, but was late.
2. She was too grief stricken and needed time away.
3. Something horrible happened to her or to Mr. Sampson.
4. Either she, or Mr. Sampson, was angry at Mr. Putnam for escorting Abigail home so late last night.

Option One seemed implausible to him – she was never late before, in fact she was typically early.

Option Two seemed unlikely. While Mrs. Sampson certainly seemed sad yesterday, she was comforting others. It made more sense for her to come to school today to help comfort the children. She would certainly know they needed it.

Option Three also seemed unlikely. When parents had any type of emergency, someone always came to the school to take the child. Certainly, if something happened, Mr. Putnam would know by now.

Option Four was the only one he could not explain away. Nothing unseemly happened between Mr. Putnam and Abigail – it was all quite innocent and, under the circumstances of yesterday, nothing seemed inappropriate. Still, an adult man escorting a young woman home at night could anger the family. And the fact Mr. Putnam was Abigail's teacher could make one pause when thinking about any courtship. But Mr. Putnam was not considering courtship, not at all. Abigail was a kindred spirit in pursuing knowledge. They understood each other. Mr. Putnam was not oblivious to Abigail's attention for him. Other students showed similar interest in the past and he could either ignore the infatuation or have a simple talk with the student to clear up any confusion they were feeling. Still, this was different. He didn't have romantic feelings for Abigail, but he certainly felt more understood by her than by any other student. Mr. Putnam wanted to spend time with her. He wanted to read books with her and then discuss and debate their meaning. She was one of the few people he knew could change his mind on a subject. He respected her.

This was exactly what he needed to say to the Sampsons. Regardless of how they would react, they needed to know he respected their daughter, and he was not trying to take advantage of the teacher/student relationship. Perhaps they would forbid him to see her again, but at least he would be honest with them – adult to adult. Surely they would respect that.

Lunch was almost over, there were still another three hours of school left because of the late start, and tonight he needed to grade papers, mostly because Mrs. Sampson was not there to help. So he would go to the Sampson house tomorrow after school, to have the discussion with Samuel and Willa.

Abigail and Mr. Putnam stayed after school for a little while to continue discussing their theories. But it was getting late and Mr. Putnam had many papers to grade, so he wished Abi a good evening and left.

When Abigail arrived home, she remembered her mother did not come to school that day as normal. "Mother – why didn't you come today?"

"I'm sorry I couldn't make it, dear. Your father and I needed to discuss many things. He didn't get to the field until after lunch and that's the first time I was able to finish the chores. I certainly hope Mr. Putnam did not miss having me there today. I'll try to go an extra day next week."

Chapter 14

Friday was nearly a normal day at school. Christina was still not back in the classroom, which was understandable, but also unfortunate. Mr. Putnam was concerned she would fall behind in her studies. His concern was mostly for selfish reasons, as he would need to spend his personal time providing private instruction until she was back at the same point as the other students. And these days, there were other matters to occupy his interest, mainly understanding the Tobias Warnock matter and, of course, spending time with Abi to help solve the mystery.

But there was only one concern on William's mind today. After school, he planned to go to the Sampson house to speak with Abi's parents. He was resolute in his conviction, but admittedly, he was nervous. Fathers resorted to violence for lesser infractions, and while Samuel was not prone to lose his temper, it was common knowledge that he was stronger than he appeared. William was certain the situation would not escalate to where he'd have to find out Samuel's actual strength. At least he was somewhat certain.

There was one thing he knew for sure. It would be unhelpful if Abi were home during the encounter. She was mature for her age, but she was headstrong, short-tempered, and not skilled in the diplomatic arts. If she felt the discussion was not going in her favor, she might resort to less-than-effective measures. William was keenly interested in ensuring a positive conversation, and therefore, a positive outcome. He was not looking to engage in a fight – whether the fight was physical or verbal. So he devised a plan to help both the Sampson situation and the situation with Christina Anderson. But he knew how Abi's mind worked, and in order for the plan to succeed, it would need to be Abi's idea, not his.

During recess, he called Abi over. She stopped playing with the other girls and jogged over to Mr. Putnam, who was sitting under a tree grading assignments.

"Christina has been absent two days in a row. Have you spoken with her, or heard how she's doing?"

"No, I have heard nothing. And to be honest, I've been concerned about her."

"Yes, so have I. She's falling behind in her studies. You know, I've noticed she doesn't seem to get along with the other girls. Do you know if she is friendly with any of them outside of school? I'd like to send someone over to visit with her."

"Not really. Most of the other girls don't speak to her too much. They think she feels superior to them. The truth is, she is quite shy. I can relate to that – there are times I'd rather read a book than play with the other girls. Christina feels the same way."

"It seems to me you might be her best friend in school, perhaps her only friend. Is this right?"

"Yes, I suppose that is true."

"Well, maybe when she feels well enough to return, you could help her get caught up in her studies. I just don't know how long she'll be out. I wish there were some way to see how she's doing."

Abigail became excited and her shoulders visibly rose. "I could visit her. I think she might like to see me. At least she'd have someone close to her own age to speak with. And I could even bring her work with me and help her with the lessons. Would that be all right with you?"

Knowing his plan worked, Mr. Putnam smiled widely. "That's a wonderful idea. You are so considerate of your classmates. I know they all appreciate it. And I'll do my part to help. After school, I have some errands to do in town and I need to pass right by your house. I'll stop there and let your parents know you'll be at Christina's for the afternoon. That way they won't worry, and you can spend as much time with Christina as you'd like."

"That would be so helpful. Thank you, Mr. Pu... Will." Abigail gave Will a wry smile. Will smiled back, but realized he would need to put an end to Abigail's infatuation. However, this was not the time, especially since he was successful in convincing her to go to Christina's. Now, if only his conversation with the Sampsons would go as well.

At three o'clock, Mr. Putnam dismissed the class for the week. The students formed a line in front of his desk so each student could hand in their work for Mr. Putnam to grade over the weekend. Abi was last in line, as normal, so she could talk with Mr. Putnam for a few minutes. When it was Abi's turn, Mr. Putnam took her work and placed the pile of papers into his satchel to take home. "Let me get Christina's assignments for you," he told her. He rifled through some papers on his desk and put together a stack of about eight pages for Abi to take to Christina. He thought, "This should be enough to keep them occupied for at least a couple of hours. I can't imagine I'd need any more time than that."

Abi concocted a plan of her own. She looked at all the papers he packed in his satchel. "That's a lot of papers to grade over the weekend, isn't it?"

"Well, it's about the normal amount I review each weekend. It looks like it will be another uneventful two days for me," he acknowledged with a heavy sigh.

"What if I stop by your home tomorrow and I could help?" Abi asked excitedly.

He knew he could not allow her feelings for him to deepen. "I'm not sure that's a good idea, Abi. But I certainly could use some help. What if we met in the town square tomorrow at noon? We could bring a lunch, sit on a public bench and go through the papers together. It might even provide a splendid opportunity to discuss everything going on with Tobias. How does that sound?"

Abi did not like the idea of meeting in such a public place – she wouldn't be able to hold Will's hand in public. But she understood his reasoning, and it made sense to her. She mustered a smile and said, "Yes, that sounds fine. I'll bring sandwiches for us both and you bring the papers to grade."

"Wonderful!" he replied with a wide smile. "That will be so helpful. I'll see you then. Now I'm off to do my errands. I'll be sure to stop by your house and let your parents know you will be at Christina's. Off with you now. Please send Christina my regards and let her know I look forward to seeing her back in school soon."

They said goodbye as each went their own way, completely unaware this would be the last time they would ever speak.

Chapter 15

It was a beautiful late spring afternoon. The flowers were almost in full bloom and the sweet smell of nectar overwhelmed William's senses when he walked the path in the woods toward the Sampson home. It was a traumatic few days, and this was the first time in a while he felt at ease. "Nothing soothes the soul like doing the right thing," he thought. He was proud of his decision to be proactive with Abi's parents. They would respect him for this, he kept convincing himself. And having such an enjoyable stroll on the way to their house only confirmed to him Mother Nature herself was giving him a pat on the back – a cosmic nod of approval.

Abi ran the entire way to Christina's house. She was excited to see her friend, mostly because she so enjoyed playing the role of teacher. They would first spend a little time with pleasantries, then go through the lessons together. Hopefully, she might get some more information from Christina about her encounter with Mr. Warnock. The effort of trying to figure out his plan was still near the top of mind for her, though other thoughts certainly took precedence of late. "What if Christina asks me about boys I'm interested in?" she mused. "Maybe I'd tell her I'm not interested in any *boys*, only a particular *man*," she gleefully thought. "No, I mustn't. Will would be angry if I told anyone, or even hinted at anything. I can't risk it at this point. I'll just spend my afternoon enjoying my time with Christina and then I'll see Will tomorrow for lunch." The thought thrilled her.

When Abi arrived at Christina's house, she raised her fist to knock on the door. But she paused as she realized Christina was not expecting her. "It's rude to show up to someone's house unannounced," she realized. She thought she could say she was there to drop off her class work, though others lived much closer than Abi, so maybe it would have made more sense for them to bring the work. Then again, the other girls didn't speak with Christina too much, so maybe Abi bringing the work actually made more sense. But before Abi could raise her fist again to knock, the door opened.

"Abigail Sampson, is that you?" Mrs. Anderson asked.

"Yes ma'am, hello."

"It's nice to see you, dear. What brings you all the way over here? Does your mother know you're here?"

"Yes ma'am, she does. I apologize for coming unannounced. I came to bring Christina the classwork she's missed and to see if she'd like some company. We've missed seeing her in school the last couple of days. Do you think she'd be interested in having a visitor?"

"That is so nice of you, Abigail. Yes, of course. Please come in."

Abi was never inside Christina's house. It was nice, larger than Abi's house. They owned a large bookshelf filled with books and sitting in front of the bookshelf were two sets of chairs with two small tables in between each of the sets. Each set looked directly across at the other two. Both tables held an unlit candle. The one on the left looked like most of the wax was gone, the one on the right was younger, fresher. In between the two sets of chairs lay a large bearskin rug. It looked very comfortable, but Abi did not dare to get near it. Her father despised cruelty to animals of any kind and he had a keen sense of smell. If he smelled the rug on her shoes, he would be very upset. She was nervous even being in the same room as the rug for fear her father could sniff it out.

Abi imagined the four Andersons – Mr. and Mrs. Anderson, Christina, and her younger brother David, all sitting in the chairs at night, candles glowing, with all four reading. "That is my definition of Heaven," she thought. "A family reading and gathering knowledge together."

"Christina, Abigail Sampson is here for you. Put on your robe and come out," Mrs. Anderson beckoned.

Christina came out from the back room in her pajamas and robe. It was obvious she was in bed all day. "Abi? What are you doing here?" Christina asked.

"Hi Christina. We've all been so concerned about you. I wanted to come over to keep you company. And I brought the classwork you've missed. Mr. Putnam asked me to bring it – he sends his regards."

Abi immediately wondered if she said that last sentence with too much pretense. "Was I blushing when I said his name? Did she notice? Did my voice change when I spoke of him?" Her heart beat heavier, not out of love, but out of fear and dread that Christina would uncover her secret. "That's so nice of you, and of Mr. Putnam," Christina responded. "Whew!" Abi thought to herself as her heart's thumping calmed.

"Mother, is it all right for Abi and me to go into my room?"

"Of course, dear. Just let me know if either of you would like anything to eat or drink."

"Your mother is so generous and kind," Abi said to Christina as they entered her room and closed the door.

****

William followed the path through the woods and made it to the clearing which led to the Sampson house. He planned to knock at their door and make small talk with Mrs. Sampson. He would tell her Abi was at Christina's and then ask her to fetch Mr. Sampson from the field for an important discussion, as he was surely still working at this time of day. Then he would ask them both to sit and he would explain the situation, adult to adult. It was a good plan, and he felt confident so easily convincing Abi to go to Christina's at lunch earlier in the day.

As he approached their house, he heard something he did not expect. Mr. Sampson was not in the field – he was inside the house, having what sounded like a rather heated discussion with Mrs. Sampson. William quickly wondered if he should cancel his mission, but this opportunity was too perfect. When would he be able to get Abi away from her house again? He was hoping to have this conversation behind him the next time he saw Abi, and since they were meeting at noon tomorrow, the time was now. "No," he decided. "I'm here and I must continue with the plan."

The closer he got to their house, the better able he was to hear the conversation inside. He didn't intend to eavesdrop, but he couldn't help himself. They clearly meant the conversation to be private, but he was feeling confident and a bit voyeuristic. He focused his hearing on them and subconsciously, if not intentionally, slowed his pace so he'd have more time to listen.

"I know he's near. I've sensed him for a while," Samuel said to Willa.

"But you have no proof. How could he have found us? It's been so long," she responded.

67

"I don't know. I don't know which one he is. He could be hiding inside any of them. He could be our neighbor for all I know. But I can't let him get to you or Abigail. She is a pureblood. She is too valuable to the Order."

The discussion fascinated William. "A pureblood? The Order? What are they talking about?" He leaned down a bit as he continued to slow his pace.

"Willa, can't you see how close he is to us now? He got to the Porters. He's closing in on us. He must know. We are not safe here. My powers are weak because of our covers. I can't risk it any longer."

William froze. "His... powers???"

"Samuel, is it at all possible you are wrong? What if you're imagining all of this?"

"If I am, then I'll admit I'm wrong. We would be someplace else and you'll both be safe. But if I'm right and we do nothing? That is not an option I can even conceive of."

"What are we to do, Samuel? Just disappear to some other territory and start over? What would we say to Abigail? Have you thought about that? How could she possibly process everything? She knows nothing of who we are – of who she is. Maybe it's time we tell her the truth about her and the prophecy. Maybe now it's finally time."

"No, not yet. She is still too young. She could not possibly understand her responsibility to the global covens."

William was now at a full stop in front of their door. He was too busy processing what he just heard – he forgot why he was even there.

"Purebloods, the Order, powers, covens??? What could this all mean? It certainly sounds like they are speaking of witches, but that can't possibly be correct. Witches are not real. It's not possible." Without realizing, because he was so deep inside his own thoughts, he unconsciously knocked at the door.

Samuel and Willa immediately stopped speaking and looked at each other with worry in their eyes. They had plans in place for many scenarios. They always had to be cautious and prepared in order to remain safe. But this situation was immensely more complicated because of two realities. First, they were careless and spoke too loudly so anyone outside could hear, they now realized this. And second, Abigail was not home – they could not protect her. They would have to be prudent with their next steps.

Chapter 16

Willa opened the door and saw Mr. Putnam, who looked flabbergasted. "Good day, Mr. Putnam. What a pleasant surprise. What can we do for you?" She paused briefly and continued with a higher pitch and more tension in her voice. "And, if you're not at school, where is Abigail? Is she all right?" When he heard that last question and the worry in Willa's voice, Samuel looked up and became concerned about his daughter, considering the gravity of the situation.

William stammered. "Uh, yes. Abigail is just fine. Um, she went to Christina Anderson's house to help her get caught up with her classwork." Samuel's shoulders lowered as he calmed down with the explanation Abigail was all right.

Willa responded, "Oh, that's very nice. Thank you for letting us know. Please, won't you come in?"

William paused before entering. If Samuel was the one to invite him in instead of Willa, he would be wary. But he knew Willa so well he did not have the same concern. Still, he could not make sense of what he just heard, and he was feeling lightheaded and hot.

"Yes, uh, thank you," he said while walking through the doorway. Samuel stood and nodded to William. "Hello," is all he could muster to say. It was not the most welcoming greeting he ever provided, but he was concerned about their visitor.

"So what brings you by today, Mr. Putnam?" Willa inquired. "Surely you didn't come all this way just to tell us Abigail is at the Anderson's, did you?"

"No, that's right. I wanted to speak with you both about…." William paused and scratched his forehead, pushing his hat back a bit in the process – the hat he forgot to remove upon entering their house because his mind was elsewhere. "I'm sorry. I apologize for eavesdropping, but when I was approaching your house, I overheard the strangest conversation. It sounded like you were speaking of…. I'm almost too embarrassed to say it, but it sounded like you were speaking of witchcraft. Surely I'm not correct."

Samuel turned, slowly stepped to the back of the room, and began pacing, looking at the floor and rubbing his chin.

"Why Mr. Putnam, whatever do you think you heard?" Willa did not consider denying it, though it was likely her best option.

"It sounds crazy, I know. But I heard you speak of bloodlines and covens."

Samuel turned his head toward William, trying to process his intent. He crossed the room toward the front door, still deep in thought. Then he turned around toward the back of the house and began pacing again.

William continued, "And then something about Abigail's role and her not knowing about the prophecy? What is this all about?" He continued further, too engrossed to realize he was actually making an outright threat, "I respect your entire family and everything you do for our village, but as I'm sure you are aware I am the biggest witch skeptic in all of Salem, save maybe for Abigail. How would Tobias take it if I, of all people, accused someone of being a witch?"

Samuel heard enough. This was a direct threat to his family, and he needed to mitigate it immediately. He and Willa needed time to figure out what to do next. Willa knew what was about to come. It was a protocol they discussed – and Samuel was right to do it.

With his back still facing William, Samuel spotted his special candle from the corner of his eye, and this comforted him. It had been a long time and though he felt unease over what he was about to do, he knew it needed to be done and there was no hesitation in his mind. He brought his hands to his chest and touched the tips of his three middle fingers from his right hand to the tips of the same three fingers on his left hand. Samuel closed his eyes and felt his emotion growing. He let his arms fall, still with the fingers touching, so his arms created a circle in front of his body. The energy within him flowed faster and faster through the circle made from his body, leaping through his fingertips, from his left arm to his right. After a few moments, his eyes opened suddenly. There was a quick, sharp flash of electricity in the room, as if lightning struck the house. Samuel put his hands down to his sides. William now lay on the floor near the front door, motionless.

"Samuel, you didn't kill him, did you?"

"Of course not. He's in stasis." Samuel shook his arms briefly to release the remaining tension and rolled his head around his neck. It had been a long time since he allowed his energy to freely flow through his body, and it felt good. "Really, Willa. I have killed no one in over two hundred years. You know I don't do that anymore."

"That's a relief," she said. "He's a good man, he really is. I don't think he meant to threaten me – I don't think he realized what he was saying. How long will he be out for?"

"I put him out for three days. He'll wake on Monday morning and by then his memory will have completely faded. I figured nobody will notice him missing over the weekend. He's always home grading assignments on Saturdays and he rarely attends Church on Sundays. That should give us time to determine our next move." Samuel learned the routines of as many of his fellow villagers as possible, exactly for this type of situation.

"Good thinking, Samuel. We need to be more careful about when, and how loudly, we speak from now on. And we need to discuss when to start Abigail's education."

"Yes, you're right, Willa. We will discuss it all. But for now, I'll take Mr. Putnam back to his house and set him up comfortably in his bed. He'll have a nice nap. I'll fetch Belle."

Samuel went to his bedroom closet and put on an old, long, dark cloak that wrapped around his body almost two full times. It had a tall, stiff collar which stood straight up with a black chain and a clasp to keep the cloak around his neck and secure it in place. He referred to the cloak as `Belle` because the main body of the cloak extended out in the shape of a bell. At least he thought it did – Willa thought `Belle` was a ridiculous name for the cloak, likely named after an ex-girlfriend, though Samuel was not the type to do something as sentimental as that. In reality, she never understood why he called it `Belle`.

"Help me get Mr. Putnam to his feet," Samuel asked his wife.

They pulled William up from the floor and rested him inside Belle, with his head resting on Samuel's right shoulder. Once Samuel was certain the cloak was covering William's entire body, he again placed his hands near his chest. This time, instead of touching the tips of his fingers together, he clasped his hands together with his palms fully pressed against one another. The action he was about to perform needed significantly more energy than the previous act, so he needed a wider stream of energy flowing through his body. With his hands firmly clasped, he closed his eyes and lowered his arms into a circle, making sure he held William captive within his encircled arms, and he let his emotion fuel the energy flow. Within seconds, his eyes opened suddenly, and with a small puff of smoke, the two men and Belle were gone.

They immediately reappeared inside William's house with an equally small puff of smoke. Samuel unclenched his hands, making sure he still supported William. He placed the limp body over his right shoulder and carried him to his bed, where he lay William down, removed his boots, and covered him with the blanket from the bed. "Sweet dreams," Samuel whispered, mostly to amuse himself. He then stood, made sure Belle was completely covering himself, tightly clenched his hands and closed his eyes for focus. This time, it took a couple of extra seconds to build the energy flow he needed, as he was out of practice and no longer used to such extreme expulsions of power. When the energy reached the tipping point, his eyes snapped open and, with another puff of smoke, he was gone. He reappeared back in his house, where Willa was beginning the preparation of dinner. There was a patina of smoky dust emanating from Belle's surface due to two quick trips after so many years of inactivity and storage. Samuel lightly removed the remaining vestige from her exterior and carefully returned her to her dedicated space in the bedroom closet.

A few minutes later, Abigail returned home just in time for Mother's delicious tomato soup and homemade bread.

"Mother, I'm meeting a friend for lunch tomorrow. Would it be all right if I made us a couple of sandwiches before I leave?"
"Of course, dear. Who are you meeting?"

Abigail felt uncomfortable lying to her parents, but in this circumstance, it was the only prudent thing to do. "I'm meeting with

Christina. She still needs some help to get caught up with her schoolwork."

"That's very nice of you, Abigail. What a kind and thoughtful young woman you've become. Isn't that right, Samuel?"

He grumpingly sipped the soup from his spoon and uttered a barely perceptible grunt of agreement. Samuel was too busy thinking about how to keep his precious family safe and ensure the bloodline stayed intact. There was no time to think about lunches with friends.

Chapter 17

Saturday began with the hope of new beginnings for Abi. The birds were chirping so loudly and happily she was certain they must know it was a weekend. The air smelled fresh and clean and there was an ocean breeze providing relief from the heat of the day. In the morning, Abi helped her mother with the chores while Father went to work in the field. "There's always work to be done and there's no rest for the weary," Mother told her. Father left for the field without his hat, which Abi thought to be rather unusual. He never forgot his hat, but it was too nice a day to give the hat much thought.

The major chores were complete by ten thirty and the newly washed clothes were hanging on a line outside, drying in the breeze. "Is there anything else I can help you with?" Abigail asked her mother. "No, dear. You've been a big help. You should go enjoy yourself outside until you need to leave to meet Christina."

"Oh, right. Christina," she thought. Abi forgot the story she told her parents, but she was relieved her mother remembered, even though she felt a tinge of guilt for lying.

Abi took her mother's advice and went outside. She considered going to the ocean, but decided against it. The walk from the Sampson home to the water was only a few minutes, but Abi knew if she sat by the sea for any amount of time, she would want to let the breaking waves spray against her face. She did not want her clothes or hair to get wet before her lunch with Will, so she thought it better to stay home. Abi found a comfortable patch of grass not even a minute from their house. She laid down to enjoy the glow of the sun for a few minutes. At first, she sat face up, leaning back on her bent elbows, to let the sun's warmth bask onto her face. After a couple of minutes, she turned over and laid face down with the sun beaming on the back of her head.

"This is such a rejuvenating feeling," she thought. "Ha! Another 're' word to explain how much I love the sun!" She did not know she was not the only Sampson being rejuvenated by the sun today. Samuel lived in predictable routines and would never forget his hat for a day in the field.

A little after eleven o'clock, she stood and brushed herself off. She wanted to make sure there were no signs of grass on her clothing. That would be unladylike. She went inside, and with her mother's help, made two egg sandwiches for her and 'Christina'. She packed the sandwiches in a satchel, along with a couple of apples and some fresh berries Mother picked earlier. Mother gave her a blanket for the girls to sit on while they ate.

"Have a pleasant lunch, and say hello to Christina for me," her mother told her. And with that, Abi left in an excited frenzy to meet Will.

****

Saturday was Tobias Warnock's errand day. He was always busy during the week with village matters and Sunday was for church. So any personal business needed to be done on Saturdays. They were always the busiest of days for him. He made it a point to stop by every business in the village and spend at least a few minutes with the shopkeepers. He hadn't announced it yet, but he hoped to be selected by the Church as a freeman to join the colonial Council of Assistants, where he would have a say in who became the Governor of the Massachusetts Territory. Eventually, he would be eligible for consideration for the office, and upon winning the seat (he believed there was no way he could lose) he would have the influence needed to rid the colonies of all witches. Tobias was skilled at executing long-term plans based on even longer-term visions.

On this particular Saturday, he was making his normal rounds in the village center. He already stopped in to see Thomas Miller, proprietor of Miller's Apothecary. Most residents of Salem regularly visited Miller's, so Thomas was always a superb source for the local gossip. Today Tobias learned James Patton was taking medicine normally prescribed to prevent uncontrolled shaking. Often this was a sign of possession by the Devil. "We'll see if the medicine helps Mr. Patton," Tobias schemed. He planned to keep that information stored away in case it ever became useful to him.

Tobias' favorite store was Cooper and Cabinets, coincidentally owned by Albert Cooper. He made many types of furniture and containers for various uses, like buckets, barrels, desks, cabinets, and caskets. The latter was of particular interest to Tobias. While most people possessed a natural fear of anything related to death and dying, Tobias was more curious about it. He was not at all looking forward to dying, quite the contrary, he intended to live as long as possible. But the idea of a body being placed in a box underground waiting to rot away fascinated him. If he was going to spend his post-living life in a box, then he wanted to do it in a box made by Albert. He was possibly the most talented carpenter Tobias ever met.

****

Abi arrived for lunch a few minutes early. She found a place to sit, which was conspicuous enough for Will to approve, but still under the shade of a large sycamore tree so they would not get too hot. She laid the blanket down, took the food out of the bag and tried a few different sitting positions to determine which Will would like the most. "I can't believe I'm being so silly," she smiled to herself, but she couldn't help it. She wanted everything to be perfect when Will arrived.

A few minutes passed, and Abi was wondering when Will would show up. She peered out, looking in the direction leading toward his house, to see if she could see him coming. But there were only other people walking back and forth, doing the things people normally did on a Saturday.

After thirty more minutes, she was upset. It was a mix of anger and hurt. It was a feeling she had not felt before and she did not like it one bit. "Why would he not show up? I thought he liked me, but even if he didn't, he mustn't just not show up like this." She was having a distraught conversation inside her head, but her face could not hide her feelings.

Mr. Warnock left Cooper and Cabinets and was on his way to visit Milner's Milliner, to see if there was any new clothing or hats since last weekend. On his way, he passed by a large sycamore tree and noticed the uncomfortably unhappy expression on Abigail's face. He saw the food for two on the blanket and could clearly see she did not intend to be alone.

"Are you waiting for someone, young lady?"

He was most definitely *not* the person she wanted to speak with at that moment. She did not want him to perceive her as weak or fragile and attempt to get her to accuse someone, as he did with Christina. She felt it was safest to tell him an adult was coming to join her. It seemed safest to tell him the truth, at least a version of the truth.

"I'm waiting for Mr. Putnam. We are going to review some assignments and I am going to help him grade papers."

"Grade papers?" he asked incredulously. "This seems more like a romantic picnic lunch than some official school business." He paused for a painfully long time, waiting to see if Abigail would respond in any way to his fishing expedition. She did not. She simply stared back at him, waiting for his next comment. It was as if they were having a completely silent intellectual battle of wit and neither would allow the other to win.

"I see," he said finally, attempting to break the silence. He thought to himself, "There is another way to see if..." He was always on the lookout for personal details he could use in the future.

He continued, "Well, I'll be on my way then. Please pass on my regards to Mr. Putnam." Tobias then leaned in and fixed his stare on Abigail's face to make sure he did not miss even the slightest twitch of a muscle. "He *is* quite a man, is he not?" he asked Abigail.

Abigail's demeanor softened as she smiled and replied, "He most certainly is." Tobias leaned back with a satisfied grimace. He got the answer he was looking for. Abigail's face gave away her true feelings about Mr. Putnam. Tobias set the perfect trap, one Abigail could not resist, and she walked right into it. Tobias decided to save this bit of information for a time he might need it. He could not have realized that time would be just hours away.

"Good day, my dear," he said as he nodded his head and walked away, leaving Abigail still angry, curious, and most of all, worried about Will.

Chapter 18

It was almost one o'clock. Will was an hour late. Abi didn't know if she should be worried or angry, and, she admitted to herself, she felt both. She stood and started for his house to confront him. "Maybe he just lost track of time," she thought, trying to find some logical reason to forgive him. His house was a ten-minute walk from the village center. She left her blanket and food under the tree and headed off, assuming she would return with Will shortly for their belated lunch.

As she walked, she wondered whether she might run into him, scamping down the trail to meet her, hopping as he was putting his boots on along the way. Or maybe she would find him laying down on the ground. Perhaps he fell and hurt his ankle and could not get to her. Now she felt bad for being angry with him.

By the time she got to his house, she realized none of that would happen. She knocked at the door. There was no response. She knocked again. "Mr. Putnam, are you home? Will? Are you there?" Still no response. She wasn't sure what to do, and many thoughts flooded into her head. "Maybe he thought we were meeting at one o'clock and he's there now, wondering where I am. Or maybe he ran into a friend and didn't realize how late he was." In either case, she needed to get back to the sycamore tree as quickly as possible to meet him. She turned and ran as fast as she could.

She arrived back at the tree a few minutes later. The blanket and food were unmoved from when she left. He was not there and appeared never to have been there. Now she became worried.

She walked back to his house, this time taking a more circuitous route in case he traveled a different way. But when she arrived back at his door, there was still no sign of him. She knocked three times, paused, and then pounded her fist as hard as she could another three times, albeit at a slower tempo. "Will! Are you there?" She was now feeling a blend of anger, frustration, worry, and anguish. Even though it went against her better judgement, she entered his house to see if she could find any clues to his whereabouts.

She opened the door slowly and peered inside with the least amount of intrusion as possible. She was nervous someone might see her and wonder why a student was entering her teacher's home. But she was worried more about him than she was about being caught.

His house was a complete mess. It wasn't dirty, there were no clothes strewn out on the floor, but it was a mess, nevertheless. There were gizmos and gadgets and partially built contraptions all around. Nothing seemed complete – as if he had many ideas for starting things, but no plan to finish any of them.

"Will?" she begged. There was no response. She slowly and cautiously stepped into his house and tiptoed around, trying not to disturb any of the mess.

Around the corner of what seemed like a junk pile with school papers balancing on top, she saw the foot of his bed. She crept closer, uncertain what she was looking for. Then she saw him. He was sleeping? She was just pounding on the door. "How could he be asleep after the noise I made?" she wondered. "Will!" she vocally prodded. "Get up – you were supposed to meet me an hour and a half ago! Will!" She walked over to him and pulled the blanket down to his feet, hoping the sudden change in temperature would wake him. "He's still in his clothes from yesterday? What did he do last night?" Her anger was back, beating down the worry which was winning only a few moments earlier. "Will!" she demanded again while shaking him violently enough to jolt him from his sleep. But instead of waking, his arm fell limp to the floor. He was completely motionless. It was as if he were….

"Oh my God! Will! No!" She shook him hard now, still trying to wake him but also trying to verify if he was really dead. His body was completely limp – there was no response. "NO!" she screamed louder and with more emotion than she ever emitted before. She ran back to the front door and yelled as loud as she could. She could barely hold herself up between the door and its frame. "Help! Help me. He's dead!" She was hoping someone would hear her – anyone. She ran back to the village center as fast as she could. When she arrived, she was out of breath, but she frantically yelled again, "I need help! Mr. Putnam, he's dead! Please, help me!"

People looked out from the shops. Others who were walking through town stopped in their tracks and looked back at Abigail. Everyone ran to her aid immediately, asking what was happening, trying their best to help with what was quickly escalating into a major fracas. Tears were streaming down her face now that others were involved. Her emotion put itself on hold until she could find help, and now that she did, it was free to be released.

"It's Mr. Putnam," she relayed through loud sobbing. "We were going to review papers. He never came. I looked for him. He's dead in his house." She was virtually unintelligible and unconsolable. Once everyone comprehended what she was saying, the crowd, which was growing larger by the second, started off in a mad rush toward Mr. Putnam's house. Tobias heard the commotion and joined near the back of the group. He scurried behind them as they made their way down the path to Mr. Putnam's abode. When they arrived, Tobias was out of breath, but he forced himself to refrain from heavy breathing so he could hear every word, every sound, that was about to be made. He didn't want to miss any detail, no matter how small.

The crowd collectively gasped when they entered Will's house and saw his limp body, fully clothed, almost dangling off the bed because Abi unknowingly shook him so hard. Everyone gathered around him. The doctor arrived after being informed of the situation by others who first heard Abigail's pleas for help. He hurried to the bedside, the gathered crowd respectfully making way for him. He knelt down next to the bed and put his fingers on Will's neck, searching for any signs of life. The doctor sighed deeply, stood and, while still looking down, shook his head slowly back and forth. "He's gone. May God have mercy on his soul." Everyone removed their hats to show their respect. Many gasped, and some started crying.

Abigail backed herself into a corner and fell to the floor, sobbing uncontrollably. It seemed as if her life ended. A deep void of nothingness overtook her. She always prided herself on her ability to control her emotions, becoming neither overly happy nor overly sad over any situation. But this was different. Her emotions were like a sudden severe flash flood overtaking its dam. There was nothing to prevent the rushing waters from overflowing and she could only hope the dam would hold and eventually contain the waters until the flood subsided.

Tobias, who was adept at pretending to be something he was not, portrayed himself to be distraught. But inside, he was relishing his good luck. "How unfortunate for him," he mused, "but how fortuitous for me." With a deeply somber, albeit insincere, tone, Tobias offered, "I'll inform the Minister and Albert Cooper we'll need to put together a funeral today."

As he left William's house, Tobias sensed something unusual. It wasn't a person or a thing. Rather, it was a feeling he hadn't felt for a long time. It was something from his family's past, a feeling he recalled from his childhood. He remembered the stories and the feelings. His grandmother spoke of it often. But this feeling now –

even though it was but a distant memory to him, he knew what it was. "How could it be?" Nobody outside of Tobias' bloodline was even capable. Nobody except one person. "Rennik," he thought. "For him to do this, he must be desperate."

Chapter 19

On his way home, Tobias stopped by Cooper's to make sure a casket was available and then went to the church to notify the Minister and other staff there would be another funeral today. The Minister called upon two young men from the church to go around town and announce William Putnam's death and funeral. "Tell them the funeral will begin at seven this evening and they mustn't be late," he told them. But Tobias interjected.

He was formulating a plan and needed as many people from the town to attend the funeral as possible. "My dear pastor, why so late? It will be dark out by then and nobody will want to attend a funeral in the dark. Do we not owe it to Mr. Putnam to ensure a large crowd for his final farewell?"

"Mr. Warnock, it is simply a matter of timing. We must have the funeral today to avoid any decomposition of the body. But we can't have it too early as there is simply not enough time to dig a grave. It's already two thirty and by the time the grave digger arrives, we'll be lucky to have it ready by seven o'clock. I would love to have the ceremony in the daylight, but I just don't see how it's possible."

"Please allow me to handle this detail, Pastor. I'm sure you have other, more important, matters needing your attention. My men will dig the grave straight away. I can't imagine it will take them any more than two hours – they are diligent workers and fast diggers. We'll begin the funeral at four thirty." And with that declaration, he nodded to the two boys and rushed them out to announce the time to the village.

A palpable sense of grief and astonishment fell over the town as word got out of William Putnam's sudden death. People stood silently in front of their houses as they heard the news, sharing in the communal disbelief. They hadn't yet recovered from the loss of innocent little Millie Porter just three days prior. Mr. Putnam was much beloved and respected throughout the town and his loss would leave a noticeable tear in the fabric of Salem.

He was a young, strong, and handsome man. Nobody could understand how or why he died. Was it a murder, was it suicide, or was it of natural cause? Or, even worse, was it because of a witch? There were many theories and rumors.

Thomas Harding proctored perhaps the most outrageous rumor. He was a farmer and a butcher, and a simple man who would find even the most ludicrous ideas and conspiracies convincing. His theory involved a cow, a goat, and a scorned lover. It made no sense to anyone who heard it, and even Thomas admitted the plot made little sense. But he stood by it – he said he heard it from someone who was there when William died.

Abigail was still stunned and ridden with guilt by Will's sudden death. She didn't know what time he died, but maybe if she hadn't waited an hour to look for him, she might have found him alive and been able to help. Between her spells of intense crying, she felt pangs of anger at herself for not going earlier. But all that mattered now was that he was gone. She was certain she would never enjoy life again.

Abigail made her way to the shore, walking in what seemed like a drunken stupor, swaying back and forth and often losing her balance. She sat near the waves, close enough for the mist to spray onto her face. The salty ocean water blended perfectly with her salty tears until one became the other. She thought if her tears could become one with the ocean, perhaps she should as well. Even the warmth of the sun's rays beating down on her was not enough to make her feel any better. She put her face into her hands and cried like she never had before, with an intensity that made her body jolt up and down. Her heart was beyond broken, it was completely shattered.

Within about thirty minutes, the news of William's death reached the Sampson house. Samuel was just coming in from the field and ran into one of the church messengers. After hearing the news, he stood motionless and pondered what it meant, which the messenger took as shock and sorrow. But in reality, Samuel was worried. He walked inside his house with a look of stunned disbelief. Willa turned to say hello, not yet knowing the news. She looked at Samuel's face and knew in an instant something terrible happened.

"What is it Samuel?"

He spoke slowly in a whispered tone, as if someone punched him in the gut and knocked the air out of him. "News came from the church. They found William Putnam in his home today – dead. His funeral is in about an hour."

Willa walked to the table and sat down in a chair, looking into the distance the entire time. "My God. What are you going to do?"

"There's nothing I can do." Samuel's gaunt face seemed to recess even further into his skull.

With tears welling in her eyes, Willa shook her head and pleaded, "Samuel, no. We can't leave him like this. You must wake him before it's too late."

"I can't. His memory is not completely cleared yet. He still needs two more days. If we wake him now, he'll remember almost everything and accuse you. I won't be able to protect you."

"Then *I'll* bring him out of his stasis," Willa declared.

"You know as well as I that only the initiator can end the stasis. And I won't jeopardize you and Abigail." He paused and then became resolute. "We need to educate her as soon as possible and protect the bloodline." He paused for another moment and then looked at the ceiling with a pained look on his face. "This situation has become untenable."

"So, what's your plan? Yesterday you told me you don't kill anymore."

"That's right – I don't, and I didn't kill him. But as far as anyone knows, he's already dead."

"I don't like this, Samuel. I don't like it one bit." She sighed and looked down. "But I see your point – we really have no other options. We must be protect Abigail at all costs, no matter how distasteful." She shook her head and lowered her face into the palms of her hands. Samuel put his hands on her shoulders to comfort her. Nobody liked with the situation in which they found themselves. But what could they do? William Putnam would be an innocent casualty of a war he believed was not possible.

"Who discovered his body?" Willa asked.

"I don't know. The church messenger didn't say." His tone deepened to a level of depression Willa had only heard from him twice before. "Come, let's find Abigail and get ready for the funeral."

Willa paused. "This is going to hit Abigail very hard. I think she was quite fond of Mr. Putnam."

That night, neither Samuel nor Willa could sleep. William's most unfortunate situation weighed heavily upon them both. Willa kept balancing the idea of letting an innocent man die in order to protect her daughter. The thought brought a feeling of disgust to her and she felt herself a failure as a person. But as much as she hated the idea of allowing William to perish, she knew Samuel was right to sacrifice him to save Abigail. There was nothing more to think about, but this was no comfort.

Samuel slept on his side that night, facing away from Willa. He did not want her seeing him shed tears for only the seventh time in his adult life.

Chapter 20

Everyone from the village who was able arrived at the church between four o'clock and four thirty. William Putnam did not have any family within a day's carriage ride, so none of his family even heard the news yet. All of Salem would sit in as his family today. He was much beloved by everyone, well, most everyone. It was common knowledge that Tobias Warnock and William Putnam engaged in heated disagreements over just about any topic you could think of. But today, everyone would remember him fondly.

At the stroke of four thirty, the minister walked down the main aisle of the church and ascended to the pulpit. All the pews were full, and many parishioners stood in the back of the church. In the middle of the pews sat the Sampsons. Samuel was stoic, as was normal. But Willa was deep in grief and Abigail, sitting to her left, was even deeper. All of Mr. Putnam's students were in attendance with their families. And all were quite emotional, especially James Boylan, who recently formed a connection with Mr. Putnam. A connection that now was a moot point. James pondered how Mr. Putnam's passing would affect his newfound interest in learning. "Maybe I am not meant for that life," he wondered.

Standing in the back of the church was Thomas Miller from the Apothecary. He was standing next to Tobias, who walked in just as the minister started the service. "It's an awful shame," Thomas whispered to Tobias while shaking his head. "And who is going to teach the children now?"

Tobias whispered back, "The council will need to appoint someone. We'll meet Monday morning to begin the search. In the meantime, we'll see if we can find a mother to fill in." Thomas nodded his acceptance of the response.

As the minister continued the service, Willa leaned over to Samuel. They were whispering intently to each other. Others at the service noticed their discussion, including Tobias standing at the back of the room. He leaned in toward Thomas.

"Can you believe those two? The Sampsons? How disrespectful to chit chat during a funeral." Thomas found the irony obvious – Tobias was doing exactly the same thing. Still, Tobias was an important man in Salem, and Thomas wanted to remain on good terms with him.

"You're right, it's dreadful. They should show some respect."

Tobias decided it was the right time, and he was with the right person, to execute a plan he was working on since the discovery of William's body.

"You know, Willa Sampson spent a lot of time helping William at the school. She was there multiple times each week."

"You don't say?" Thomas whispered back.

"Yes, in fact some people say there was something between the two of them."

"I am not surprised. Samuel doesn't seem to be the most gregarious person, and Willa certainly seems to be more outgoing," Thomas replied with more than a hint of sarcasm toward Samuel. Still, he actually found the idea surprising. An illicit affair with a younger man did not seem like the Willa Sampson he knew.

"Oh yes, and I happen to know her daughter Abigail also had feelings for William. In fact, they were supposed to meet for a romantic picnic lunch today. It was Abigail who found his body because he never showed for the lunch."

This made Thomas think. Could it be true both Willa and Abigail, a mother and daughter, had feelings for the same man? "And exactly how do you know Abigail felt this way for him?"

"She all but told me. I came upon her while I was in town today and saw her sitting alone. She freely admitted her feelings for him."

This news shocked Thomas. "And why are you telling me this here, now, at the man's funeral?"

Tobias leaned in even closer. He spoke slow and soft to make his point very clear. "Don't you find it odd a girl he was supposed to meet mysteriously found the man dead, when that girl's mother also had feelings for him? It all seems a bit... coincidental, don't you think?"

Tobias chose his words carefully. All of Salem knew Thomas believed there were no coincidences in life. If anyone were to find the facts of this situation pointing to a person with motive, it would be Thomas Miller.

Thomas thought for a long time and he leaned close to Tobias. "Are you accusing Willa?"

"I cannot do that. As the chief judge for the trials, it would be inappropriate. All I know are the truths I've shared with you. You can determine your own conclusions."

Thomas paid no attention to the rest of the service. Instead, he was trying to consider if Willa really could be a witch. She was so pleasant and helpful, and always had a cheerful disposition with everyone she met. That was definitely not how Thomas thought a witch would act. "On the other hand," he countered to himself, "Isn't that the perfect camouflage?" If she really were a witch, she selected the perfect costume to hide it. "All right," he thought, "so I've determined she *might* be a witch. At least I can't rule it out." But he needed to decide if it was plausible she had feelings for William and was jealous of her own daughter. Jealous enough to commit murder.

The funeral moved to the cemetery. Tobias' men dug a fine hole and did it in record time. While a typical grave is about six feet deep, they didn't have time to dig that far down, so William's grave was only about four feet deep. It was certainly deep enough to bury the casket, but just barely. What the two men lacked in depth, they more than made up for in attention to detail. The straight edges of the hole, along with the clean, tight corners, even impressed Tobias.

Thomas was still standing at the back of the crowd, now keenly watching the Sampsons, who were still talking with each other during the burial. In fact, their conversation, while nearly silent, appeared to be quite intense. Almost as if they were arguing. "It's almost as if Samuel is accusing her," Thomas imagined.

Abigail spent the entire service crying. She was so deep in her grief she didn't notice her parents' discussion. Her eyes were completely bloodshot and the areas directly below her eyes were red and swollen. Dried tear streaks stained her cheeks with a flaky whiteness from the salt they left behind. Word got out she was the one who discovered Will's body. She knew she would have to answer for why she was at his house, why Christina wasn't with her as her parents expected, and why she planned to meet with him in the first place. She did not have a good explanation for any of this. Any answer would only make her look guilty. She would need to think of the proper response for these questions – but not today.

This was a time for saying goodbye to a great, inspiring, passionate man. Tomorrow would be her day to answer the questions.

Chapter 21

The church service on Sunday morning was better attended than normal. It seemed many in the village were feeling rather distant from God, mainly because of the recent deaths of Millie Porter and William Putnam. The Minister was pleased to see so many faces staring back at him, especially because his sermon was regarding the popular story of Samson and Delilah, and using that allegory to teach the congregation how to spot the difference between good and evil in their everyday lives. "In these sad and uncertain times, the story of how evil can lure and entrap the good is even more important," the Minister said at the start of his sermon.

When the service concluded, the Minister announced he would allow the shops to open for the afternoon. Typically, Sundays were for God and prayer, but the village needed this Sunday for family and healing. The Minister encouraged all to have formal family dinners that night, and he realized many would need to purchase goods to make that happen.

Most went into town to get supplies for their supper, while others met in private at the town council's office. Tobias called an emergency private meeting of select individuals, including Thomas Miller. These meetings were unusual, but not rare. Nobody would question seeing a few people enter the council's office, even though most of these meetings ended with someone walking out in anger. Typically, that was William Putnam's role.

The Sampsons were home preparing for their dinner. They spoke very little since returning from the funeral last evening. Everyone was still coming to terms with what happened, and each of the three Sampsons was dealing with private feelings of guilt for their role in what took place.

Samuel was in his chair, staring at his candle, deep in thought. He was considering what he might have done differently, but realized there was not much that could have been different. "If only William had not overheard our discussion," he thought. "Then none of this would have happened." But Samuel was wise enough to realize nothing important happened without a reason for it to occur. He knew William overhearing them was ultimately part of a larger plan. But he could not determine what that plan might be.

Willa was also feeling guilty for what happened to William. "If only I had been quieter," she bemoaned. She knew she needed to keep her voice low when speaking of anything involving the Order. She was angry at herself for forgetting this one time, resulting in this most horrible tragedy for William.

Even though she was the only Sampson not directly responsible for William's apparent death, Abigail was feeling the most guilt. She couldn't help thinking if she did not wait so long to look for Will, she might have been able to help him. It was the unknown that was so difficult for her to deal with, the 'how comes' and the 'what ifs'. She believed in reason, and reason requires answers. But these questions have no answers, which made it more difficult for Abigail.

Indeed, all three Sampsons were carrying the weight of their own guilt on their shoulders. While guilt was nothing new for the Sampson family, the gravity of this situation certainly was. That made it all the more terrifying when, almost out of nowhere, they heard the most bone-chilling sound getting closer and closer.

Witch!...

Witch!...

Samuel stood immediately, his face displaying grave concern. This was his worst nightmare. But who were they coming for? Were they even coming to the Sampson house? Did they somehow find out about the stasis Samuel placed William in? Samuel and Willa prepared a protocol for this, but for it to work, many unrelated actions needed to synchronize on their own. Chances were, they would not.

Abigail fell out of her chair with fear as the chanting became louder and louder. She had flashbacks to the day Tobias accused Millie and could not take any more emotional situations – not now. Not for a long time. Then again, maybe they were coming to accuse her. The thought frightened her to her bones, but also seemed like a good way out. At least all her misery would be over. Though, she realized, it would be just the beginning for her parents. She could not imagine what the loss of a third child would do to them.

Willa was thinking exactly the same thing. What would happen if they accused Abigail? She feared this ever since last night when she learned Abigail was the one who found William's body. It would be just like Tobias to accuse another innocent young girl. But Willa could not comprehend losing Abigail. She was scheming how to take the blame if Tobias accused Abigail. Without their realizing it, the situation pitted the three Sampsons in a mental standoff against, and in defense of, each other.

Samuel looked out the window to see where the mob was going. His heart sank as they walked right to his front door, pitchforks in hand, voices calling out.

Tobias raised his right hand to the crowd to quiet them. "Willa Sampson," he said in a slow, deep, menacing tone. "You stand accused of performing the Devil's bidding through the use of witchcraft to commit the murder of William Putnam. You can admit your sins and face your judgement now, clearing your name in the eyes of God, or you can claim your innocence and perform the Test of Witchcraft to determine your fate. How say you?"

Samuel grabbed Willa with both hands and clasped her arms tightly. He pulled her face close to his own and looked deeply into her eyes. "Willa, you know what you must do. It's the only way out."

Abigail broke down in tears for maybe the hundredth time in the last two days. She couldn't believe what was happening. A third person now potentially facing death, each closer to her than the last. "It must be me," she thought. "I must be bad luck." But more than anything else, she was desperately trying to comprehend what was happening with her beloved mother.

Willa, still in Samuel's clutches, responded, "I know, dear. It will be all right. I know the plan."

Samuel looked into her eyes for a moment, then kissed her deeply. Abigail never saw her parents kiss so passionately. She knew this meant something terrible was about to happen.

Samuel let Willa out of his grasp. She looked at him with a confident, but weary, smile. She rubbed her hands on her skirt to pat out any creases, turned around, and headed for the door. Samuel stood motionless, watching Willa gracefully walk to an almost certain death. Abigail's crying stopped, momentarily, out of disbelief – both because of the accusation against her mother and for how calmly she was handling it. In fact, Willa was anything but calm – she knew the odds were against her, but she needed to protect her family.

Willa opened the front door of her house as if a neighbor stopped by for a friendly visit. "Why, hello Tobias. How nice to see you. Jonathan, good to see you. Henry, thank you for coming by." She greeted each person in the mob. She knew this would make no difference to the outcome, but perhaps it would add a tad bit of guilt to each person's decision about her innocence.

"Willa Sampson," Tobias continued, "You stand accused. What say you?"

"Oh Tobias, of course I'm innocent," Willa responded, as if she thought Tobias was joking. The mob normally would have jeered and booed at a claim of innocence, but Willa's gentle smile and disarming greetings dismissed the normal bloodlust out of the mob.

"Very well," Tobias responded. "We will see you at the shore this evening at six o'clock for the Test of Witchcraft."

Willa interrupted, "Actually Tobias, I believe I have the option of choosing my test, do I not? I choose the test of fire."

There was audible, yet indistinct, mumbling throughout the crowd. The request shocked each person. Samuel stood behind Willa, still motionless and proud of how his wife was executing their plan. Abigail gasped loudly, with more disbelief than she thought possible. "Mother, no!" Abigail pleaded. After everything she already endured, the thought of seeing her mother burn was more than she could bear. Samuel looked at Abigail and nodded slowly, as if to say, "Leave her be. She knows what she is doing."

Tobias pondered Willa's request for a few moments. The accused certainly had the right to choose their test, but nobody ever *chose* fire. On the one hand, he knew exactly what she was trying to do. A true witch can create a torrent to escape fire. This tacitly proved to Tobias she was indeed what he suspected. On the other hand, the villagers loved a good stake burning, and he thought this would make him even more popular. Regardless, he knew the torrent would not be possible, and even if it happened, it would reveal Rennik to Tobias once and for all.

The Witches torrent is a mystical event that only powerful witches and warlocks can initiate, and only when fire is involved. The torrent is, in actuality, a tunnel connecting the dimension of the living with that of the deceased. When the tunnel is open, the family and close friends of the witch descend through the torrent and take the soul of the witch back with them. It's a way to save a witch from burning and rescue her soul to the other side. For witches who are lucky enough to pass through a torrent, it is one of the most blissful episodes of their life, and of their death. It saves them from agony and delivers them to peace.

But torrents take a significant amount of energy to create. Of the two categories of Witches of the Order (the Wicken and the Wicked – pronounced wik't), only the Wicked have the power to create a torrent. While the Wicken can see a torrent while it is active, non-witches (otherwise known as the "Unbloods") cannot see a torrent at all. It exists in a dimension to which they are completely oblivious.

Tobias was not worried about Willa's request for a burning. He would make sure they tied her hands to her side, just as he did with Millie, so Willa could not generate the energy needed to create the torrent herself.

That left Rennik. If he were foolish enough to create the torrent, it would expose him while it was active, and Tobias could identify him. This was a no-lose situation, Tobias determined.

"Very well, Willa. We will prepare the stake for you this evening at six o'clock. My men will bring you with us for now."

Tobias' two men walked to the doorway of the Sampson's home and each grabbed one of Willa's arms. She turned back and gave a comforting smile to Abigail and then looked at Samuel with a slightly less confident gaze. Samuel nodded back to Willa, hoping their plan would work, but not at all confident it would.

Chapter 22

Abigail spent the entire afternoon sobbing, even though her body was no longer capable of generating tears. Her eyes swelled, almost to the point of being shut, and the reddening of her eyelids equaled the red in her bloodshot eyes. She had not eaten all day and was weak, but not hungry. Samuel prepared some soup for her and urged her to eat because he feared she would faint at the ceremony. That would only add to the speculation about Willa and would force people to look deeper at Abigail, potentially accusing her as well. No matter what else happened, Samuel could not allow Abigail to be accused, or even suspected.

All afternoon, Samuel was deep in thought about Abigail's future. He thought she still was not ready, but circumstances forced him to rethink his schedule. As Abigail was sipping her hot soup, Samuel sat at the table next to her.

"I know we need to leave in a few minutes. We don't have time to get into it now, but I've decided when we return this evening, no matter how we are feeling about your mother, we need to have a discussion about your future. There are many things I need to explain to you. I'll need you to prepare yourself to open your mind and take in a lot of information you may not understand. Can you do this for me?"

Abigail nodded, but was completely confused. Her father never spoke with her in such a serious tone, but she understood these were serious times. Even though she did not know what her father was talking about specifically, she innately understood he was going through a lot of pain and difficult emotions, as was she, and the best thing Abigail could do for her father was to be there for him and help in any way she could. "Of course, Father. Anything you want."

"Good... good." Samuel placed his left hand on the table and stood. "I need to explain my special book and my special candle to you, and show you their meaning to me, to each other, and to you. It will be a lot to take in, but I think you're ready." He said this even though he was anything but certain she was. As he was talking, Samuel looked over at his candle, the one Abigail watched him stare at for hours on end. He also motioned to a mysterious old book conspicuously wedged into the back of one of their bookshelves. Abigail tried to read it once. It was in Latin. She could read and understand Latin, she learned the language in church and Mr. Putnam taught it, but this book used Latin words she did not understand, nor could she read. And when Samuel caught her looking through the pages years earlier, he became irate with her – one of the few times he became angry and yelled at his daughter. She never got near the book again. It intrigued her that finally her father wanted to share the mysterious book.

After the soup was gone, they both quietly washed their hands and changed their clothes. One doesn't know what is appropriate apparel when attending the burning of a close family member. Without discussion, they put on different sets of Sunday clothes, not very different from the clothes they had on for church that morning. At about five forty, they silently left the house and headed for the town square, holding hands. Neither spoke a word on their way.

Chapter 23

Tobias made sure he was well prepared. He did not want any surprises. He knew tonight could harken the end of his hunt for Rennik. If not, at least he was closing in. His men planted the stake with enough wood and kindling surrounding it to produce a hearty fire. There was a pathway cleared in the pile, so Willa could walk to her position on the stake.

At five fifty, Tobias took his place at the top of a wooden scaffolding which was built specifically as a viewing area for the witch burnings. Rather than it being a point of good viewing for the people on the scaffold, it was a way for the crowd to have a good view of the town leaders who stood upon it, beaming with pride at their ability to keep Salem free from evil.

A few minutes before six, the two men brought Willa out from the town office where she was being held. She was not tied up yet and looked remarkably serene for someone who was about to endure excruciating pain. The men escorted her through the pathway in the woodpile to the base of the stake. There was a small step, about twelve inches in length, upon which Willa would stand. She obediently proceeded onto the step, turned around to face the gathering crowd, and put her hands together behind her back, ready to be bound for her test.

Tobias motioned for the men to come to him. They walked to the scaffold where he stood, careful not to step onto it. Tobias leaned down and whispered something to both men. They nodded in agreement and went back to attend to Willa, who was still standing with her hands waiting behind her back. "Nice try, Willa," Tobias snickered to himself.

The men grasped the three thick ropes Tobias provided for the occasion and secured Willa to the stake. It was at this moment Samuel and Abigail appeared. Willa noticed them and immediately saddened. She did not want them to see her undergo this metamorphosis.

The men first wrapped a rope around Willa's waist three times. Then they brought the rope over her shoulders and down, through her legs and back again. One man picked up a second rope just as thick, but shorter than the others. He tied the rope around the bottom of Willa's legs three times, making sure her feet could not stray even a little from the stake. Finally, each man grabbed one of Willa's hands, still behind her back, and pulled them to her side. She tried to force her hands back behind herself, but she didn't have the strength to force them to a position other than what the two men intended. They wrapped each hand firmly with the third rope, three times, and secured to the side of her body. They were as far apart from each other as they could be under the circumstance. Willa could not even wiggle her fingers. As soon as they trussed her body, the two men reorganized the wood, removing the pathway they used to bring Willa in. Now, the wood and kindling encircled her completely.

Upon seeing her hands so far apart, Samuel sighed and thought, "No…" being very careful not to make any facial expression whatsoever. Both Samuel and Willa knew things did not go how they hoped and planned. There was nothing now they could do without jeopardizing Abigail – they took a gamble and lost. As a result, Willa would burn.

The townspeople fully gathered – it was now six o'clock. Tobias raised both hands to quiet the murmurs of the unusually somber audience.

"Wilhelmina Delilah Sampson. You stand accused of being a witch. You have declared your innocence and God, through the fine people of Salem, will judge you to determine the truth. We have tied three ropes around your body three times. The 'three threes' are symbolic of the Holy Trinity – the Father, the Son and the Holy Ghost. We offer this as protection for you during your trial. Willa, may God have mercy on your soul."

Tobias forced a frown, which was hard for him to accomplish, and nodded to his two men, each of whom was holding a flaming torch. They stood on opposite sides of Willa, and as if the routine was practiced, they lowered their torches simultaneously onto the woodpile and the flames immediately ignited the kindling.

Abigail could not bear to watch her mother burn. She was still grieving for her friend Millie and losing William just yesterday was still raw – she didn't even start grieving properly for him yet. This was more than she could endure. She looked to God for some semblance of solace. Abigail clasped her hands together tightly in prayer, closed her eyes, and bowed her head. She prayed intensely for her mother's soul and hoped she would pass quickly so as not to endure too much pain. Her emotions overwhelmed her, and she began crying again.

Samuel stood as stoically as he could with his arm around Abigail's shoulders. He was watching the love of his life burn. He knew he had the power to prevent it, but in order to protect his daughter, he could not use that power. This was harder for him than even the loss of his first two children. But to preserve the life of his third, he must let it play out, as heartbreaking as it was for him. For the first time he could recall, he questioned all of his life choices that brought his family to this tragic moment.

Across the crowd, Joseph Porter was standing with his wife, Elizabeth. Both watched in horror and disgust as the flames engulfed their friend.

Willa's feet were beyond hot. They were literally on fire, and when she looked down, she could see her skin bubble and melt off her legs. As painful as that was, the fact she could not move her arms or legs and the unconscious urge to do so made her suffering even worse. She could not stand the pain, or seeing what was happening to her body, so she instinctually looked straight up, her neck fully extended as if her mouth and throat created a straight line directly to her stomach. It was then she saw it.

In the sky, maybe thirty or forty feet directly above her, she saw what looked like a small, reddish, purplish cloud form. It became darker and started flashing, as if mini bolts of lightning were shooting around inside of it. "Samuel, no. Think of Abigail – remember our plan," Willa thought, hoping beyond hope Samuel could hear her thoughts.

The cloud was mesmerizingly beautiful. Willa could not avert her gaze, and she didn't want to. As the cloud became more distinct above her head, the color changed to a deep blue. It was a beautiful shade of blue, somewhere between azure and cobalt. The torrent was the most beautiful sight Willa ever saw. It brought a sense of tranquility to her – she no longer felt the heat of the fire, even though the flames were ravaging her torso.

The cloud widened, and the center became lighter. The deep blue was still highlighting the outer edges of the cloud, but the middle now was a bright white, nearly as bright as the sun but without the blinding glare. Instead, it felt.... serene.

Out from the center appeared a face. At first it was indistinct. Willa could not make out who it was. But within a few seconds, the face came into clear view. It was Willa's beloved mother, dawning a wide smile. Seeing her mother's face doused Willa with feelings of love and belonging. She saw other figures come into focus. They were long-lost friends and other close relatives. Willa smiled and cried tears of happiness. The unbloods, who could not see the torrent, all wondered if she went mad from the flames, the devil, or both. But on the contrary, the torrent saved Willa. Her family and friends all reached out their arms, down to Willa's burning body, now badly charred and flittering away in the breeze like so many burning embers. Though her physical body could not reach up, the arms of her disembodied presence did, and when they connected with the arms reaching down for her, the torrent liberated Willa's soul from her physical presence. The torrent pulled Willa back into its cloud, along with and all the others in its tunnel. Willa was now at peace. She turned back to the earth and saw her body crumble into ashes, then took one last look at Samuel and Abigail as the cloud fully ensconced her and she disappeared.

Tobias noticed the cloud forming and immediately knew what it was. "How could he be so careless?" he wondered. He ignored the cloud and panned the crowd of over two hundred people trying to identify its creator.

Samuel saw the cloud too. "A torrent…. But how?" he thought. "And by whose command?" He looked around the crowd to see if anyone else created it. He also noticed Tobias and Joseph looking around, trying to find the source. That's when Samuel looked down at his side and noticed Abigail crying desperately, her hands tightly clasped together.

"It can't be!" His mouth was wide open in a combination of awe and disbelief. Samuel could not comprehend Abigail, who was not only untrained but also completely unaware, was powerful enough to create a torrent on her own. He never saw anything like it. He stared at her for a long time with a mix of pride and fear – too long, in fact. Both Joseph and Tobias saw him staring at Abigail and they both immediately knew she was the source of the torrent. All three men were in complete shock at what they saw. Samuel snapped out of his trance and noticed Tobias staring at him with a wry smile, like a cat who just found a hidden stash of fish. It was a smile Samuel recognized - he had seen that smile before. Luckily, none of the others in the crowd could see what the three men saw. Surely, it would cause a riot of accusations. Abigail was safe for the moment from the crowd, but not from Tobias. Samuel needed to act.

He whisked Abigail away as quickly as he could. The other villagers assumed it was out of immense grief, which would have been unlike Samuel, but certainly understandable given the circumstances. Abigail did not know what was happening – she never saw her father so panicked. She wondered if the emotion of seeing his wife burn alive was too much for him. It certainly was too much for her.

When they arrived at their house, Samuel slammed the door behind them. He demanded Abigail sit for a moment. Then Samuel placed his three middle fingers from each hand to the temples on the respective sides of his head. He closed his eyes and began thinking a message.

"Joseph, please come over right away. It's urgent. You saw what happened. Abigail is in grave danger now. Junius is in Salem and I must confront him. I need you to stay with Abigail and protect her."

At that same moment, across the village, Joseph Porter stopped mid-step, placed his fingers on his temples and closed his eyes.

"I understand, Rennik. I'll be right there."

Chapter 24

Samuel paced around the house, sweating more than usual, trying to determine his next move. He needed to think quickly, but he needed to be careful – two concepts which rarely work in unison. The plans he and Willa put in place were no longer relevant. The contingencies they thought covered all possible inevitabilities were now moot. They never imagined a scenario where Abigail's powers would be on display for all to see, especially with her not even knowing she possessed them. Joseph would be there in a matter of minutes. What could Samuel explain to Abigail in the next few minutes, and how would she react in her current state of mind?

Abigail was still in shock and not able to comprehend much of the situation. She was aware her father felt panic about something, but she was too emotionally spent from the events of the past few days to process much. She was looking forward to the end of the day. An end that would allow her time to be alone with her thoughts and to think about her mother and to mourn privately. But the situation would not allow for that.

Suddenly there was someone at the door, knocking with three rapid raps. "Samuel, it's me, Joseph." Samuel swooped to the door and opened it. "Come in, quickly." Joseph entered and Samuel shut the door immediately behind him, making sure he secured the lock.

"Samuel, how did she do it? I thought you haven't taught her yet."

"There's not time for that now, Joseph. Junius is here. I must confront him – now. I need you to stay with Abigail. Protect her at any cost. I will protect the house once I leave, but there's no way to know if Junius might send others while I'm gone. Do you understand?"

Joseph was stunned and looked away. "Junius... is here? But who?"

"It's Tobias. I didn't know for sure until tonight. But now I know it's him. He was the only other one who saw the torrent and realized she created it. And..." He paused as the memories flooded back. "I'll never forget that smile."

Joseph looked back at Samuel and said defiantly, "That bastard killed my daughter. Yes, of course. I will protect Abigail with my life, Samuel. You go. Do what you must."

"Good. Thank you, Joseph. I know you understand what's at stake. There's one other thing. I'm sorry to ask this of you, but there is no time to waste. I know now Willa was right – we should have educated Abigail long ago, but I would not allow it. Her education must begin tonight. Can you start her teachings while I'm gone?"

Joseph did not know how to respond. Of course, he would do whatever Samuel asked, especially to protect the bloodline. But he never educated anyone before – especially not a pure blood. He did not think he was up to the task. But these were desperate times, and Samuel urgently needed him.

"I'll do my best, Samuel."

Samuel put his hands on Joseph's shoulders and smiled as best he could, considering the stress he was under. He exhaled. "I know you will. Thank you, Joseph." Samuel went to Abigail, still sitting in her chair staring off into the distance, even though there was no distance to stare into.

"I must leave you for a little while. Mr. Porter will stay here with you and he will explain many things to you. I need you to listen to him very carefully." Samuel said those last two words slowly for emphasis. "Get something to eat so you have the strength to understand his words. Your life is going to change tonight in ways you cannot imagine."

Then Samuel did something he never did before. He put his open palms onto Abigail's cheeks, held her face tenderly, and put his eyes close to hers. "Abi, I love you very much. Always remember that." Then Samuel gently kissed Abigail's forehead. He stood, looked back at Joseph and nodded, and then exited the house, leaving Abigail comforted, but bewildered.

Once hidden safely in the trees, Samuel stopped and turned back toward the house. He firmly clasped his hands together, closed his eyes and lowered his arms so they formed a circle with his body. He thought about Junius. Samuel felt raw anger and hatred rising from his toes. By the time it reached his chest, his energy became great, and it was flowing through his arms and around through his body at immense speed. Suddenly, his eyes snapped open and a beam of light shot forth from his hands and raced toward his house. The power of the bolt jolted Samuel back a step or two, but quickly he could regain his balance and focus the beam. Once the beam hit the house, it expanded out in all directions, completely enveloping the structure in an orange haze. The exterior glowed momentarily and then stopped, with just an afterglow of burning dust particles falling to the ground around the house, like the first light dusting of snow in late autumn. He unclasped his hands and put them down by his sides, satisfied. "That should protect them," he said as he turned and started running toward Tobias' home.

****

Joseph did not know how long Samuel would be away. And he was unsure of how to begin Abigail's education. "Are you hungry?" he asked, mostly to stall for time.

113

"Yes, I am," she replied. "I'll fix myself something to eat. Would you like something too?" she asked Mr. Porter.

"No, thank you," he said, pleased he would have a few moments to gather his thoughts. Abigail stood and went to the kitchen. She grabbed some bread and the butter along with a butter knife. She sat at the table and spread the butter on a piece of bread, expecting Mr. Porter to explain something about how good a woman her mother was and how missed she will be. And while it was true she was about to learn new things about both of her parents, there was no preparing her for what she was about to discover.

Mr. Porter stopped pacing and drew in a long, deep breath. He slowly exhaled all his air, as if he were about to tell someone terrible news.

Chapter 25

Samuel ran for about ten minutes before he arrived at Tobias' house. He was careful to stay within the trees for the entire route. He could not risk being seen. After they burned his wife to death earlier, as most in Salem thought, seeing him running toward Tobias' house would make him appear to be a man seeking revenge. And in fact, he *was* looking for revenge. But not only because of what happened to Willa.

A little over two hundred years prior, two men were arguing over the future of the Order, as one of them was to be elected the next Master. One man, Rennik Samson from the West, argued the Order would best function in the light of day. Hidden, but in plain sight, with the members living as part of the unblood world. The other man, Junius Dracul from the East, warned of the dangers of living amongst the unbloods. Not only did it risk discovery of the bloodline, but it increased the possibility the bloodline would become contaminated and ultimately lose potency.

At first, they respectfully debated the arguments. It was almost cordial. Each man would make his respective points while the other would rebuke them – always acknowledging where the points were valid. After some time, it was becoming clear Rennik's message of hope and inclusiveness was winning the day. Junius needed to take drastic steps. As he often did, Junius consulted with the matriarch of the Dracul clan, his grandmother Chwaer. They were both ruthless in their own way, but where Junius had some capacity for empathy, Chwaer did not. She would push him to perform acts of the utmost cruelty, often against Junius' better judgement. But he never considered disobeying his grandmother. He believed she had his best interests at heart, and she knew what was best for the family. When he disagreed with his grandmother, Junius would do as she commanded and he would consider it a learning experience – his way of learning how to be a leader, how to be the Master.

Based on Chwaer's advice, Junius ultimately challenged Rennik to a duel. She was shrewd and realized a duel between the two would work out well for the Draculs no matter who won. If Junius won, then he would be the next Master, and she would make the decisions behind the scenes. If Junius lost, then Rennik was likely to use the opportunity to attempt a unification of the Order, which meant Rennik would likely spare Junius and give him a position of importance. Rennik could be so predictable. So Chwaer recommended Junius challenge Rennik to a duel, which he did.

"Only the strongest 'lock should lead the others," Junius said to Rennik, daring him to accept the challenge. Rennik ultimately relented and badly defeated Junius both in the duel and for the position as Master. But Rennik made a crucial mistake. After winning the duel, it was traditional for the winner to take the head of the loser as a trophy. Instead, Rennik stopped the killing within the bloodline to form a truce between the East and the West. Rather than taking his head, Rennik offered Junius his hand with the promise the two would work together to unify the Order for the first time since the Great Master himself. "Together, we will fulfill the prophecy from the ancient book," he said to Junius. This was exactly as Chwaer predicted.

The ancient book offered many pieces of advice and hidden, cryptic clues for the Masters to unravel. But there was one clear and concise rule – the succession of leadership. It was a rule added by the Great Master himself, many millennia after the ancient book was first scribed.

There were two, and only two, ways to change the leadership of the Order. This was unusual because the ancient book generally spoke of everything in threes. One way a change in leadership could occur was if the current leader dies *completely of causes determined by nature, not by the hand of any other man, except for self defense.* This prevented the murder of a leader by one jealous for the position, for if they caused the death of the leader neither they, nor any of their descendants, could ever become Master. The second, and only other, way was if another pureblood member of the order killed by their own hand, the three children of the current leader. It must be three children and the person vying for the position must be the one directly responsible for their deaths.

After Rennik became the Master, Junius started plotting for his eventual rise to leadership. At the time, Rennik had no children, but that was no matter. Junius would wait, hiding in plain sight, as Rennik wished for the Order in general.

Chapter 26

Samuel planned to take Tobias by surprise. He was eager to do what he should have done two centuries prior and end this once and for all.

He arrived at Tobias' house and snuck around to ensure nobody else was present. Finding no one else, he went to the back of the house, which faced into the woods, and peered through a window. There, sitting in a chair facing away from the chimney toward the front door, was Tobias, smoking a pipe and reading a book. He seemed oblivious to the danger lurking outside. Samuel thought this would be an excellent opportunity.

He clasped his hands quietly and concentrated, careful not to step on a branch, a leaf, or even a cockroach. Within seconds, his body vaporized into a thin cloud of dark gray smoke and traveled along the outside wall of the house. It looked a bit like an amorphous snake, slithering up the side and onto the roof where the smoke scurried over to the chimney, climbed the stack, whirled into the flue, and finally sank into the house. It was the most perfectly hidden entrance he could hope for. Once fully inside, the cloud reformed into Samuel's shape, while making no sound at all.

"I've been expecting you, old friend." Tobias said, welcoming Samuel into his home while turning the page in his book without looking to see if he were even there.

"You have a lot of nerve coming here and starting this up again, Junius." Samuel responded determinately. "This time, I won't make the same mistake I did before."

Tobias put his pipe and book down on the side table, stood slowly but intently, and turned to face Samuel. "And what mistake was that?"

"I never should have trusted you wanted what was best for the Order. You only wanted power, and I should have taken your head after I defeated you."

Tobias responded in a remarkably matter-of-fact tone, "Yes, I suppose you should have. What you thought was a righteous and valiant display of unity the other members viewed as weakness. They felt you turned your back on protecting the bloodline. And they were correct."

"That was only how you and your family thought – only the Draculs. Ever since your father embodied your uncle, the destiny for your familial line has been destruction and chaos."

"Ah, yes. My dear Uncle Vlad." Tobias was now slowly pacing through his house in a large circle with his hands clasped behind his back – a detail not lost on Samuel. "How I miss his reign in 'ole Trans. Actually, I miss everything about my old country." Tobias' face melted into a look of homesickness. "Do you miss your old country, Rennik?"

Samuel responded carefully, knowing Tobias was toying with him like a cat playing with a mouse before devouring it. "I miss my friends and family, yes. But I do not miss the memories I have of Coventry. The memories you forced upon me."

Tobias feigned a look of sadness. "Yes, that was most unfortunate. Your two boys were such fine lads." Tobias faced up and smiled in remembrance. "They had great potential, you know. They would have been strong warlocks. It saddened me that the prophecy, how should I say, impeded their being alive."

Samuel redirected the conversation. "Why are you here now? What do you want?"

Tobias was finished playing with Samuel. "You know exactly why I'm here. I need to fulfill the prophecy. I need to kill your third child. And since she revealed herself this evening at the burning…" Tobias swung around quickly to look at Samuel, complete with a sarcastic pout, "by the way, my condolences about Willa. She was a fine woman." He then swung back to his pacing and continued, "once I kill your daughter, then according to the ancient book, I will become Master of the Order. Your wretched reign will be no more."

"It will be more difficult than the first two, Junius." Samuel wanted to imbue fear into Tobias' eyes, but he received no such satisfaction.

"Excellent. I enjoy a challenge."

"As you know, I won't let you harm her. You'll have to kill me first. You couldn't do it the first time, you won't be able to now. And besides, if you kill me, then you won't be eligible to become Master."

Tobias stopped pacing but didn't face Samuel. Instead, he looked straight at the wall, still with his hands clenched together behind his back. "Oh come now, Rennik. Surely you remember the words 'except for self defense'? It would be perfectly understandable that a man, even the Master himself, would want to take vengeance for his wife's death." He continued with a significant amount of sarcasm, "I'm quite afraid of what you might do to me right now, and I fear for my life." He changed back to his normal tone of voice, "Now then, before we begin, shall we relieve ourselves of these dreadful shells?"

120

Samuel snickered, "You mean you no longer want to be Tobias Warnock? By the way, I've been meaning to tell you, the name you selected was quite brazen – only changing one letter from 'warlock'. I see you truly hid in plain sight."

"And what about you, Mr. 'Samson'? Only one letter difference for you as well. You also were hiding in plain sight."

Samuel curled his lips into a wry smile as he thought to himself, "In more ways than you realize."

Chapter 27

When he was twenty-five, about a year after his defeat at the hands of the more senior Rennik Samson, his grandmother summoned young Junius Dracul to a large room in their home. On most days, she paid little attention to the young man – she had no patience for his immaturity and lack of skill. He was but a means to an end for her. Junius was merely her vehicle to achieving power over the Order – the power was rightfully hers ever since her brother had perished many years prior. She considered Junius nothing more than a feebleminded idiot, but in this case, that was a good thing. It made him malleable. She had complete control over him, and she knew how to use that power wisely. The key was to make sure Junius constantly needed her approval. She purposely deprived him of any acknowledgement with masterful skill. The more she disparaged and ridiculed him, the more he would seek her attention and confirmation. She often ignored Junius for days, which only made him acquiesce to her desires even further.

"Yes, Grandmother?" he asked while catching his breath. He ran to her as soon as she summoned him and he hoped his quick responsiveness pleased her.

Chwaer glowered back at him. "Rennik is showing the Order exactly what kind of fool you are. Your loss to him sullied our family's good name. Tonight I will explain a plan to you. If you execute this plan properly, you will be Master."

"Tonight I shall become Master?"

Chwaer despised his need for immediate fulfillment. With squinted eyes, she shook her head at him. "No, you nitwit!" She turned away from him. "If I cared for any of the members of the Order, I would feel guilty for inflicting you on them as their leader! Luckily for you, I do not care for them."

Junius hung his head in shame – a position he often took when in his grandmother's presence.

She continued through a deep sigh, "Not tonight. My plan will work, but it will take time. I understand you are not patient, nor are you disciplined, but I will guide you. If you can wait until the right time and execute my plan exactly as I dictate, you will eventually become Master."

Junius looked up at her, knowing his grandmother would help lift his spirits.

Chwaer walked to a chair at the back of the room and sat. "But for now, I have something new to teach you. This is a maneuver I've learned over the years – only your father and I know of it. Now it is time you learn as well."

Junius quickly sat cross-legged on the floor in front of his grandmother. She sat in her teaching chair which meant he was to sit in his learning position. These were his most favorite times, when he was the object of his grandmother's complete attention.

"What will you teach me today?"

"A faster way to disembody from a host. For most, this process can take many seconds – perhaps even a full minute. This is time wasted during a duel. I know a secret method to reduce the disembodiment time, giving you an advantage. Listen carefully, this might save you one day." She turned away from Junius in contempt. "Though I'm uncertain that saving you is necessarily good for anyone."

"A faster disembodiment? But I thought the speed depended on the elastic quality of the ground where you stood, which is why we hold our hands parallel to the earth so we can bounce our energy back into our palms and begin the process."

Chwaer snickered, "You thought?" Her face grizzled with disdain. "As usual, you thought wrong."

Chapter 28

The two men slowly backed into opposite corners of the room as if they staged it, though it was completely by coincidence. Each put their arms down to their sides and pointed their hands flat out so their palms were parallel to the floor. They faced up, not straight up, but as if they were looking at someone who was about one foot taller than they were. They closed their eyes and their bodies shimmered and ultimately glowed.

It was at this moment Tobias recoiled from his stance. This was his chance to use the method his grandmother had taught him many years earlier. He practiced this dozens, perhaps hundreds, of times and was confident he could pull it off. He was more skilled than his grandmother gave him credit for.

Samuel felt something unusual. His eyes were closed, but something seemed off to him. He peered through small slits in his eyelids to see what Tobias was doing. It shocked him to discover Tobias took himself out of the normal disembodiment stance and was doing something odd. Rather than using the energy between his flat hands and the ground, which is how all witches normally disembodied their hosts, Tobias crossed his arms across his chest. In record time, Tobias' facade seemed to melt away. Samuel was only halfway through his disembodiment, but Junius already completed his.

Tobias, who was now Junius inside and out, looked as different from his former self as you could imagine. He was a tall, slender man, significantly hunched over from years of being trapped inside Tobias' skeleton. His hair was brown, thick, and long – falling halfway down his back. Junius had distinctive features, which included a nearly triangular nose resulting in an almost perfect forty-five-degree angle, dark – almost black – eyes, and a wide, but thin mouth. His most distinctive feature was a large pothole scar on his left cheek, similar to a burn mark, which was a gift to Junius with regards from Rennik during their duel two hundred years prior.

Junius stood tall, relieving his slouched posture, and flashed a licentious smile at Samuel. It was the same smile Samuel remembered from that awful night many years prior. And just like that previous time, Samuel was helpless to do anything. Completely immobilized, Samuel was still peeling away his outer persona, not yet ready to be Rennik fully. He immediately knew he was in trouble and dread overtook him.

Junius planned for this exact moment for years. It felt good to have it play out precisely as his grandmother expected it would. Knowing he had time and the clear advantage, Junius slowly brought his hands together in front of him, staring at Samuel with a curled smile the entire time. He clasped his palms together and held his arms in front of him. His smile changed. It turned from a taunting glee to a haunting fury, his eyes angry from years of hatred and malignancy. With no hesitation, Junius' passionate rage welled inside him and from his clenched fists shot a fierce bolt of energy, headed directly for Samuel's gut. Samuel's eyes grew wide as he realized his impending doom.

At the precise moment Samuel realized he lost, Junius' beam of energy froze, just mere inches from Samuel's stomach, as if time itself stopped. Junius, too, looked frozen in his posture of attack and disdain. Samuel tilted his head in bewilderment, and as he looked closer, he could tell the beam was still moving toward him, but at an incalculably slow pace. As the beam moved each fraction of an inch, Samuel heard a faint popping sound, as if the beam were cracking through something solid in the air. Samuel was able to move at his normal speed, but each movement he made also produced the popping sound. He was in an unfamiliar state, now frightened both by Junius' gamesmanship and the time distortion going on around him. "I have to get out of the energy beam's path," he realized, as he forced his body down and to the right, breaking through the popping sounds seeming to fight against his movements. As his right arm extended down to the floor with his left arm flailing back behind him, Samuel leaned back just enough to avoid a direct hit from the bolt. But he didn't have enough time to retract completely, and he watched in shock as the left edge of the beam brushed across the left side of his stomach. It was moving slowly enough that he witnessed the beam gorge across his skin, with painful heat cauterizing the wound as it was being created. As soon as the beam passed by his body, normal time resumed and Samuel fell to the floor – injured, but still alive and able to fight. He did not know what just happened and there was no time to think about it.

From his vantage point, Junius saw Samuel move with lightning speed to avoid his energy burst. He saw no one move like that before. He stood straight, baffled and amazed by the Master's brilliance. The momentary pause was just enough time for Rennik to complete his transformation out of Samuel and stand so he could face Junius, injured but still in the game. It was the first time they saw into each other's eyes in nearly two centuries. Rennik saw what just took place caused bewilderment for Junius. It bewildered Rennik as well.

Rennik, now bereft of Samuel's body, was merely a pleasant-looking man. He was of average height – shorter than Junius, but not as short as Tobias. He had non-distinct features, nothing to would make the normal passerby look twice. What was most notable about Rennik was his eyes. There was deep determination locked into their deep blueness. He was known for being able to disarm, and to dis-arm, an opponent just with his stare.

Amazingly, both men looked very much younger than their previous embodiments, even though they were very much older.

Rennik quickly clasped his hands tightly together. He did not need time for his emotions to stir his energy. He was already highly emotive at the sight of a man he had not seen for two hundred years and despised for the entire time. A thick bolt of energy shot out of Rennik's hands directly toward Junius. But he was quicker than Rennik expected. He tucked down and rolled to his right, avoiding the bolt completely, though it narrowly escaped hitting his left shoulder as it continued on to the dining room table, completely disintegrating one leg causing it to fall over, taking an iron plate and silverware with it.

Junius' roll to the side resulted in his landing in an offensive position on one knee, directly facing Rennik. He clasped his hands together, generating a bolt aimed directly at Rennik's head. Rennik turned sideways, to his left, and watched the bolt pass right in front of his eyes – exactly where his head was less than a moment before. The sudden turn inflamed his injury and reminded him of its presence. He couldn't spend any energy trying to heal the wound – he knew he would need every bit of energy to fight Junius. The bolt missed Rennik but crashed right through a window, shattering all the glass and continuing on to a tree outside the house, taking down a large branch with it.

As in any battle, taking a higher position provided an advantage. So both men took to the air. Unlike the manufactured myths about witches, there was no need for a broom or any other type of object in order to levitate. Their immense energy could form a field around their body, allowing them to move in any direction in three dimensions, and to change direction in a flash, literally, as any sudden change of momentum caused electromagnetic sparks. The result, when there were two highly skilled purebloods engaged in a duel, was a three-dimensional, high-speed dance of light and energy.

The two men shot around the room, each trying to take the higher position. From their perspective, everything was moving at normal speed. They could clearly see the other's position and direction and had time to adjust accordingly. But to an outside observer, it was nothing more than two entities moving so fast they were but a mere blur. They were not moving as fast as Rennik did earlier, when he moved out of the path of Junius' direct hit. Neither knew how Rennik performed that feat.

There were bolts of lightning blasting off in rapid succession, sometimes hitting their target, sometimes missing wildly. Both men flew through the air at amazingly high speeds, flipping and darting around with precision and flair. These were two masterful fighters, neither willing to lose.

Eventually, the confines of the house were too small for the battle, and Junius escaped through a newly formed hole in the roof. Rennik also fled to the outside. He would be an easy target if he remained in the house. But he was careful to exit through a window on the opposite side from where Junius escaped. If he followed Junius out the same exit path, Junius would be certain to be waiting for him.

While the damage to Tobias' house was real, the raucous noise and the amazing light show from the battle was taking place in a separate dimension only members of the bloodline could hear and see, just as with the torrent. Because of this, the two men did not concern themselves with how loud the battle was. The villagers would not hear or see anything. The two warriors completely focused on destroying their opponent.

The battle was now taking place at a much larger scale than the house could accommodate. The two men were buzzing past each other high above the trees. Bolts of energy shot past them, each with a number of wounds already inflicted against their body. When he wasn't shooting bolts at Rennik, Junius used his energy to hurl large objects toward his enemy – rocks, trees and even large boulders came hurtling toward him. This was no problem for Rennik, he could avoid them easily, but bodily harm was not Junius' plan. His strategy was to distract Rennik, just for a moment each time, so Junius could take another shot, moving closer with each distraction. The strategy worked, as he got closer to Rennik bit by bit. He was getting close enough to take his kill shot.

Just as Rennik saw another large boulder headed his way at high speed, he ducked and spun to get his body just below the boulder and come out from underneath, almost as if he gracefully swam out of its way. He emerged from under the boulder facing Junius directly, who was now just a few yards in front of him. Junius did not expect this amazingly physical act by Rennik and it took him by surprise, the aggressive move altering the angle of Junius' kill shot at the last moment.

Both men, feeling like they now owned an advantage over the other, dug deep into their well of emotion and formed the most powerful and focused beam of energy they could summon. Simultaneously, powerful, focused beams of light shot out of their hands, directly aimed at their opponent's body, only a handful of feet apart.

It struck both men hard, forcing them backward a great distance. The combination of the release of energy to create their own bolt, along with being struck by the other's high energy beam, knocked them both out cold. With no internal force to keep their protective fields active, they fell to the ground, like stones falling off a rocky outcrop into the cold, hard ocean. They landed hundreds of yards apart, not within sight of each other, crashing hard into the ground, which would have been certain to cause great pain if they were conscious to experience it.

After a few minutes, Rennik came to. He placed his hand on his forehead, trying to relieve the pain he was feeling. He tried to stand, but could not. Rennik placed his hand on his left side and then pulled it to his face. Blood covered his hand. A strike must have reopened his original injury. He was badly wounded and the hard landing on the ground only made matters worse. He was in agonizing pain, too weak to use his powers, but he knew he needed to get up. Rennik did not know Junius' status, and if he were well enough to find Rennik, he would surely take his head. He crawled to a nearby tree stump and used it for leverage to slowly and shakily stand. He picked up a moderately thick branch laying nearby. "This should work." With his right hand covering his wound and his left leg dragging behind him, he used the branch as a cane and started back for his house to warn Joseph and Abigail. He didn't have enough energy, and was too weak to send Joseph a message. He did not know if Junius was right behind him or not.

Junius suffered a similar fate and did not know how Rennik fared. He couldn't know this, but he landed at least a half mile away from Rennik. Junius was already standing and able to walk, albeit not steadily. While both of his legs were working, he was also too weak to use his powers. He retreated to the woods so he could rest and heal, hoping Rennik was not out looking for him. With the morning sunlight he would feel stronger, be able to find Rennik, and fulfill his destiny.

Chapter 29

Joseph started Abigail's education, still unsure exactly where to begin. So he started with the first thing to come to mind. "Tell me about…" He paused for a moment trying to guess how Abigail might react to his question. "…your hair."

"What an odd question," she thought. "My hair? What about my hair?"

"Have you ever noticed anything unusual about your hair? How do you feel about it?"

"Well… um…." She looked down and squinched her eyes, unsure how she was supposed to respond. "I quite like my hair. It's thick and long, but I wish my parents would let me cut it." Her tone slowed and dropped in pitch. "But they never allowed it."

Joseph looked at the floor and smiled while shuffling his right foot a bit. "No, I don't suppose they would."

He continued, "Let me ask this a different way. Do you enjoy being outside on a warm, sunny day?"

"Well of course I do. Who doesn't?" She was not at all clear where this line of questioning would take them.

"Does the sun ever make you feel… energized?"

She looked up, smiled slightly, and stared at nothing in particular. Her mind immediately flashed back to her days at the shore, basking in the sunlight. She remembered how she loved sitting by the water, letting the waves splash onto her face and soaking her hair in the sun. "Yes, it does. In fact, I came up with several 're' words to describe how I felt – renewed, reinvigorated, reborn, refreshed. I even created my own 're' word best describing how I felt: re-alive."

"Re… Alive?" Joseph looked a bit stunned, and the word caused him to pause. "Interesting," he said while rubbing his chin, pondering the new word and its potential implications. He continued to pause, then broke his own concentration. "Well, there's no time for that now."

"Tell me Abigail, are you familiar with the story of Samson and Delilah?"

"Of course, I learned about it in Sunday school – and the minister's sermon this morning was about that story."

"Yes, yes. It was a fine sermon." Joseph paused some more while pacing slowly, still gathering his thoughts and trying to figure out how to move the conversation forward in some coherent way. He quickly realized there was no way he could continue in any fashion that would make sense to Abigail, so he decided to just keep going.

"What you know about that story is only *part* of the story."

Abigail's eyes widened, and she sat up straighter.

"It's true Samson was a fierce warrior and his hair gave him great strength. But it wasn't anything magical. His strength came *from* his hair, directly from the sunlight *through* his hair."

Abigail was silent, her mouth open wide as she listened intently. Her left eyebrow rose, and she squinted her eyes as she looked up at the ceiling, trying to comprehend.

133

"How can I explain this better?" he said out loud but to himself. "You see, Samson was born with an extremely rare mutation. His body was physically different from everyone else – not in appearance, but in its physiology. His hair, well, it wasn't hair as you and I know it. It was more plant-like than actual hair. He had very fine tendrils growing from his head."

"Wait, are you saying Samson had plants on his head instead of hair?"

"No, not at all. It was still human hair. But it possessed an extra mutation, allowing his hair to harvest energy from sunlight just as plants do, and he could store the extra energy in his body. *That* is what made Samson stronger than anyone else – he had an immense amount of extra energy created from his hair and he learned to harness at will. It made him incredibly powerful. In fact, the literal translation of the name Samson is 'Man of the Sun'. In his case, the name had a dual meaning."

Abigail's mind did not believe this story even for a second, but her heart knew it to be true. It felt real to her. Somehow it felt familiar, but in a way she could not explain.

Joseph continued, "It's true the Philistines cut off his hair." He swallowed hard and looked away, imagining Samson's torment. "It must have been excruciating for him. Each strand firmly rooted to his scalp. Each was an appendage, like a finger – it was that much a part of his body. They must have used very sharp blades to cut through each strand. I can't imagine the pain he must have endured. It was the cruelest form of torture they could have imposed on him, like having each finger violently slashed off your hand thousands upon thousands of times over."

Abigail, always eager to display her knowledge of a subject, interjected, "And that was all because of Delilah, who betrayed Samson and turned him over to the Philistines."

"Not exactly," Joseph said, causing Abigail's shoulders to diminish in stature a bit. "Despite the story as you've heard it, Samson and Delilah were very much in love. In fact, she was pregnant with Samson's child, well, actually children. She gave birth to triplets. They both understood the importance of Samson's mutation and they agreed to keep their children, and therefore the bloodline, hidden and safe. They concocted the story of her betrayal to protect Delilah, the children, and the truth. This, too, must have been very painful for Samson. But he knew the importance of the bloodline and did everything in his power to keep it safe."

"But didn't Delilah die with Samson at the temple of Dagon? They gouged his eyes out and they all died when he collapsed the temple on all the Philistines, including Delilah."

"That is what you were to believe. The truth is much murkier. When something important needs to be protected, reality becomes shaped in a way allowing for that protection. What might appear to be the truth can often hide the actual truth, which might be closer to you than you realize." Joseph paused, "Does this make any sense to you?"

She thought for a solid ten seconds to make sure she understood what Mr. Porter was saying. She knew by the eager look in his eyes he was hoping for an affirmative response. "No, it most certainly does not make sense. You are asking me to believe quite a lot. A biblical hero with plant hair, a pregnant traitor who actually was also a hero. I'm not sure I understand what any of this has to do with me."

Joseph smiled widely and slowed his pace. "A great deal, actually. You see, after Delilah gave birth to her three children, they were separated to keep the bloodline safe. One child went to Northern Africa, one went to the East, and one to the West. Those who knew of the bloodline and vowed to protect it cared for each of the children. Over the centuries, the family lines grew deep and wide. Many centuries later, about one thousand years prior to us right now, a direct descendant of the bloodline from the West discovered he was actually a pure blood – he traced a direct line back through his family history, which was well documented in an ancient book, all the way back to both Samson and Delilah. His blood was completely pure. Over the millennia, there were certainly others with this pure bloodline. But what made this man unique was his hair."

"I'm sorry, but I still don't understand what any of this has to do with me," Abigail said, though she had an inkling.

"I'm getting there. This man was a bit of an amateur scientist and had done many examinations on various aspects of his body. When he discovered the plant-like qualities of his own hair – soaking up energy from sunlight – it caused him to research his family history. He wanted to learn how he came to have that special type of hair. This led him to discover the ancient book and the secret of his past. It turns out both of his parents were direct descendants of Samson and Delilah. This was the first known instance of a dually descended person since the original triplets. This made him quite unique. His name," Joseph paused for a bit of dramatic effect, "was Myrddin Wyllt. You may have heard of him as Merlin the Magician, though he never had an association with King Arthur – that was a story created by the Order to protect him."

"The Order?" Abigail asked, as if *that* were the important question.

"I was just getting there. When Myrddin discovered the ancient book, where he learned the truth about Samson, there was something else he discovered. There was a full lock of Samson's hair, perfectly preserved, with thousands of individual strands. There was no way to know if it was the lock cut off by the Philistines, or if they took it after Samson's death. But Myrddin examined the hair closely and noticed it possessed the same qualities as his own hair. He ran tests to verify the strength of the hair."

"One strand, though stronger than normal hair, could still tear with great pressure applied to both ends. He could also tear two strands, but it was quite difficult to do. However, he found three strands together were virtually indestructible. In fact, if he wound the third strand around the other two, he could find no way of destroying the hair. Not even fire could damage it. Because of this, the number three is very important to the Order – anything done in threes or associated with the number three has more strength and power than anything else."

"And also because Samson and Delilah had three children?"

"Yes, it's all tightly connected. There are no coincidences. During his time, others thought Myrddin to be a magician, not because he could perform actual magic, but because he learned how to harness the power stored by his hair and use it to generate incredible amounts of internal energy, just as Samson himself had done. He learned to use the energy to perform superhuman acts, and many people of his time could only describe it as magic. He found the key to harnessing the energy was his emotion. The stronger his emotions, the faster the energy would flow through his body and the more powerful he became. He ultimately found the true key to his strength had nothing to do with being stronger than others, but everything to do with being able to control and harness his emotion. That was the key."

Abigail immediately connected this with her ability to lock away any emotions when she needed to. Her inkling was growing into a suspicion.

Joseph continued, "Myrddin spent most of his long adult life searching for other members of the bloodline. He found twenty-nine others scattered throughout the known world. He called them all to meet in the first coven, in what would later become Coventry, England."

"Mother and Father are from Coventry." She paused for a moment of realization. "Wait, a coven in Coventry? Is that how Coventry got its name?"

"Yes, that's right. It was there Myrddin taught the others about their lineage and showed them the strength of the hair. He divided the lock equally amongst all thirty and instructed each member to give three strands to each of their children and to pass the hair down through the bloodline. To keep the hair safe, Myrddin suggested using the wound strands of three hairs as candle wicks, since they could not burn. Ever since then, each member of the Order has had a candle containing a wick made of three strands of Samson's hair. They are invincibly strong and will never burn down."

"Just like Father's special candle," she realized.

"And this is where the Order got its name – the Order of the Wick. Those who are partially of the bloodline are called Wicken. Pure bloods are called Wicked (wik't). The word 'witch' itself is a derivation of 'wick', though what people these days consider a witch is nothing of who we are. True witches of the Order are merely members of the bloodline who have learned how to control and harness their emotion to perform acts of incredible strength. Some Wicked can perform superhuman feats, like traveling long distances through the air. Over the centuries, the unbloods have heard bits about the Order, and along with the actions of the Dracul clan, some have created their own stories about how witches act and live. They concocted fanciful stories of cauldrons, spells, 'eyes of newts', broomsticks and other silliness. None of that has anything to do with genuine witches. We allowed these misguided interpretations to flourish because it provided cover to the real members of the Order. We were hiding in plain sight, just as Myrddin suggested we do with the candle wicks."

Abigail interrupted, "We? Are you saying you are a member of the Order?"

"Yes, I am. And so are you. We're both witches, but not the type of witch Salem is intent on destroying. Those witches don't exist. The witches of the Order do not perform magic. We use our internal energy to protect the secret of Samson and his bloodline. And based on how you've been able to manage and compartmentalize your emotions over the last few horrific days, shows me you are going to be a powerful witch."

Abigail looked to the side to think for a moment, then looked back and asked, "Earlier you spoke about three strands of hair making up the candle wick. Are you sure it's three?"

"Yes, I'm very certain of it. Why?"

"Because Father's candle has six strands."

Joseph jolted up in surprise. "What? Are you sure? Show me."

Abigail fetched the candle from the side table next to her father's chair.

Joseph stared through the clear wax and looked intently at the wick. To his astonishment, he saw six strands. There were four straight strands with two wrapped cylindrically around them. "Dear God," he said. "The only way this could happen would be…" He paused, pondering what this discovery meant for what happened earlier in the day.

"It could only happen how?" Abigail asked slowly, but in an insisting way.

"It could only happen if each of your parents had their own set of three strands and joined them together to make six."

"What does that mean?" she asked.

"It means both of your parents are direct, pureblood descendants from both Samson and Delilah. Only one other person *ever* has had that distinction."

"Who was that?" she asked.

He looked her dead in the eye. "The Great Master – Myrddin himself." Joseph cocked his head slightly and stared at Abigail, wondering if he was looking into the eyes of the next Great Master. Could she really be? Who *was* this person Samuel charged him to teach and protect? And why didn't Rennik confide the truth to him?

He snapped himself out of his thoughts and continued on with his teachings, not wanting to make too big a deal over the revelation he just learned. It was important for him to build her confidence in her abilities, not scare her away with the weight of responsibility.

"Anyway, using the hair as a wick would keep the hair hidden in plain sight. And that is a key tenet for protecting the bloodline – *Semper Invisibilia Huc*. That's Latin for…"

Abigail interrupted him, staring blankly at the wall, soaking in everything Mr. Porter was saying as her mind started connecting many small dots into a larger picture that was taking shape. "It's Latin for 'Always Invisible Anywhere'."

"That's right," Joseph confirmed. "And in fact, legend says past masters have inscribed the acronym AIA multiple times in the ancient book to underscore the importance of this concept to the Order, and to highlight the prophecy."

Abigail listened closely, still intellectually believing very little of what was being said. It was too fantastical to be true. But she noticed something familiar about the acronym. "Did you say AIA?" She paused, making sure her thought made sense. "That's also the initials of my brothers and me – Archibald, Ichibad and Abigail."

The statement stopped Joseph dead in his tracks. Until this point, he enjoyed sharing the story of the Order. He never spoke of it so freely, and doing so brought him great joy. But Abigail's realization sent chills up his spine, tingling all the way to his fingertips. He stared down at the floor, but wasn't really looking at it. His eyes were darting from side to side, as if he were quickly assembling a jigsaw puzzle in his mind. The pieces were now falling into place for him – pieces he never realized were part of a puzzle in the first place. "Dear God, Abigail. Your father was right." He met Abigail's eyes with his own. "You *are* in grave danger."

Chapter 30

At that exact moment, the house shook. Then it shook again. Joseph experienced earthquakes before, and this was not one. During an earthquake, the house would shake and shimmy constantly for a period of time. This felt more like the house was being hit by some type of large projectile. Something was hitting the house, sort of. Joseph motioned for Abigail to get on the floor and hide behind a chair as he quickly extinguished all the lit candles, drawing the house into pure darkness. He quietly stepped to a window and ever so carefully peered through the curtain. It was hard to see anything in the darkness. Every few seconds, out of the pure black, he would see what looked like the form of a man lighting up brightly, as if he were being zapped briefly by fire. Everything would then go black again for twenty or thirty seconds, and then he'd see the zapped figure again.

"Rennik's protection is working. But who is that man?" Joseph squinted to get a better look, but he still couldn't see anything. In reality, it wasn't one man, but two. Tobias' two men, in fact. He sent them to the Sampson house to capture and return Abigail, but they did not expect the protection field Rennik left for them. Eventually, they figured out what was happening, and instead of torturing their own bodies, they started throwing rocks toward the house to weaken the field. The field of electricity surrounding the house repelled each one. And with the number of rocks being thrown and rejected, Joseph could identify there were two men. He immediately realized who they were.

"We're safe as long as your father's protection holds up," he assured Abigail. As if planned, right after that assurance, a rock made it through the protective field and hit the roof with a loud and unexpected thud. Both Abigail and Joseph ducked down in fear at the sudden sound.

"I think we should get out of here," Abigail said.

"Yes, I agree with you. But how can we get out without being seen?" Immediately, there were two more thuds. Joseph thought through a plan, but his ideas all depended on Tobias' men being idiots. "It might work just for that reason," he thought.

Thud!

As Joseph shared his plan with Abigail, another thought entered his mind. It was unlikely, but worth a try, considering who her father was.

"Does your father have any cloaks? I'm thinking of one that would be quite old, with a tall collar? It would be black."

The thuds were happening more frequently now. It was only a matter of time before the electricity field was completely down and their protection was gone. Joseph knew the only way they could break the field this easily was if Rennik were seriously hurt and could no longer sustain the field. Or worse. He knew there was not much time before the two men would be in the house. In fact, their slow progress pleasantly surprised him.

"Do you mean Belle? That old thing is in my parent's bedroom, in the closet."

"Belle? Can you show me now? And fetch anything important you need in case we have to leave quickly."

"Father said he wanted to discuss his special candle and his old book with me. I suppose I should take them."

"All right. Gather them as fast as you can and then take me to… Belle."

The two of them stayed as low to the ground as they could. Their eyes were adjusting to the dark, and they could see a little better now. Abigail grabbed the candle and then scurried to the bookshelf and grabbed the old, dusty book. They hurried into the bedroom, and Abigail led Joseph to the coatrack and pointed up. More thuds, now louder and even more frequent.

"What do you want with this old thing?" she asked.

Though there was no time, Joseph paused in awe. "Could it be? I can't believe I'm actually holding it. Abigail, if this is what I think it is, what I hope it is, it's going to save us tonight."

Joseph only heard rumors about the cloak, he never saw it. It was a relic from the Great Master himself and passed down only to other masters through the centuries. He was hoping beyond hope two things would now be true. First, this actually *was* the legendary cloak and not some random cloak Samuel acquired over the years. And second, that he, a non-Master, could harness its power and save them both.

Joseph wrapped Belle around himself. "Come here. Stand next to me, fully inside the cloak, I mean Belle. You'd better close your eyes for this." Abigail hopped into Belle and huddled in next to him. The thuds stopped, but this was not good news. Joseph could see through the bedroom window the two men were feeling around in the darkness for holes in the protective field. A leg from one of them was dangling through. Joseph needed to hurry.

He knew this was going to take all the energy he could muster. Joseph clenched his hands together tightly, connecting his palms as

144

much as possible. He put the circle created by his arms around Abigail and he started thinking of his sweet, departed Millie. This brought out extreme emotions for Joseph – sadness, longing, and of course, immense anger. He closed his eyes as he felt his energy gathering speed through his arms. Suddenly, his eyes snapped open, and poof.

Nothing.

They both stood in the same position. Abigail still huddled at Joseph's side. "Can I open my eyes now?" she asked sarcastically.

Joseph completely deflated. Not only were they at risk from the two intruders, but he also apparently failed to discover the real ancient cloak. His shoulders drooped and his face grew long. "Yes, you can open your eyes," he replied. He looked out of the bedroom window and saw one of the men made it almost completely through the hole in the invisible field. Both of his legs were on the other side and he was trying to fit his torso through. His partner was attempting to shove him into the hole from outside the invisible field.

As Joseph removed Belle from around his body, now certain it was not the cloak he hoped it was, Abigail noticed an inscription on the inside in bright red letters. "I recognize this inscription," she said. "Sunt alii. That's Latin for 'There are others'. That's what Mother always said to me."

Joseph's head perked back to life and a wry smile grew on his face. "Willa, you clever one," Joseph said with glee. It immediately made sense to him. The cloak was giving him a message through the salutation of the Order – 'There are Others'. And in this case, there were, in fact, others – at least there was one other. While Joseph was not a Master, Abigail was only the second person ever born, and to survive, whose parents were both pure bloods and of the direct line of descendants. In all of history, it was only Myrddin and Abigail. So if the cloak were not to work for Joseph, perhaps it would for her. At least it was worth a try.

"Let's switch positions. I want you to put Belle on. I'll explain what you need to do."

Quickly, Joseph unclipped the cloak from his neck and put it around Abigail's. "It's a good thing you're so tall, otherwise you might collapse under the weight of this thing," he said. He peered over his shoulder and saw the first man was completely through the hole. He was pulling the second man through, though he was larger and they were having a difficult time with it. In fact, how much trouble they were having surprised Joseph. It was almost as if they were purposely trying to stall for time.

Once Belle's clasp was secure around Abigail's neck, Joseph continued, "Now give me the candle and the book and put your arms around my waist. Clasp your hands together tightly. Make sure the flat parts of your palms are completely touching each other."

He looked down to ensure she was doing it properly. "Good. Now, close your eyes and picture my house. In your mind, imagine the route from your house to mine. Make sure it's very clear in your head. Do you see it?"

With her eyes still closed and her hands tightly gripped together, Abigail nodded and murmured, "Mhm."

"Right. Now I want you to take a deep breath and relax. Think about something deeply emotional for you. What am I saying... think about your dear mother. Think of how much you love her and how sad you are about what happened to her. Now imagine how angry you'd be if you found out someone did that to her on purpose."

146

Abigail was feeling immense sadness until Mr. Porter's last comment. She never considered the accusation against her mother was for nefarious reasons. That would make her death a murder. She felt an intense anger rise from the pit of her stomach, like a sleeping dragon suddenly awakened after a decade's long slumber. Her emotions were building on top of each other – sadness, agony, anger, vengeance.

She was trying to keep her hands clenched together but was having difficulty. She could feel the energy growing and flowing within her. The energy was so strong it was forcing her hands apart. She almost could not overcome the resistance, but she ultimately forced her hands to remain clenched.

Her energy was reaching a boiling point when, suddenly, her eyes snapped open on their own. With a small puff of smoke, the two of them were gone.

The two men made it through the hole in the protective field, which was now quickly deteriorating. They ran to the front door of the house and used their strong shoulders to break through the lock and force the door open. The men entered the house, and to their surprise, nobody was there. They saw the lit candles when they first arrived and they saw the candles go out. There was no back door to the house. The only possible ways out were the front door, which remained closed the entire time, and the chimney. They would have easily seen someone on the roof. They considered maybe they escaped through a window, but all the windows were securely in place. Somehow, inextricably, they lost their target. Tobias wanted them to bring the girl to him unharmed. They knew tonight he would be gravely disappointed.

Joseph stepped out from under Belle to see where they were. They were not inside his house, that was for sure, but still Abigail impressed him and he was more than a little relieved. "Why are we outside my front door? Did you not imagine inside my house?"

Abigail giggled slightly. "Mr. Porter, Millie and I were friendly, but I was never inside your house. I do not know what your house looks like on the inside, so when I imagined the route, I had to stop at your front door."

"But," Abigail continued, her voice much higher pitched, "what just happened???"

"Come, let's get inside quickly. There will be time later for an explanation."

They opened the door and entered. At that moment, Joseph looked down at the candle and the book Abigail handed him before they transported. He did not recognize the Latin words on the cover.

"Abigail wait. What did you say the name of this book was?"

"I don't know. Father always referred to it as his 'ancient book'."

For the third time tonight, Joseph found himself in deep awe. First, he discovered Abigail was the only dually descended since the Great Master himself. Next he used, or more precisely helped Abigail to use, the ancient cloak. And finally, he possessed another relic. This one, however, was not from the Great Master. This relic was many millennia older than that. He was holding the mystical ancient book. The relic both Delilah, and Samson himself, both once held.

What a day this had been, and it was far from over.

Chapter 31

Rennik was hobbled but making progress getting back to his house. The pain was of no concern to him, his only goal was to make sure Abigail was safe. He made it to the edge of the woods leading to the clearing where his home stood. Suddenly, two men ran out of the house heading into the woods. Luckily they were not entering close to where Rennik was so he darted behind a tree to hide, just in case. He looked around the side of the tree and could just barely see the two men. He thought he recognized them, but more importantly, he could see they were alone. Abigail was not with them.

As soon as they disappeared into the woods, Rennik made his move. He walked as quickly as he could, considering his wounds and makeshift cane. He made it to his house and swung open the door. Rennik was afraid of what he might find. He was fearful he might see two bodies lying dead on the floor. But upon inspection, the house was empty. He immediately noticed the missing candle and looked on the shelf for the book. It was also missing.

"Hopefully you have all three of them, Joseph," he thought to himself. "Now, where are you?"

Joseph just settled Abigail at their table, and Elizabeth Porter was making some tea. Elizabeth was an unblood, not of the bloodline at all. Joseph explained a bit of the Order to her – she needed to know because their daughter, Millie, was a Wicken – she possessed the bloodline, but they did not educate her in the Order. Elizabeth needed to know what it meant to be a member of the Order, in case Millie ever needed her protection. She was feeling immeasurable guilt over her inability to protect Millie, and she was feeling even more hatred toward Tobias for what he did.

"I need to contact your father. He won't know where you are." Joseph said. In reality, Joseph didn't know whether Rennik was in the heat of battle, or even still alive. But he needed to attempt contact.

Joseph pressed his middle three fingers from each hand to their appropriate temple on the sides of his head, closed his eyes, and thought, "Rennik – where are you? I have Abigail, we're safe at my house. Please get here as soon as your can."

Rennik immediately received the message and put his three middle fingers to his temples, barely generating enough energy to send a message back.

"Joseph, I'm happy to hear you and Abigail are safe. Thank you for protecting her. Do you also have the candle and the book?"

"Yes – and we also have the cloak," Joseph responded. "It's how we escaped. And I have many questions for you about all three of them."

Rennik smiled, "I'm sure you do. But now is not the time." His smile wiped itself away. "Joseph, I'm badly injured. I don't have the energy to make it to your house. I'm barely able to keep up this conversation. Can you use the cloak to come get me?"

"No, I can't. The cloak does not work for me. But we can send Abigail. She's the one who used the cloak and save us both."

Rennik was stunned. "But how did she… She doesn't even know what it is."

"I walked her through it. Rennik, she's quite amazing. I've never seen such natural power and ability to harness one's emotions as she possesses. I'm certain she can fetch you."

"I suppose we don't have a choice. Yes, send her but let her know…" At that point, Rennik drained the last of his energy. There was nothing left in his reserves, and the sunrise was still hours away. There was no way for him to regenerate until then. He never got the chance to remind Joseph he no longer had Samuel's embodiment. Abigail would not recognize him. Rennik slumped to the floor, weak and in great pain.

"Rennik? Rennik?" There was no response. This could only be bad news. Perhaps Rennik suffered a grave injury, or perhaps Junius found him. Whatever was going on, they needed to get to him right away.

"Abigail, put your tea down. Your father needs us. He needs *you.* He's back at your house and we have to get there right away. We need you to use the cloak again. You'll need to do two more trips. Do you think you can do it?"

Abigail immediately stood. "What's wrong with Father?" After just losing her mother only hours before, the prospect of also losing her father frightened her. But then her Sampson obligation took over, and she focused on the issue at hand. "Of course I can do it. Not that I know what exactly I'm doing. But if I did it once before, I can do it again."

"Great, let's go straight away. There's no time to waste." Joseph grabbed the cloak he laid across the back of a chair not three minutes prior and put it back onto Abigail's shoulders. She fastened the clasp herself and raised a side of the cloak for Mr. Porter to enter. Abigail put her arms around his body and clasped her hands together tightly, making sure her palms were completely flat against each other. She closed her eyes and thought about her mother. Abigail's inner dragon woke again, and within a few moments, a puff of smoke appeared and they were gone.

Elizabeth Porter dropped the teapot on the floor in horror and amazement. Even though she knew about the Order, she never saw its magic before. She found it interesting how comfortable Abigail appeared in her new role. Elizabeth wondered how long Abigail knew she was a witch, and she wondered how long it would be until someone accused her publicly.

Chapter 32

Abigail and Joseph appeared from nowhere inside the Sampson house. There, slumped on the floor, they could see the silhouette of a man.

Joseph ran over and knelt next to the figure, "Rennik. Can you hear me? Are you all right?"

Rennik wearily raised his hand and placed it on Joseph's shoulder. "I'm weak and badly hurt. Please help me up."

Joseph looked at Abigail, "Here, come help me with your father."

She rushed over and put Rennik's other arm around her shoulder and together they helped him stand. But something didn't feel right to Abigail – her father should be much taller and thinner. She looked at Rennik's face and backed away in fear, almost causing him to fall back to the floor. Luckily, Joseph caught him.

"Who are you? You are not my father."

Joseph intervened, "Actually Abigail, this *is* your father. This is his actual body – his genuine face. The man you've known your whole life, Samuel Sampson, was a facade – a costume. He embodied that man to hide his true identity. Your father is the Master of the Order of the Wick, Rennik Samson."

Again, this day showed something to Abigail which by itself would be too much to digest. And logic, of which Abigail was a fan, would dictate multiple unbelievable events and facts, being exposed all in one day, would be too much to handle by any person. But this new, inconceivable fact actually gave Abigail some sense of solace, as if everything bad was happening for a larger purpose. She still did not like that it happened at all, and the reasoning behind it completely escaped her, but there seemed to be some underlying logic and order at play, regardless of whether she understood it. This made her less fearful of this stranger than she otherwise might be.

Abigail moved in closer to Rennik's face. She wanted to get a good look at this man. But as she looked closer, she realized he wasn't really a stranger. She saw his face before. She rubbed her chin and furled her forehead. "Where have I seen him?" Suddenly, it occurred to her. She ran off to her parents' bedroom.

Joseph called to her, "What are you doing? We need to get your father out of here."

Abigail ran back into the room, holding a picture. It was a drawing of two people dressed for a wedding. She held the picture next to Rennik's face. He was breathing heavily and still slumped over, hanging on to Joseph's shoulder for support.

"This is you, isn't it? Mother told me this picture was of my grandparents, but it's really you. Right?" By the tone of her voice, Rennik couldn't tell if she was excited at using the clue to solve a mystery or if she was angry for being lied to her entire life.

"Yes, that is your mother and me on our wedding day. Abigail, there is much you cannot understand yet. For one, that drawing is from the year 1446. That is the year we were married. This will be impossible for you to understand but I am almost three hundred years old. I realize this all must shock you, but please, don't be angry. We don't have time for this right now – you must harness your emotion and focus on what matters." He coughed and wiped some blood from the corner of his mouth. "Take me back to the Porter's

154

house so we can talk. You have much to learn and too little time to learn it."

Without thinking, Abigail put the drawing down, grabbed the cloak and put all three of them underneath it. Joseph objected, "You can't transport three people with the cloak. Only two can go. I just came along to make sure your father was all right. You take him back with the cloak, I'll run back to my house and meet you there in a few minutes."

Rennik looked at Abigail and nodded. Through coughing he agreed, "He's right Abigail. Belle can only transport two people. Thank you, Joseph. We'll see you in a few minutes."

Abigail repeated the steps to activate the cloak, but this time she knew what the inside of the Porter's house looked like, so she could imagine it and deliver Rennik directly inside.

Just as Abigail was preparing to close her eyes, Joseph grabbed her shoulder and said, "Tell my wife to engage Plan Three A. She'll know what it means."

Abigail nodded her understanding and closed her eyes. It was difficult for her to keep her arms around Rennik as he slumped over so much. She clenched her hands as tightly as she could and began her energy cycle.

Rennik struggled to stand in order to help ease the load and said, "Thank you, daughter."

"I have to say, it's weird hearing those words come from *that* face. It will take some time to get used to."

Rennik smiled as he laughed and coughed simultaneously. Abigail closed her eyes, felt her energy build and as soon as her eyes popped open, they disappeared.

After making sure they were safely on their way, Joseph left the Sampson house and started running back toward his own. He just needed to make one quick stop along the way.

Tobias' house was not too far from Joseph's, perhaps at most a five-minute walk. Even running at a great speed, it would take him seven or eight minutes to arrive. He wanted to see how Junius fared during the battle.

Running out of breath, Joseph reached Tobias' house in near record time. He slowed as he approached, panting heavily, and what he saw surprised him. The house looked as though a tornado made a direct hit. He walked by the shattered glass from the windows and tried to count how many gaping holes he saw in the house's structure. There were almost too many to quantify – holes of varying sizes covered the walls, from a couple of inches in diameter, to five or six feet in diameter. Around the house were trees split in half, branches were down and thrown all over were large rocks. He opened the door, which took some doing because it was hanging partially off the hinges, and slowly entered. There was no sign of Junius, but the house was a disaster. Nothing was in its proper place. Strewn throughout the home were dishes, silverware and glassware, broken into many pieces. Overturned chairs were on display and somehow a rug was hanging from the mantle. "This must have been some battle," he thought. "I wonder if Junius survived."

Chapter 33

Abigail and Rennik appeared in the Porter's main room. Elizabeth did not see them materialize – she was in the kitchen cleaning the dishes from the day so her back was turned to them.

"Mrs. Porter," Abigail said gently not wanting to startle her.

The sudden voice from an unexpected guest nearly gave Elizabeth a heart attack. She jumped in the air and screamed. She turned to face Abigail with her right hand now covering her heart from the fear. "My dear. You mustn't scare me like that."

"I'm sorry ma'am. This is urgent. Mr. Porter asked me to tell you we need Plan Three A."

Her fear turned into nervous seriousness. "Really? Three A? Are you certain that is what he said?"

"Yes ma'am."

Elizabeth ran to their bedroom as fast as she could and came back carrying a small black bag. Abigail was helping Rennik sit down in a chair at their table. He needed to lean against it to help prop himself up.

"And who do we have here? Who is this mystery man we're helping tonight?"

"Oh, that's right. You're in the same position I am," Abigail said.

"Based on what I've seen tonight, I highly doubt that, dear."

"You will not believe this, so don't even bother trying. This is my father. The man you knew as Samuel Sampson was not real. It was a costume. This is Rennik Samson – he is my true father."

Elizabeth's face almost turned gray from the shock. Abigail commiserated with Mrs. Porter and said, "I know. It's unbelievable, isn't it?"

"Not at all, Abigail," Mrs. Porter responded. "Not after what I've seen tonight. I'm just shocked I finally have met the Rennik I've heard so much about over the years. And to think I've known you all along."

Elizabeth was buzzing through the black bag. "Three A… Three A…. I need the herbs… the mushrooms… and the hair."
She pulled various ingredients out of the bag, along with a paper with written instructions upon it, almost like it contained several recipes. Even though she was rushing to get everything together, she appeared to be quite calm. When most people would need to prevent their hands from trembling under the pressure, hers were completely serene, seemingly at peace with the task they were undertaking.

"Rennik, it really is a pleasure to meet you. I wish it was under different circumstances, though."

Rennik grimaced in pain. "Elizabeth, I might look different but it's still me. Samuel was a part of who I am. You've known me all these years."

Elizabeth leaned backward in her chair and turned to Abigail. "Be a dear and grab a wet towel. Then carefully wipe the blood and dirt from your father's face." Abigail obediently complied, coming back to dab Rennik's face lightly to not cause him any undue discomfort.

"Now Rennik, show me that wound on your stomach."

For the first time, he removed his hand from his right side. His hand became somewhat stuck to the skin and the act of pulling it off seemed to cause even more pain for him, like he was separating skin which grew attached. It was the first time Abigail could see how badly hurt he really was.

Elizabeth did her best not to show any reaction. But what she saw appalled and disgusted her. "Well, that must hurt a good bit," she said.

"Abigail, go out in the front and gather some dirt from the yard in that bucket." Elizabeth motioned to a bucket sitting by the front door. "Bring it in and add some water from the basin to it. We need the mud to pack onto the wound."

While Abigail was performing the chore, Elizabeth started mixing the various herbs and mushrooms together with a mortar and pestle, based on what she was reading on the instructions. Soon the mixture became a paste, and a foul smelling one at that.

"Let's see," she said out loud but to herself as she was reading the directions. "Mix the items together until they form a paste. Done. Place the hair around the edge of the wound, careful to ensure no hair actually gets into the wound itself." She looked into his face, "Rennik, I do not know if this is going to hurt or not."

He winced in pain even before she reached over. "I'm fine," he told her in a tense and pained voice.

Elizabeth carefully placed the hair along the edge of Rennik's wound. The hole in his body was too large for just one strand, so she reached back into the bag to grab another. Together, the strands now encircled Rennik's injury. Elizabeth beckoned to Abigail, "How are you coming with the mud?"

Abigail was coming back into the house with the bucket of dirt when Joseph ran up. He was sweating profusely and very much out of breath. Abigail was so involved in caring for Rennik she didn't notice Joseph arrived ten minutes later than he reasonably should have.

Joseph slowed his pace to a walk in order to catch his breath. His hands were on his hips as he struggling to get back to normal breathing. "How is Rennik?"

"I think he's in a lot of pain. His wound looks bad. Mrs. Porter is…" Elizabeth cut her off calling her name, wondering what was taking so long.

"I'm sorry Mr. Porter. I have to get this dirt inside so we can pack his wound with mud."

They both entered the house and Abigail immediately took the bucket to the water basin and poured some water in. She put her hands into the bucket to mix the mud. Abigail knew the best mudpack was thick, but not too thick – wet, but not too wet. She massaged the mud to the right consistency and then brought the bucket to Mrs. Porter.

Elizabeth continued reading out loud, "Take the mixture and pack it into the wound, as deep as possible. Then cover the wound, mixture and hair with mud to keep it in place." Without hesitation, Elizabeth scooped a large handful of the mushroom and herb mixture and spread it into the wound. Rennik buckled over in pain and gasped loudly. His face contorted to show just how much pain he was in. Elizabeth gooped another handful into the wound and then spread Abigail's mud over the entire area and tightly packed it in.

That was enough for Rennik. He nearly passed out from the pain and he needed to let his body rest, and hopefully heal. If he could hold on until sunrise, he could get outside and let the sun re-energize him. That would give his body the strength it needed to heal fully.

Joseph and Abigail helped Rennik move from the table over to a bed so he could be more comfortable, and also so the mud could lay flat on his wound to help with the healing.

Rennik was exhausted, but he felt an urgent need to impart as much information to Abigail as possible. He motioned for Joseph to join him. Joseph gently sat down on the edge of the bed, careful not to cause too much motion so he would not disturb Rennik.

In a whispering and pained voice, Rennik said, "We need to teach her as much as possible, as quickly as possible. Even though it goes against my better judgement, I think she needs to know exactly who she is, and exactly what her role within the Order will be. She needs to know who she can trust, and who she cannot. Can you help me with this?"

"Of course, Rennik. I will help any way you'd like."

"Joseph, I need to know you will always protect her as I would, no matter what."

"You have my word."

Joseph called for Abigail to join them and he asked Elizabeth to go to the other room. "We have important, private business to discuss with Abigail, darling. For your own protection you cannot know anything of it." Elizabeth understood and retired to the bedroom for the evening.

Chapter 34

Joseph explained to Rennik what he already taught Abigail, which was not very much, but it was a significant amount considering the lack of notice he had and the short time they spent together. There was much more Rennik needed to impart to his daughter, and even more he didn't have time for, so she would need to learn much on her own. Luckily he put a plan in action to help with that.

"Abigail, come sit next to me," Rennik pleaded. "I know what you've already learned must seem unbelievable. But every word is the truth. I know how logical you are and you must turn off your scientific disbelief. Normally, being skeptical is a good thing. But right now I need your mind to dispel all of that and just soak in every word like a sponge. You must accept it as truth for now, and experience it to believe it later. Can you have that kind of faith for me, and in me?"

She realized this unfamiliar looking man was certainly her father. He knew how her brain worked, and he also knew how to pique her interest so she would listen to what he needed to say. "Yes, of course. Anything you need, Father."

"I'm going to give you a brief history lesson." It turned out the word "brief" was a rather subjective term.

"You already know the truth about Samson and Delilah, about his hair, and their plan to protect the bloodline. For the next seventeen hundred years or so, the history is mostly of the bloodline spreading throughout the world, from the original three pockets – Africa, the East and the West." Rennik glanced at Joseph, "Did you explain the threes to her?"

"Yes, a bit. She knows three is the most important number to the Order."

"Good." Rennik turned back to Abigail. "The number three is more important than you know. Whenever there is a mystery, or something you cannot figure out, see if the number three is a key to solving the problem. More often than not, it will at least help you unravel things and lead you down a path to a solution. You will find many aspects of our lives naturally revolve around a pattern of threes. Always trust that."

Abigail nodded her understanding though she didn't really understand at all.

"The next major event in our history was Myrddin's discovery of the ancient book. That is a relic going back to Samson himself. It is the book you brought with you tonight from our house. This is one of our most sacred relics, it is quite fragile so you must handle it with great care, always. That book is the rightful property of the current Master of the Order, right now that is me. Only a Master can read the book. For anyone else, they will only see encoded letters so they cannot read from the book. When a Master takes the book, the letters rearrange themselves just for the reader. There is great knowledge and power in that book. One day, maybe one day soon, it will make itself readable to you. Read it carefully and heed its messages. It will become a reference to help you make any tough decision and it will guide you down the path best for the Order and for you."

What Rennik was saying enthralled Abigail, and she wasn't paying particular attention to the true meaning of his words – one day, maybe one day soon, *she* would become the Master. Even though everything she was learning was incredibly outlandish, that was simply too unrealistic for her to even consider. Her ears simply ignored it.

"I know Joseph already explained about Samson's lock of hair. Each child of the bloodline has three strands. As you've likely realized by now, you have six. That is because I am a direct descendant, as was your mother. Only Myrddin himself has had that distinction. This makes you a very special person, and it puts you in great danger."

Abigail's look became more serious. She sat straighter and leaned in closer to her father.

"When I was a nominee to become Master, I was the candidate chosen from the West and the African delegation supported me. My opponent, the candidate from the East, was Junius Dracul."

Abigail jumped in, "Oh, is that the election you won over him which you've felt guilty about ever since?"

"In a way. It wasn't really an election, it was a duel. We held different ideas on how the Order should move into the future. I thought we should live amongst the unbloods, proffering peace between our two people. With our protection, the unbloods could live happily and with prosperity, and that would benefit us since it would make it less likely they would try to destroy or undermine the Order."

"But the leading clan from the East, the Draculs, had a different strategy. They wanted to remain hidden and separated from the unbloods. They felt the bloodline would become contaminated if our two peoples lived amongst each other. And they were fearful the unbloods would look to destroy us out of ignorance. The majority of the Order agreed with me. This enraged Junius and he challenged me to a duel with the prize being the title of Master of the Order." Abigail interjected, "He sounds like a horrid person."

"He is. In fact, he has only one redeeming quality I can think of. He would do anything to get what he wanted, as I'll explain in a moment. But he made a point of making sure everyone knew he would never physically harm any member of his family. They were all afraid of his grandmother – she ruled the family with violence and disdain. This brought the family members closer together, and they swore never to harm each other. It's funny, the only good thing I can say about this man is he wouldn't harm his own family. That seems like a rather low measurement of human quality."

Abigail didn't know how to respond. She just nodded slightly in agreement.

Rennik continued, "It was the first time in the Order's history there had been a duel where the outcome would determine the next Master. In the past, the changing of the Master was a joyful, peaceful event. But Junius could not accept his ideas were not as popular as mine. It was a fierce battle. I won, and he was badly scarred."

Joseph's face lit up, "It was the greatest battle I've ever seen. The Order viewed your father as a hero after that. And with good reason. Instead of killing Junius, he offered his hand in partnership to unify the branches of the Order. Junius pretended to accept."

Rennik put his hand on Joseph's shoulder and patted it. "That was a long time ago, old friend. I would not be so arrogant today."

Abigail asked, "What ever became of Junius?"

"Well, he went back to his family in the East – in Transylvania. His father, Mircea, was a slithering fool of a warlock. He believed keeping the unbloods in constant fear was the only way to protect the bloodline. He felt if they feared him, they would leave him and his family alone. So he embodied his brother, Vladimir, much like I embodied Samuel. Vlad was much weaker in spirit than Mircea and so Mircea could easily embody him."

"Embodying Vladimir, Mircea tormented the unbloods in unspeakable ways. He became known as 'Vlad the Impaler' and took to cheap trickery to make the unbloods even more fearful. He would often embody the recently dead and open their coffins from within, acting as if they had come back to life. The unbloods concocted many myths around this seemingly 'undead' persona. No other branch of the bloodline can perform an embodiment of the dead, only the Draculs and the Master have that knowledge. They can embody anyone of the same gender, alive or not. His stunts led the unbloods to believe many silly notions, like Vlad would drink the blood of his victims, or he was invisible to a mirror, or sunlight would kill him. That last one always struck me as odd, because as a Wicked with the mystical hair, the sunlight would actually rejuvenate him. But he never objected to the fanciful myths. He felt the misinformation protected him, which made him more invincible."

Joseph interrupted, "Abigail, do you recall when your word 're-alive' startled me? This is the reason. It reminded me of the Draculs' ability to embody the dead and it immediately made me wonder if you had some Dracul blood in you."

"Of course she does," Rennik said amid a terrible fit of coughing. "She is only the second living convergence of all three branches of the bloodline. She has a part of every member of the Order in her." He rubbed her shoulder in a proud, loving, parental way.

Rennik regained his composure from the cough and wiped a bit of blood from his mouth. "This is where things get very serious. Junius never forgave me for defeating him in the duel, and instead of joining me to unify the Order as he promised, he and his family devised a plan to create a self-fulfilling prophecy. They aimed to prove to the Order's general assembly the Draculs were right about living apart from the unbloods. Their reign of terror aimed to show just how irrational the unbloods could be. And they accomplished their goal. Once Junius had the proof he was right, such as he saw it, he embarked on a campaign to take the role of Master away from me."

"How? Did he try to kill you?" Abigail asked.

"Well, yes, he tried. But he could not have become Master if he was successful. The only way he can legitimately do that...," Rennik paused, trying to decide if he should continue his thought but immediately realized he needed to give Abigail as much information as he could. "The only way for him to do it would be for him to kill all three of the Master's children. It is so written in the ancient book."

There was dead silence in the room. Even the air seemed to stop moving in order to reap the gravity of the moment.

Abigail looked down with a very serious look on her face. It wasn't quite fear, and it wasn't quite determination. It was an unconscious blend of both.

"So Archibald and Ichibad? They didn't die of natural causes?"

"No," Rennik said somberly. "I wasn't exactly sure what happened when Archibald died. It happened at night, we were all asleep. When we discovered him in the morning, we thought he somehow just lost consciousness during the night. There were no signs of a struggle. He was just laying there, a dead fifteen-year-old, otherwise healthy boy."

"But Ichibad was a different situation. Ever since Archibald's death forty-five years earlier, I became a very light sleeper. I always kept one eye open, fearful something might happen to your mother, and when Ichibad was born, I was fearful for his safety too. One night, when he was fourteen, I heard a faint scratching sound coming from one of his windows. I went to Ichibad's room and his window was open with Junius levitating outside. He already held the boy in his arms, under some kind of trance. I did what I could, but I was too late. I could only watch as Junius snapped his neck, smiling his hideous smile at me the whole time. Through his evil grin he said to me, 'That's number two.' I've never forgotten his horrible smile."

"This devastated your mother and I, as you could imagine. We waited a very long time before deciding whether to have a third child – we understood the risk. When we finally decided, we knew we needed to leave Coventry and take on new embodiments. It was the only way to keep you safe. At least we thought it was. I'm not sure how Junius found us, but he's here now. And he intends to kill our third child so he can become Master."

Rennik started coughing heavily. This time, a significant amount of blood came up. Joseph rushed to the basin to grab a towel and water while Abigail moved to her father's side and propped up his head so he wouldn't choke on the blood. Rennik was sweating quite a bit, he clearly had an awful fever.

"My dear daughter," Rennik said with a struggling voice, "do whatever you must to survive. After me, you are the next rightful Master. You will lead the Order in the right direction. Junius cannot become Master, no matter what. For the good of all people – unbloods, Wicken and Wicked, you must see to it."

After her father stopped coughing, Abigail made him comfortable while saying nothing. She put a pillow under his head and wiped a cool, wet towel across his forehead. This morning she woke a young girl with her family intact. Tonight she would go to sleep with her mother dead, her father possibly dying and the weight of the world literally resting upon her shoulders.

While Rennik rested, Abigail talked with Mr. Porter, seeking any advice she could get. "What about Belle? Could I take him to a place where the sun is already out?"

Joseph shook his head. "No, unfortunately. The cloak can only travel short distances. The sun is probably just by the Old World at this point. You wouldn't get anywhere close."

Abigail was silent for some time. Then she came to a realization. "I've been thinking about the 'threes' you and Father both mentioned. Do you literally mean the number three is as important as you say?"

"Actually, it's both. Members of the Order often find the literal value of threes in everyday life. Other times it's more figurative. But it is a constant thread through everything. Why do you ask?"

"Well, Millie died on Wednesday – the third day of the week. Do you think it was a coincidence?"

"No, I do not."

"All right." She paused for a moment to connect her thoughts. "And so far three people close to me have died – Millie, Mr. Putnam and my mother. Are you suggesting this also is not a coincidence?"

"That's exactly what I'm saying."

"So that means Father won't die, not tonight. Because three already have."

The idea made Abigail feel a little better, and it might have been true, had three people close to her actually died.

She fell asleep sitting on the floor next to her father's bed, her legs tucked underneath her body. She folded her arms on the side of the bed with her head laying in them. Abigail was as close to her father's face as she could get while still having most of her body on the floor. She could hear him breathe, which comforted her. There was much for her to think about, and more emotion to deal with than anyone could expect of her. But for now, all she cared about was sleeping – happy this horrid day was finally over.

Chapter 35

He opened his eyes – slowly. His throat was dry but somehow there was enough moisture for him to dampen his mouth by creeping his tongue around. His tongue felt… sticky. "Uhhh, my head. It feels like my sinuses are going to burst." He wanted to put his right hand onto his forehead, just to wipe the hair and sweat away. He thought the pressure of his hand against his forehead might ease the pain. But he couldn't. His arm was laying across his chest with very little room to move. He could only lift his arm maybe five or six inches before it hit something solid. He tried to move his arm down to his side, but hit something solid just to the right of his body. The pace of his breath increased.

It was dark. Too dark to see what was there. He tried moving both arms, and neither could move. "Dear God," he thought. Panic grew in his chest and tightened against his heart. He could not move and he could not see. "Am I trapped?" He could feel the sweat drip down the side of his face, but he was unable to wipe it away and relieve the discomfort.

His legs could not move too far upward. He estimated he could only raise his legs four or five inches at most. They could barely move side to side. He banged his legs as hard as he could up and down, trying to determine what was confining him. All he could tell was he was not on a bed of any kind, but on something hard and in something confining.

He started screaming for help, which gave him more clues to his surroundings. His screams had no echo and he could tell he was boxed into very close quarters. His lack of motion in all directions confirmed this to be true. The thuds made by his kicking produced no reverberation whatsoever. He was in a dead space. His panic grew more intense, and he began screaming uncontrollably.

His mind was racing, and his breathing was rapid. "Where can I be? Am I being held hostage? I'm not tied up, so that's unlikely. What was the last thing I remember? Uh, I don't know – I can't recall." He no longer cared about his dry mouth or throbbing sinuses. He just wanted to get out of wherever he was. It was hot – stifling hot. His perspiration made the small space even warmer from his own self-induced humidity. He could only assume he was somehow buried alive, which was always one of his deepest fears.

He did not know what time it was, nor the day. His ears heard no sound. He did not know how he got there, how long he'd been there, and most importantly, how he might escape. He devised a plan, though it was flimsy. It was his only option – it would be better to die trying to escape than to die not trying at all.

"Think William, think," he urged himself. "Graves are dug about six feet deep and a standard coffin is probably two to three feet deep. If I'm correct and someone has somehow buried me alive, that would mean I need to escape the coffin and dig through three to four feet of earth to get to the surface."

He couldn't know Tobias' men did not have the time to dig a full six-foot-deep hole. His grave was only four feet deep, so in reality the top of his coffin was only about twelve to eighteen inches underground. It was still a lot of earth to dig through, especially in the state of panic and anxiety in which he found himself, but it was certainly more achievable than three or four feet.

Logic and reason abandoned him – an unfamiliar feeling for William. His only thought now was escape. He was able to wedge his arms onto his chest and turn his hands upright. He felt like the walls were

172

closing in on him, compressing onto his body and preventing him from taking deep breaths. This caused a combination of even more panic and less logical thinking. He started scratching and clawing at the surface just above his face. It was too dark to see if he was making any progress, but there were bits of wood and dirt falling onto his face and into his mouth each time he scratched. "Progress," he realized nervously.

He was scratching at the surface like a dog digging to hide a bone – fast and ferocious. William used both hands simultaneously and his fingers were moving faster and faster as he made more progress. He could feel wood splinters pushing into the skin under his fingernails. It was painful and caused him to scream with even louder agony, but his mind was beyond the pain. He was only thinking about getting out. His fingers dripped blood onto his face as his panic grew to pure horror. The air in his confinement was thick and heavy but every bit was precious. His hard work and fear were using up the oxygen too fast, and he knew it. Awareness of one's plight makes it even worse. It is true ignorance can be blissful.

When the pain from the splinters in his fingers was too much, he paused the scratching and tried pushing his body against the surface above him. At first there was no movement. But each time he pushed, he tried to get more force into his arms, even pressing his elbows against the surface beneath him for leverage as he pushed his full body with as much torque as he could muster. His face writhed in pain and he grunted a loud, sustained moan as he summoned as much power as he could to push against the surface.

Finally, on the third try, he felt some movement. It was heavy and still very difficult to move. But it was enough to give him hope. He needed every ounce of hope he could find. He started scratching again, but not for too long as the splinters were creating a significant amount of pain as they crept deeper and deeper into the tender skin below his fingernails. Newly formed splinters entered the soft under-nail skin behind the splinters that came before. His face bulged with anguish. He went back to pushing on the surface, since it involved less pain even though it was a more intense struggle and weakened him faster.

Every minute or so he paused to rest his muscles. He was making slightly more progress each time, but found himself unable to catch his breath. The air inside his box was stale and seemed to thin. He was sweating heavily now and could feel the wood beneath his neck becoming damp. There was little for him to do except to keep trying. His chest tightened. Either he would escape or he would suffocate from the lack of air.

He pushed as hard as he could each time, using every bit of energy he could muster. He was feeling dizzy from the combination of extreme exertion and lack of fresh oxygen, but he needed to keep trying.

Finally, with one large push as his body became drained, he forced the surface up a full inch or two. The dirt rushed in through the gaps he created like water filling a hole. The area he scratched gave way and collapsed onto him. This happened right above his face and the dirt filled and covered his mouth completely. Still unable to move any part of his body other than his hands, there was not much he could do to stop it. He frantically tried to sweep the dirt away from his mouth and eyes, but each swipe led to a frenzy of more dirt filling in behind it. William could not keep pace with the deluge. He sapped all his energy and his lungs felt heavy from the earth pressing down on top of him. His horror turned to terror, his panic to dread. He tried to breathe, but was unable. He attempted to force himself to cough but nothing happened, which was the most horrific moment for him. There is no fear like when your mind can think, but you cannot force your body to perform even the simplest of functions. It's being aware of your plight that makes it so frightening. He immediately realized he lost the battle. Not knowing how he got there or why, his life was ending in a most horrible manner. The ground filled his throat. He felt the rough, gritty feeling of dirt packing his esophagus. William could not swallow because there was not enough room for his Adam's Apple to move. He was suffocating while desperately trying to reach toward the sky, his outstretched hand unknowingly a mere six inches from the surface. He died with his eyes open revealing the fear of his final moments.

Chapter 36

As soon as the sun showed itself in the east, shimmering over the waters of the Atlantic Ocean, Junius stood. He stayed awake most of the night, keeping watch in case Rennik came looking for him. When he saw the first sign of the sunrise, he moved to a clearing in the trees and turned his back to the east. He wanted his hair to soak in every beam of light the sun could deliver to him. Once the first beam of that delicious sunlight touched his hair, he immediately felt rejuvenated. Within just a matter of minutes, he was strong enough to walk a few steps. He started back for his house, or more precisely, Tobias' house.

After about ten minutes, he arrived home. It was much worse than he remembered or expected. Luckily it was still early in the day. Nobody would stop by just yet, and he conducted almost all of his business in town. He had some time. He would not clean everything on his own, instead he planned to wait a bit longer and build more strength from his hair. Once he was back near full capacity, he would use his energy to get everything back to normal. Plus, he would need to embody Tobias again. If he didn't, people might wonder where Tobias disappeared to.

After about thirty more minutes in the sun, he was feeling almost his old self. First, he would re-embody Tobias. That was important to do first in case anyone happened to stop by. He clasped his hands together, let the energy flow through him, closed his eyes and thought deeply about Tobias. He imagined his short, stout body, and his fat, red, bumpy nose. Junius imagined every detail and as each thought crossed his mind, his body morphed closer and closer to Tobias' visage. Within a couple of minutes, Junius was no longer visible and Tobias was back.

Tobias waited a few more minutes to allow his hair to harvest more energy from the sunlight, since he just used a good amount for his re-embodiment. Once he felt strong enough, he clasped his hands back together and undid all the damage to his house and property. A few minutes later, everything was back to normal. Tobias felt good – everything was back in order. He reckoned he must have badly injured Rennik since he never came looking for him. And now he finally knew the identity of the child keeping him from becoming Master. His multi-decade plan was near fruition. Monday promised to be a good day.

Things were not as happy at the Porter house. Rennik did not react well to the medicine Elizabeth applied. He slept very little, was quite feverish and the area around his wound became bright red and swollen. It was too painful for anyone to touch. The lesion was badly infected and there was nothing they could do – it was happening faster than anyone could believe. "I've never seen a wound abscess so quickly," Joseph whispered to Elizabeth. She shook her head in agreement. For obvious reasons, they could not consult a doctor. Their only hope was Rennik would survive the night and with the rise of the sun, use its energy to heal.

To pass the time while he couldn't sleep, Rennik talked to Abigail. He explained more about the history of the Order. Abigail's favorite part was when he talked about what it was like to be Master. At first, Rennik talked about the great responsibility and obligation of his position. "Speaking about obligation is a very Samuel thing to do," Abigail mused. By three in the morning, however, the conversation turned to the pleasures of his role. He talked about some pranks he pulled on his friends. Having access to the relics had its benefits.

There was one time late at night when he put Belle on, grabbed three medium-sized rocks, and then transported to his friend's house. His friend was fast asleep. Rennik stood directly above him and dropped the stones at exactly the same time he transported away. His friend woke from three stones falling on his stomach with nobody around to blame. Rennik recalled laughing himself to sleep that night. He also admitted to Abigail he needed to practice the maneuver about a dozen times to ensure the timing was just right.

Abigail was happy to spend this time with her father, but it saddened her it took so long to reach this point, and that it was under such unpleasant circumstances for them to have this rapport.

But the night did not go well. By four thirty, well before sunrise, Rennik took a turn for the worse. He was in a lot of pain, his fever was entrenched, and he was consistently coughing up a significant amount of blood. Abigail was doing her best to comfort him, while Elizabeth and Joseph tried to keep clean towels replacing the bloodied ones. At four forty-five, Rennik motioned for Abigail to come close to him. He motioned for her to put her ear next to his mouth. It was a great struggle for him to speak and he could only muster a forced whisper.

"I'll be leaving soon. But know I will always be with you, as will the others. There are always others."

Abigail tried to stop him from talking – she wanted to will him to remain alive. If he didn't speak about dying, perhaps death would not notice him.

But Rennik assured her, "It will be all right. You will be the Master now. It may take time for the rest of the Order to see you as the Master, but Joseph will tell them what he's seen in you. They will support you." He coughed some more. "You have two primary responsibilities now – first, you must remain alive, at any cost. Second, you must go to England and call a global coven. You must make all members of the Order aware of your inauguration. When they see you reading from the ancient book, they will know the book has revealed itself to you, proving you are the new, true Master. I love you Abi, this will forever be true. And always remember, there are others."

With the salutation of the Order contained in the last six words he would speak, the great and revered Rennik Samson, fifth Master of the Order, drew his final breath. Abigail collapsed onto his body, weeping. For the first time in her life, she was alone. Both parents were gone, within one day of each other. She stood, with the Porters standing behind her, and watched in astonishment as Rennik's body disintegrated into dust and a sudden breeze which mysteriously entered the house swept it away. They all looked up and watched the body of dust float away. Joseph, though sad, smiled widely as he knew this was the way of the Masters. Rennik's soul was being taken to a place where he would join the other Masters in eternity. It was a bittersweet moment for Joseph and entirely bitter for Abigail. A few moments later, Tobias received a message. He placed his three middle fingers upon the temples on his head and said nothing. The person on the other side simply said three words, "Rennik is dead."

Tobias removed the fingers from his head and smiled. "This day is looking up, indeed. Just one more to take care of."

Chapter 37

Abigail was confused. She found herself in a chasm between deep despair and, although she hated to admit it, anxious enthusiasm. She missed the life she knew just two days prior and could not think of a word dark enough to describe her sadness. The 're' words from her days at the shore were of no more use to her. At the same time, she was exhilarated by the new world which had been revealed to her and she looked forward to her new life, and new role as Master, with innocent naiveté.

"Mr. Porter, I need your help. I don't know where to begin, what to do, or even how I'm supposed to grieve." She paused, trying to figure out if she should ask her next question. "You were smiling as my father disappeared into dust. Why?"

"I don't expect you will understand this, but what happened to your father when he died was a beautiful experience. His soul joined the souls of all the other Masters. He is now unified with them, and together they will look after you. One day, hopefully many, many years in the future, you will join with them and you will be with your father forever."

This was a wonderful thought. The idea lifted Abigail and filled her with hope. She smiled through her tears at Mr. Porter. "Thank you," she said slowly and with great sincerity.

"And another thing, Abigail. You must stop calling me Mr. Porter. You will soon be the Master of the Order, I am merely your humble servant. I am here for you however you need me. So please, call me Joseph. But in public, please continue to refer to me as Mr. Porter, otherwise people will become suspicious."

"I will try… Joseph." It was hard for her to call him that and she giggled awkwardly. It strangely reminded her of the time she called William Will, but not in every way.

She continued, "I want to know what happened to my father. How do I find Junius, and how do I confront him myself?"

"Whoa, whoa, not so fast," Joseph cautioned. "Junius has great power and knowledge and comes from a long line of witches. You are not ready to confront him, not yet. Especially since you'll likely see him as soon as you leave the house."

"What do you mean?"

Joseph immediately realized Abigail did not know Tobias was the embodiment of Junius. As the soon-to-be Master, she needed to know, but he was uncertain how she would react.

"Well," Joseph continued gingerly, "only yesterday Rennik discovered Junius has been in Salem for quite some time. He's been hunting your family, looking for your father – and for you."

Her eyes thinned with a lack of understanding. "He's been here? Where?"

"Apparently he was using the trials to force you both out of hiding. He randomly targeted various women and girls and closely scrutinized the reactions of their families and friends. As he got closer to you he focused in more. He is a keen observer of human behavior and apparently he kept detailed mental notes as clues. The torrent you unwittingly created for your mother finally exposed you."

Abigail looked astonished. She was aware of Tobias' almost maniacal attention to detail – she experienced it under the sycamore tree. But she did not realize her own actions led directly to the death of her parents. Her stomach felt like a void and she needed to step back to avoid stumbling over at the revelation.

Joseph continued, "Do you remember how your father explained how embodiment was only available to the Dracul family and to the Master? Junius Dracul has been embodying someone here in town for a while."

Abigail spoke slowly and firmly, and her eyes glared with determination. "Who…. Is…. He?"

Joseph knew it was pointless to delay. She was going to find out eventually. He took a deep breath, looked at the ground and said, "Tobias Warnock."

Much like the vision of the escaping tunnel Abigail saw when Christina explained how Tobias tricked her into accusing Millie, Abigail's view again narrowed and became focused. She thought for a few seconds and said to Joseph, "You're right. I'm not ready to confront Junius. But I'm more than prepared to confront Tobias." She ran out of the house and headed for town.

Joseph followed behind her, pleading, "Wait, Abigail. No, you can't. Not yet." But just like her father, she was headstrong, determined and more than a little stubborn. When she made a decision, there was no way to change her mind. This was a trait which would serve her well as Master. Joseph hoped she would live long enough to make use of it.

Chapter 38

Abigail stormed defiantly toward the town center with Joseph trying to keep pace behind her. Her confident stride made it appear she had a plan, but Joseph did not know what it could be. He wanted to stay nearby in case Abigail tried something more advanced than she should, which was just about anything at this point. Luckily for them both, Abigail was no fool.

She arrived in the town square within a few minutes. She passed right by the stake where her mother burned just hours before. Abigail slowed her pace and walked past the stake as if it were sacred ground, staring with remembrance. The charred wood was still smoldering. Her mother's ashes were strewn about and the smell of burnt flesh still permeated the air. After a few moments of reflection, her determination was restored, and she continued on to the center of town.

"Tobias Warnock!" she yelled as loud as she could while turning in all directions so everyone could hear her voice. "Tobias Warnock – where are you? I summon thee!"

Some villagers turned their heads and started over to see why Abigail was yelling. A few people came out of the shops when they heard the noise. Abigail was drawing attention, and a crowd was forming, but Tobias was nowhere to be seen.

"Tobias Warnock! Please come out!" She continued to turn and yell, which drew more people over.

Joseph was concerned. He examined the entire town square, trying to determine the angle from which he might need to defend Abigail. "What is she doing? She's going to get herself accused and killed."

He knew this could only end badly, but there were no other options. He had to trust she knew what she was doing, but he was fearful she did not. After about ten minutes the crowd grew to about thirty people and others started calling out for Tobias so they could see what this was all about.

Tobias finally entered the square from the direction of his house and made his way to the crowd where Abigail was still calling for him. The crowd grew to almost fifty people now.

"Young lady, what is this all about? Why are you making such a commotion?"

"Mr. Warnock," she said glibly while also trying to catch her breath. "Thank you for making yourself available. I have something very important I'd like to say to you in front of my fellow villagers."

"This is quite unusual, my dear child. I can't imagine what you feel you need to say to me in such a public fashion. There are procedures for you to make inquiries to the village." But internally this turn of events pleased Tobias. Abigail was making herself a pariah and this would make her soon-to-be disappearance easier to manage.

"Oh, this is not regarding the village, my dear sir," she said mimicking Tobias' way of speaking. Everyone understood her mockery and several people laughed openly because her tone and delivery were quite accurate.

With her hands clenched behind her back, she started pacing in front of the crowd. "Mr. Warnock, I've summoned you here today in order to accuse you." The townspeople gasped in unison. It was almost too ridiculous to consider, and yet everyone immediately considered it.

184

Tobias was stunned by her nerve. "She does not understand the wrath she is about to bring onto herself," he thought. He did not understand what game she was playing, and as a result he underestimated her move.

Abigail continued, "Earlier this week, you killed an innocent child, Millie Porter. Yesterday, you killed my mother."

Tobias interrupted her and made the mistake of talking down to her like a little child. The other villagers did not appreciate his tone. "My dear girl, as you know, Millie Porter exonerated herself, as did your mother." Tobias knew Willa did not, in fact, exonerate herself. But the villagers could not see the torrent and therefore thought she died and was exonerated. The villagers were his audience, not Abigail. He knew he just needed to win them over. "They were both legitimately accused and underwent the prescribed tests." He chuckled smugly as if to show her accusation was ridiculous, yet another mistake. "By the way, where is your dear father this good day?"

Abigail stood even straighter, her chest pushed forward with pride. "He died early this morning." There was another collective gasp from the crowd. "And before he passed away, he told me *you* were his killer!"

Joseph smiled inwardly. "This is brilliant," he thought.
With an overly feigned look of surprise, Tobias said, "Your father? Samuel Sampson… is dead? My poor dear child, where is his body? We must arrange for a funeral right away."

Abigail realized she did not have an answer for this, it was a clever move by Tobias. But she did not show any concern in her face. Instead, Joseph rose to her defense, and he quickly diverted attention away from Tobias' request.

"The same thing happened with Millie," Joseph exclaimed, pointing at Tobias but speaking to the crowd. "The night before he accused her, Millie confided in me she thought Tobias Warnock was out to get her and something bad was about to happen to her by his decree."

Two people now publicly accused Tobias. This never happened before – there was no precedent. The crowd started mumbling indistinctly, but it was clear the mood was turning against Tobias.

He spoke in his own defense, employing a warm, friendly tone as he extended his arms in a disingenuous attempt to welcome the entire crowd to his point of view. "Good people of Salem, please consider what is happening here. Two people who are... emotionally distraught... are lashing out at the person they feel responsible for the deaths of their loved ones. This is a normal part of the grieving process and we mustn't hold them to account for what they say. Instead, we should take pity on them and help them through their time of... emotional distress." Tobias intentionally used the terms 'emotionally distraught' and 'emotional distress' because they implied insanity. If he could get the townspeople to buy into the claim, it would be easy for him to have Joseph committed to an asylum. He was not worried about Abigail, she would be dead before tomorrow's sunrise.

Amid the internal debate taking place from within the crowd arose a solitary voice. It was soft at first, but grew louder.

"Excuse me? Excuse me? I have something to say."

Christina Anderson stepped onto a rock so everyone could see and hear her. "Excuse me, I have something to say," she repeated louder. The crowd grew silent and turned to face her.

"It's all true. Mr. Warnock tricked me into accusing Millie. He wanted someone to accuse her and he enticed me to do it. When I realized what he was doing, he threatened to accuse my mother and me if I ever said anything." She turned to look directly at Tobias. "You are a wicked man."

This was not a good turn for Tobias and he knew it. Still, he couldn't keep himself from thinking, "Actually, it's pronounced *wik't*."

Everyone in the crowd turned to face Tobias, clearly believing Christina.

Thomas Miller heard enough, and he stepped forward to the front of the group, just in front of Tobias. He glanced at Tobias briefly and then turned to face his fellow townspeople. "It happened to me too." There were more gasps – a *fourth* public accuser! "Tobias forced me to accuse Willa. He spoke ill of her to me in church, trying to turn me against her. Then later in a private meeting he told me I must accuse her or he would accuse my wife. I feel awful about it, Abigail. I am truly sorry."

This was more than enough evidence for the villagers. Three of the townsmen stepped forward and grabbed Tobias by the arms clasping him tightly. Abigail climbed to the top of the scaffold where Tobias witnessed her mother's death. She held her hands in the air and quieted the crowd.

She continued in a tone mocking how Tobias spoke. "Tobias Warnock, you stand accused of performing the Devil's bidding through treachery and lying against the innocent, resulting in their murders. You can admit your sins and face your judgement now or you can claim your innocence and perform the Test of Purity to determine your fate. How say you?"

Abigail completely invented the Test of Purity at that moment. Tobias was not being accused of witchcraft, so they could not use that test for him. She thought this would work equally well and if Tobias tried to protest, the crowd was already against him. "Such brilliance," Joseph thought.

Though he was being held, Tobias stood straighter as a form of defiance. "You have no authority to..." Abigail cut him off abruptly, "It is not *I* who accuses you, it is *we* who accuse you. There are others." Joseph wanted to punch the air in victory with her pronouncement but contained himself. Abigail continued with a menacing, Tobias-like tone, "What say you, Mr. Warnock?"

Tobias realized it was no use fighting. The longer he did the more the crowd would turn against him. The girl outplayed him, at least in this round. But he already had an escape plan forming in his head. He might lose this battle, but the war would still be his. "I am innocent, and I choose fire for my test."

"Very well," Abigail responded. She was becoming quite good at mimicking Tobias. She nodded to the men holding him. "Take him and hold him until noon, when we will have the Test of Purity here at the stake where this wretched man murdered my beloved, *innocent* mother." The crowd applauded Abigail and booed Tobias as the three townsmen escorted him away.

Abigail climbed down from the scaffold, and Joseph congratulated her with a hug. "Such a brilliant move. Your father would be proud of you."

Abigail also impressed Tobias. She was bold, decisive and willing to take daring action. "That will make killing her much sweeter," he thought as they took him away.

Chapter 39

Elizabeth Porter was not in town to witness Abigail accusing Tobias. When Joseph arrived home, he excitedly told her all about it. "You should have seen her, Elizabeth. I've seen no one comport themselves so well under such pressure, except perhaps Rennik. Tobias, or should I say Junius, was no match for her. She completely out-maneuvered him and set him up."

The story of Abigail's performance impressed Elizabeth. "It sounds as if she will do a fine job as Master, from how you tell it. Do you think the others will support her?"

"You can never be sure how the Order will react as a whole, especially the Dracul clan. But if she continues to behave as I witnessed today, she may become the most revered Master since Myrddin himself, and she might unite the Order as Rennik wanted."

Elizabeth was pleased Joseph was so excited. "I wish I could stay and hear more, dear. But I have errands to run in town. Do you think the crowd has cleared – would it be safe for me to go there?"

"Yes, I'm sure most have dispersed by now. You should have no problem."

"I'll be off then." She kissed Joseph on the cheek and headed to the town square. Joseph did not ask what errands she needed to run, nor did Elizabeth offer to tell him.

****

Abigail returned to her house to rest before Tobias' test at noon. She was not a violent person, and she did not condone violence of any kind. But she would have no mixed emotions about ridding the world of Junius for good. Still, she did not like the idea of being responsible for another person's death. This guilt was a feeling she knew she would have to overcome in her new role. There might be times where she would need to spill the blood of others in order to save her own blood. The bloodline was more important than any one person, including her. She knew it would take a while for her to come to terms with the need to use violence when necessary.

She was wary of Tobias, however. Her father tried to rid the world of Junius for many years, decades even. And her father was much smarter and stronger than was she. It seemed too easy this morning. She could not believe how easy it was to outwit Junius with mere words and accusations. She couldn't decide if it explained more about how easy it was to outplay Junius, or if it said more about how gullible the good people of Salem were. But either way, she knew she would have to remain vigilant until she saw his dead body. Until then, nothing was certain.

When Abigail arrived at her house, she stepped in and looked around. It was eerily quiet. She could not remember a time when she was home alone. Even if her mother were the only one there, some sound was being made. Whether she was doing laundry, dishes or preparing a meal, her mother always had something going on and there was always a cheerful noise in the house.

But now, the air was dead quiet. The only sound Abigail could hear was her heart beating – it appeared the beating came from inside her ears. She walked around, letting her hand fall upon the table, then the bookshelf. For the first time, she was thinking about how much she missed her parents. How was she going to survive now, with nobody to take care of her? And most important, how was she to go about convening a global coven and getting to England? There was much to figure out – all on her own.

She came upon the drawing of her parents on their wedding day she left behind the day prior. "I can't believe I grew up always thinking they were my grandparents. I missed out on so much." She left the drawing in its frame on the table. She kept it in her family home instead of taking it to the Porter's. They generously asked if she wanted to stay with them as they had an extra bed now – Millie's old bed. Abigail was happy not to be alone.

It was only about ten o'clock – Tobias' test was still two hours away. Her eyelids were heavy, and she struggled to keep them open. She decided an hour-long nap would help. She laid down but could not fall asleep. The entire time she was worried she would oversleep. If she did not show up, it's possible Tobias would sweet-talk his way out of the test. She could not allow that.

****

Mrs. Porter was in town making rounds in most of the shops. In some shops she needed to purchase goods, while in others she stopped in just to say hello to everyone. Especially in the current climate, it was important to maintain positive social connections. She missed the commotion from earlier, so in each shop she asked what happened. She was looking for any inconsistencies in the recollections from various people. It's in the inconsistencies where the true story lives and where one can find the easiest path to advantage. But each story she heard was remarkably consistent. In fact, the level of consistency surprised her. It seems Joseph was not the only one visibly impressed with Abigail. And most were equally in awe of Christina Anderson's bravery and Thomas Miller's honesty, though most felt Thomas should have known better than to allow Tobias to pressure him into accusing an innocent, costing her life.

There was one stop Elizabeth made that was not a shop. She was in the town hall for about five minutes, the location where Tobias was being held. She entered and left having drawn no particular attention to herself. Nobody thought anything of it and Elizabeth continued on to the other shops. About thirty minutes later, she headed home. She would have just enough time to freshen up and prepare to come back to town by noon on Joseph's arm, for Tobias' test.

Chapter 40

Abigail arrived at the town square at eleven thirty. She could not sleep and was feeling exhausted, both physically and emotionally. When she arrived at the stake, she found Tobias' two men stacking the wood and kindling. It surprised her to see them.

"What happened to the others who were holding Mr. Warnock?"

One of the men replied in a strange accent Abigail could not place, "They couldn't stay, they needed to get home to their families. We were asked to take over the duties, since, ya know, we have experience doing this already."

They were referring to Abigail's mother's death. Abigail did her best to ignore the taunt, though her expression showed she could not ignore it. "Who asked you?"

"I don't know who she was. A pleasant woman stopped by and asked us to take over the preparations."

The other man spoke to the first one, "I think it was the girl's mother. You know, the girl who drowned in her test last week?"

"Yeah, that's right," the first man said.

"Mrs. Porter?" Abigail wondered why Mrs. Porter would have been interested in having the men take over, but she only wondered for a moment. Perhaps she was walking by and heard the first men talk about having to leave. It would be just like Mrs. Porter to step in and help solve a problem that wasn't her own.

"What about Mr. Warnock?" Abigail asked.

"Oh, he's not going anywhere," said one of the men. "He's chained to the wall inside the town hall good and tight."

"Excellent," Abigail responded. "Please finish this up quickly. You'll need to bring him out right at noon."

Abigail walked toward the Town Hall building as the two men got back to work. "That felt strange," she thought. "I've never given a command to an adult before. They just accepted it and did as I asked." She smiled. "I could get used to this."

Abigail entered the Town Hall and checked to see who else was inside. The only one she saw was Tobias, sitting in a chair with both of his hands chained, more than his body width apart, to a firmly ensconced brace on the wall with both of his feet shackled together.

Tobias looked at her. "You've come to gloat, I assume?"

"Not at all," she responded. "I find no pleasure in carrying out my obligations."

"Hearing a Sampson talk about obligation is like hearing a cow moo or a dog bark. It seems to be what comes naturally to your kind."

Abigail stepped closer, cautious not to get too close. She leaned in so she could look closely into his eyes. "And what comes naturally to your kind? Killing just to get a title you want to have?"

Tobias looked aggrieved. "Killing? What are you talking about, child? What title do you think I am after?"

"It doesn't matter what I think or what you say. I'm the Master of the Order now."

194

Tobias' face curled into an evil grin and his tone grew more sinister. "So he told you all about it, did he? And you think *you're* the Master now?" Tobias laughed louder than even he intended. "You know nothing of our people, of the prophecy, or our relics. There is no way you could ever become Master. You are but a child. The Order would never allow it. You'll never be in control of the Witch's Toolkit." He turned away from her with utter disdain.

"Witch's Toolkit?"

"I see. So he never explained the Toolkit to you? It seems perhaps he did not trust you with that knowledge." Tobias' lips curled as he turned away from her, his arms still struggling against the chains. "The Master controls the Toolkit. They are his tools allowing him to govern the Order."

Abigail looked dubious. "And what exactly is in this Toolkit?"

"The Toolkit contains just three items. They are the only tools the Master needs, other than his own abilities. The Toolkit comprises a book, a candle and a bell."

Abigail stood and walked to the other side of the room, looking down and thinking deeper with each stride. "A book, a candle and a bell?" She immediately realized the book was her father's ancient book. "The candle must be Father's candle. But I don't remember ever seeing a bell." She continued walking and thinking, trying to picture every item she ever saw in her home. Tobias glanced over his shoulder at her, trying to determine what was going through her head.

He taunted her, "Trying to figure out what to do with your life now that you realize you'll never control the Toolkit? Don't worry I have my own plans for your life."

Abigail stopped in her tracks and looked up. It wasn't because of Tobias' threat – she wasn't paying attention to him. But then it hit her. She had the book, and she had the candle. And she also possessed Belle – Father's cloak. That must be the third tool from the kit. Her face glowed as an enormous smile overtook her. "He hid them in plain sight. *Semper Invisibilia Huc.*"

"My dear Junius. I may not have realized what the Toolkit was, but I already possess all three items."

Tobias sneered and looked away from her again. "That was a feeble attempt. I expect more from you."

"Oh, but it's true. I have the book – Father's 'ancient book'. I have the candle – Father's special candle with six strands of hair as the wick. And I have Belle – Father's old cloak I've already used twice to transport between my house and the Porters."

Tobias tried not to display any outward emotion, but this news shocked him and he looked at her with a bit of surprise in his eyes. He heard rumors about a cloak used for transportation, but it never occurred to him the cloak was the famous 'bell' from the Toolkit. "The Cloak is not in the New World. Not even Rennik would be that foolish."

Abigail knew she should have revealed none of this information to Junius – he was certain to use it against her. But he was soon to be dead and besides, she wanted Junius to know he was up against a true rival. She needed him to take her seriously. This was a character flaw and mistake she would not soon forget.

Tobias sat motionless for some time staring blankly at the wall. "Why would she transport to the Porters?" he pondered. Then, without warning, an ominous smile took over his face.

196

"Your candle has *six* strands? So your mother? That would mean...."
He paused, thinking a bit more. "Oh, this is just too good to be true."

Abigail expected her comments to fill Junius with fear, not pleasure.
His reaction surprised and confused her.

He continued, "You realize all I have to do is kill you with my own
hands, like I did your brothers, and then I'll be the rightful Master."

"That *was* true while my father was still alive. But since he is no
longer the Master, I no longer represent the third child. Killing me
would only confirm you to be a serial killer."

"Oh dear girl, you have much to learn. You are not the Master until
the global coven inaugurates you. That is assuming they actually go
forward with inaugurating you, which they will not. Until then, the
Order still considers Rennik the Master – even in death. Your murder
at my hands will make me the Master at any point until the Order
inaugurates another."

One of the men opened the door. "Excuse me ma'am, we're done.
And it's nearly noon."

Tobias glared at Abigail. "Consider my words, my dear. I will become
Master – it is my destiny. Until then, I believe we have an
appointment to keep. Shall we?"

Chapter 41

Abigail stepped outside and saw a large gathering of townspeople. She nodded to the two men to unchain Tobias and bring him out, while Abigail ascended to the scaffold where, just one day earlier, Tobias directed those same two men to burn her mother alive. Most villagers made note of the irony, many of whom felt Tobias' impending death would close a grim chapter in their shared history.

The two men escorted Tobias from the Town Hall, past the scaffold, through the clearing in the wood and kindling, and finally onto the step at the base of the stake. They took a thick rope, placed Tobias' hands together behind his back, and bound him tightly to the stake. First, they wrapped the rope three times around his body, and around his chest. Finally, they tied the rope around his legs, all the way to his feet. The rope constrained Tobias, and he had virtually no wiggle room. The two men placed the wood on top of the open path they created as they backed away from the stake. Everything was ready.

Abigail was dreading the next part, and she wanted to get it over with as quickly as possible. She raised her hands to silence the crowd. "Tobias Warnock, you stand accused of treachery, lying and murder. The citizens of Salem provide you with one last chance to admit your guilt and accept our judgement, or you may continue with this Test of Purity where God himself will be your judge. How say you?"

"I proclaim my innocence, and only ask once my body has shown me to be an innocent man, the village should know those I condemned were truly guilty."

"Amazing," Abigail thought. "He's about to meet death and all he cares about is turning the table on those already exonerated. There truly is no bottom to this man's soul."

The townspeople hissed in response to his plea.

Abigail responded to Tobias and to the entire crowd simultaneously. "You are in no position to make demands. You will begin your test." And with a perfect impression of Tobias himself, she continued, "May God have mercy on your soul."

With that, Abigail nodded to the two men who were standing on opposite sides of Tobias, lit torches in hand. In unison they lowered their torches and set the kindling ablaze.

Elizabeth Porter took longer than usual to get ready for the burning, so the Porters were a few minutes late. They arrived just as the flames spread through the woodpile. They moved as close as they could to the front, and then Joseph realized something terrible. "Oh no," he thought. "His hands – they are behind his back…. In contact with each other." But it was too late. The flames were already growing on their own accord. There was no way Joseph could stop the ceremony and separate Tobias' hands. The unbloods would not understand. Abigail's unfamiliarity with the Order gave Tobias an opening he somehow, inextricably, took advantage of. It was not her fault, Joseph understood this. She only knew of the Order for less than one day.

Abigail could not bear to watch someone burn alive, not even Tobias. Yet, she understood she could not turn away. Many in the crowd were now looking to her for moral strength and she could not portray any weakness. Instead of watching Tobias suffer, she gazed upon each in the crowd with a look of somber confidence. It was as if she was saying to each person, "I know this is difficult, but it's the right thing to do and our town will be better off for it." Each person responded with a look saying, "Thank you for being here for us."

Tobias could feel the heat on his feet. It was quickly becoming unbearable. But he needed to wait until the last possible second to make his jump. Once he did, Tobias' body would shrivel. If he jumped too early, it would appear Tobias' body was a limp balloon and the death would appear to be fake. If he waited too long, he would suffer great pain and potentially not be able to make the jump at all. Timing was the key to this endeavor, and it's the main teaching Junius' father, Mircea, passed down to him. "If Father and my cousins could do this, then certainly I can do this too. I just need to wait a bit longer. The flames from the burning wood pile need to reach the same height as my face." His flesh was flaming red and his face was contorting in five different directions as he attempted to deal with the excruciating pain.

Finally, the flames reached up to his head. At long last it was time – he was as hidden from the unbloods behind the flames as he could be. He closed his eyes and clasped his hands tightly behind him. Fear was the dominant emotion driving his energy. He pictured exactly what he wanted to happen next and suddenly his eyes popped open. With that, the essence of Junius escaped Tobias' body for the last time.

From the crowd's perspective, it looked as if Tobias reached the point of death. His eyes, which were been tightly closed, suddenly snapped open and his body slumped forward as much as it could within the tension of the rope. Tobias' reign of terror ended in a blaze of guilt and shame for all those in Salem.

Junius' soul had little time. If a soul remained disembodied for too long, it would be too weak to embody another. Luckily for Junius, he had a plan, and a fresh body. He careened through the air, like the mist of a cloud, by the church and flew into the graveyard. There he found William Putnam's freshly dug grave. The dirt still looked like it was only recently filled back in, which in fact it was. Even though it seemed much longer, it was only two days since it was dug, and then filled, for William's funeral.

Junius' spirit swooped down into the grave, through the few feet of dirt and into the partially collapsed coffin. This would be a tricky embodiment since it appeared William attempted a failed escape from the grave. Normally, the spirit would enter the new host through the mouth or nose, embody the heart first and then spread throughout the rest of the body. But in this case the nose, mouth and throat all appeared completely blocked by dirt. Junius would need to enter through the ear and carefully find a passage down to the heart and then envelop the rest of the body as normal. It's always more dangerous to be near the brain before the heart is taken over. Even though Junius' current state appeared to be a simple mist, in reality the mist contains a strong electrical current keeping Junius' mind and thoughts intact. One wrong move in, or even near, the brain could cause irrevocable damage to the host body and ultimately to Junius.

Still as mist, Junius carefully found, and entered, the left ear. It would be a shorter trip to the heart than if he went through the right ear. The speed of the mist slowed down, careful to remain against the far left side of William's skull as it slowly made its way into the ear and down the neck toward the heart. Junius kept his thoughts to a bare minimum to keep the electrical current as low as possible during the journey. He could not risk any type of electric charge jumping into William's brain – he wouldn't have time to find another host. The mist carefully crept inside William's ear and followed the ear canal past the eardrum. It couldn't go into the eustachian tube, since dirt filled the throat and nasal cavity. So instead, he carefully needed to pass through the membrane just before getting to the eustachian tube and follow it down to the carotid artery. Being careful to remain on the left side of the artery, the mist slowly followed down to the heart. Once there, Junius allowed his electricity to go back to full capacity, and he enveloped and controlled William's heart. The mist then filled the rest of the body as it normally would. Junius slowly opened his dirt-covered eyes, now as William embodied.

Junius anticipated what was to come next, but he could not entirely prepare himself for the death from which he was about to emerge. He saw William's hand, nearly at the surface and his face deluged with the earth. Before taking a breath, Junius forced his hand the last six inches into the air and was able to reach his second hand to the surface as well. He forced himself into a sitting position, further breaking through the lid of the casket. The surface was now around his chest and he immediately coughed all the dirt out of his nose and throat. It took several deep coughs before he could breathe but ultimately he cleared his lungs enough so there was room for the oxygen. William stood, wiped more dirt from his face and body, and stepped out of the grave.

He could feel the pain from the many splinters below his fingernails. He wouldn't have the strength to use his energy to remove them until after tomorrow's sunrise. For now, he would need to suffer and pull out as many of the splinters as he could. That would be difficult considering how bloody his fingers were.

He thought to himself, "I appreciate you were trying to save your life, but you could have left things in better working order for me. Now I will need to wait until tomorrow to kill Abigail and become the Master."

Just then, the two men arrived carrying shovels, prepared to exhume William's grave and retrieve the body. They were surprised to find William standing before them, covered from head to foot in dirt, but very much alive.

William looked at them, acknowledging they needed an explanation for why he was already out of the grave. He spoke while continuing to wipe dirt off his face and body. "He did most of the work for me. Poor man, he didn't realize just how close he was to the surface. He almost made it." He coughed out some more dirt. "Now get this cleaned up, so it looks like an undisturbed gravesite. I'm going to William's house to get some new clothes and then into the woods to find a stream and clean myself so I am presentable. Young Miss Sampson has quite a surprise in store."

Chapter 42

After Tobias' test, Abigail went back to the Porter's house with Joseph. He asked Elizabeth to give Abigail and himself a few minutes alone. Elizabeth obediently obliged and retired to the bedroom. Joseph got close enough to Abigail so he could whisper, "You did great today. You really did. But do you remember how a witch generates their power?"

"They put their hands together and build their emotions?"

"Yes, that's mostly correct. There is a lot more nuance, but that's basically right. Depending on how much energy they need to generate, based on what they want to do, they actually create a circular tunnel in their body for the energy to build speed. If they need to do something small, say to move a rock from one location to another, they don't need a lot of energy. They might only touch one or two fingers together. The energy flow would only be as thick as their finger. If they need to do something of moderate energy, they would touch three or four fingers together. This would generate a thicker flow of energy. Make sense?"

Abigail nodded.

"Good. So if a witch needed to do something taking a lot of energy, like using Belle, or embodying someone, they would place their palms together so the energy flow would be as thick as the full surface area of their palms, essentially as thick as their arms. The thicker the connection point is, the thicker the energy flow will be. Once the witch establishes the circular tunnel, the emotions fuel the energy and make it go faster and faster until it builds enough power to generate what the witch wants to do. This is all done quite intentionally while you are learning, but once you have it down, you never have to think about it again – it's just a habit. Just remember the diameter of the energy flow matters and since the energy flows through the witch's heart and around their body, the emotions act as the fuel. Do you understand?"

"Yes, I think so. Why are you suddenly going over all this with me? I am eager to learn, but It's been an emotional few days and I really need rest."

"It's important because I know you believe Junius is no longer a threat."

"That's right, we all saw him burn today."

"Did we? Did you notice someone tied his hands differently then your mother's hands were tied?"

"They were?"

"Yes. Your mother's hands were tied down her side, so there was no way for her to connect her hands and create an energy flow. But they tied Tobias' hands behind his back, clasped together."

Abigail's eyes opened wide. "What? How? Who?" She suddenly paused and glanced toward the bedroom. Could it be? No, it made no sense. But clearly the two men knew to put his hands behind his back, not down the sides – they were the same men who tied up her mother so they knew to keep *her* hands apart. And the only reason those two men were there to prepare Tobias instead of the three townsmen who originally took him was…. Elizabeth Porter.

Abigail looked at Joseph as if another person close to them died. "What is it?" Joseph asked.

"I can't be sure yet, maybe nothing. Back to what you were saying…. So Tobias had his palms together, which meant he could generate a large energy flow. Are you suggesting he escaped somehow?"

"I'm merely suggesting it's possible."

Abigail stood suddenly and started pacing around the room, looking at the floor and deep in thought. "Joseph, is there someplace we can go to speak in private?"

"We're alone here – Elizabeth is in the bedroom."

"No, I mean truly in private."

Joseph looked down and thought for a moment. "There's a place in the woods where we would sometimes meet for secret covens. Only the members of the Order know about it."

"Members? You mean there are others?"

"Of course – there are always others."

"I mean, there are others beside you, my Father, Junius and me?"

"Yes – there are others. You must learn to trust that."

"Does Junius know of this private place?"

"I don't think so – we didn't know he was here, so we never contacted him about it."

"Let's go there so we can speak in complete privacy."

Joseph nodded then knocked gently on the bedroom door, "Elizabeth, Abigail and I are going into town. She needs to meet with some of her friends."

"That's fine, dear. I'll see you both later." Elizabeth sensed she was being lied to and peeked her eyes out the door as they were leaving. Something did not feel right. She considered following them but decided it was too risky. If they caught her, it would be difficult to explain why she was following them. She couldn't be sure they were suspicious, but following them would certainly make any suspicions real. She chose to be prudent and stay home.

Abigail and Joseph walked through the woods for about twenty minutes. During the walk, Joseph asked Abigail a number of times what she wanted to discuss. "Not here, not yet," is all she would say. The fact was she was stalling for time trying to figure out how to discuss the topic with Joseph.

When they arrived at the location, Abigail could see they used it as a gathering spot. The grass was flat, and they dragged fallen trees to form a shape close to a circle. While the woods were fairly dense in this general area, the canopy above this specific location was clear. One could see to the sky and the sunlight shone directly down.

Abigail was the first to speak. "How many members of the Order meet here?"

"The number varies based on the day, the time and how far in advance the meeting is called. It can be anywhere from five people to about thirty. They come from other towns and villages nearby too, like Beverly, Marble Head and Lynn."

"I did not know there were so many."

"Of course you didn't. You've only known about the Order for one day." He paused for a moment. "So why are we here now? What were we unable to speak about in my home?"

Abigail wasn't sure how to begin the topic, so she just started talking. "Please take no disrespect from what I'm about to say."

Joseph sat down on a tree stump and looked at Abigail. He thought he was about to be reprimanded by the new soon-to-be Master. "What is it?" he asked.

"You told me Mrs. Porter was an unblood, but one who knows of the Order. Is that right?"

"Yes, that's right."

"How did she come to know about the Order?"

"I told her. Since Millie was a Wicken, Elizabeth needed to know about the Order to help protect her. We decided not to educate Millie about her heritage in order to keep her safe."

Abigail walked around Joseph with her fingers rubbing her chin, seemingly deep in thought. "But that didn't work out as you intended, did it?"

With that question, Joseph furrowed his brow and crossed his arms. He raised one eyebrow and glared at Abigail. He felt immense guilt ever since Millie died for exactly that reason, but he responded anyway. "No, it certainly did not. What are you getting at?"

Undeterred by Joseph's aggravation and motivated by bluntly getting to the deeper truth, Abigail continued with her line of questioning. "You said you and Mrs. Porter decided together not to educate Millie about being a Wicken, correct?"

"Yes, we made the decision together. But we both agreed she would still need protection."

"Of course. That's perfectly logical. But how did Mrs. Porter even know Millie was a Wicken in the first place? She would have to know you were a warlock yourself, which meant Millie was part Wicken and part unblood."

Joseph's face contorted a bit as he tried to remember the sequence of events over fifteen years earlier. "I suppose I told her I was. I recall feeling like she had a right to know since we were having a child together."

"Again, that's perfectly logical, although I also suspect it's against some core tenet of the Order to identify yourself to an unblood. But that's not what I'm interested in right now. Do you recall how Elizabeth reacted when you told her that her husband, and her unborn child, were both witches?"

"Elizabeth is a remarkable woman. I remember clearly how calm and rational she was about the whole thing. She wanted to know more about the Order so she could help with the protection. She reacted much better than I ever could have expected."

"Perhaps she reacted too calmly?"

"What do you mean by that?" Joseph was becoming more agitated. Abigail sensed his disapproval and got to the point.

"It was fifteen years ago, you said. That was around the time the accusations of witchcraft started in Salem – certainly before the trials began in earnest, but there was surely an anti-witch sentiment throughout the colonies. And I presume Mrs. Porter had a religious background growing up – a Puritan background. Isn't it a bit strange a Puritan woman, in the midst of witchcraft accusations, learns her husband and child are both witches and has virtually no reaction to that news? I would think she would be quite upset by this realization."

"Well, yes. I suppose that makes sense." Joseph had to agree.

Abigail continued, "But she was not upset – not even a little. Instead, she wanted to learn about the Order. She wanted to delve deeper into this world that could potentially put her and her family in jeopardy."

"I insist you tell me directly what you are insinuating."
Abigail was still pacing. "Of course, I'm sorry. I'm still trying to connect all the clues in my head. Earlier today, prior to Tobias' burning, I went to make sure everything was in order. Instead of seeing the three men that originally took Tobias for holding, I saw the two men who took my mother and Millie before her. When I asked what happened to the other men, they told me Mrs. Porter instructed the others to go home and directed the two men to take over Tobias' watch. At first, I thought little of it. But as you pointed out, these two men tied Tobias' hands behind his back, even though they tied my mother's hands to her sides. Perhaps Tobias instructed them to keep his hands together. But then, at the burning, you arrived late. Too late to do anything about his hands being tied together. If you arrived even five minutes earlier, we could have addressed that. It's as if the timing of your arrival was intentional. Tell me, why were you late?"

Joseph stared blankly into the dirt and spoke in a slow, deliberate tone, as if he was realizing something he didn't want to consider might be true. "We were late because Elizabeth could not find the dress she wanted to wear. It was hidden in the back of the closet and took her a long time to find." He looked at Abigail. "Are you suggesting Elizabeth planned Tobias' escape? That she is working with Junius Dracul? She hated Tobias for what he did to Millie."

"I don't know. But if you're saying you were late because she couldn't find a dress, it seems rather deliberate to me, don't you think? The dress she wore did not differ from any other dress of hers – or any of us. Any dress would have been fine for the occasion. It certainly seems like she was planning for you to be late, keeping you from seeing Tobias' hands until there was nothing that could be done. Unfortunately, it all adds up."

Joseph could not tolerate the accusation. He stood and barged into the path of Abigail's pacing. His face was mere inches from Abigail's and she could feel the heat of his breath grunting against her.

"What you're suggesting, what you're accusing my wife of, is unconscionable. That would mean she was somehow involved in Millie's death. You saw her that day – she was devastated. She felt nothing but disdain for Tobias. You're accusing the woman I love of being nothing less than a monster."

"Believe me, I don't want it to be true. But my father said I needed to protect the bloodline *at any cost*. If there's even a possibility it might be true, we need to take it seriously and explore it. Joseph, if I can be frank with you, I'd rather investigate this, be wrong and have you hate me for all eternity, then to ignore it and it turn out to be true. We owe it to my father to make sure we're doing all we can to protect the bloodline. We both gave him our word."

Joseph backed away – he knew she was right. He sighed deeply and regained his composure. "You will be a great leader for the

Order. Your intentions are just and true. I don't like these accusations, and I hope with every fiber of my being they are false. But I will work with you to investigate the possibility, no matter where it leads."

Abigail put both of her hands on Joseph's shoulders. "Thank you, Joseph. I pray I am wrong, but I fear I am not. Come, let's head back, and for now let's be cautious of what we discuss around your wife."

Chapter 43

Abigail and Joseph arrived back at the Porter home just in time for dinner. Elizabeth was in the middle of preparing a chicken for the three of them. They did not eat meat often, but Abigail went through so much over the past few days and Elizabeth felt having a hearty dinner and a good night's sleep would be beneficial for the girl, and indeed all of them. It was not lost on her that perhaps a full belly might also help dispel any potential suspicion.

They walked in the door and immediately felt the warmth of the bird cooking in the oven and the distinctive scent of the spices cooking into the skin. "That smells delicious," Joseph enthusiastically exclaimed. "A nice chicken dinner is exactly what we all need. Thank you, Elizabeth."

Abigail joined in, "Yes, it smells wonderful. Thank you so much for preparing such a delightful meal."

"It's my pleasure," Elizabeth replied. "I thought we all could use a nice dinner and a good night's sleep. Abigail, how are your friends?"

Abigail remembered the excuse Joseph invented for them to leave the house. "Oh, they're fine, thank you. Everyone is still getting over the shock of Millie's death. She was a friend to all."

"Oh, that's sweet of you to say," Elizabeth replied. "It will take a while for us to come to terms with her loss and what Tobias did to us all. Thankfully, Abigail, you've brought us some justice." Elizabeth dried her hands on her apron which was tied around her waist and approached Abigail for a hug. She put her arms tightly around the girl, first around her back and then up to embrace Abigail's head, with both of her hands feeling around Abigail's hair, as if she were looking for something.

Joseph paid no attention to the hug, it seemed rather normal to him. But for Abigail it was something altogether different. Mrs. Porter never hugged her before, that alone was odd. But the way she was clutching Abigail's head, like she was searching for something in Abigail's hair – or worse, trying to see what Abigail's hair felt like. Should she worry, or should she give Mrs. Porter the benefit of the doubt?

She remembered back to Millie's funeral, when Will gave Tobias the benefit of the doubt for not attending. Look where that got Will. In all the disarray of the last few days, Abigail almost forgot about him. It had been some time since she thought about Will – at least a few hours, she couldn't be sure. She missed him again, deeply. She could use his logic and reason right about now to help her think through her next steps, but she knew Will wouldn't understand, nor approve of, the new life into which Abigail was flung.

She needed to figure out if Junius was still alive or not, discover what was really going on with Elizabeth Porter, and most of all she needed to figure out how to call a global coven so the Order could inaugurate her as Master, preventing Junius from taking the role. That alone was a tall enough order, but in addition, she needed to learn how to *be* the Master. She got lost in her thoughts and anxiety. Once she realized she drifted off to some other place, she immediately forced herself back into the here and now.

She realized she was still in Mrs. Porter's embrace. She put her arms around Mrs. Porter as Mrs. Porter whispered in her ear, "We will always be here for you – always."

"Thank you. That means a lot to me," Abigail replied as she pulled herself away from Mrs. Porter's clutch.

Mrs. Porter put her hands on the tops of Abigail's arms, not quite onto her shoulders, and smiled in a completely disarming way. "Oh, she is good," Abigail thought. "She is Willa Sampson good."

Joseph interrupted, "Abigail, would you like to continue your education while we wait for dinner?"

"I would, but I'm so tired. I'm not sure how much I would remember. Could we do it tomorrow?"

"Of course. You're right – a good night's rest will help you learn more tomorrow. That's a good idea. I'm just excited to impart as much information to you as I can."

"Me too. How about I go to my house in the morning to fetch some clothes and a few other things and then we can spend the rest of the day talking. Would that be all right with you?"

"Of course. In fact, why don't I go with you to help carry some things back. Elizabeth, maybe you could come help us too?"

"Why of course, I'd be happy to help," Elizabeth responded. She realized this would be a splendid opportunity to see what else might be in the Sampson house.

Joseph continued, "Since we still have a few more minutes before dinner, why don't you see if you're able to read anything from the ancient book."

Elizabeth had her back to both of them as she was attending to the meal, but she made sure to listen intently showing no outward interest.

Abigail, noticing Mrs. Porter turned away, scowled at Joseph for mentioning the book in front of his wife. It was a scowl Samuel Sampson would have been proud of, silent and menacing. Along with the scowl, Abigail tried to direct Joseph's attention to Mrs. Porter with her eyes, as if to tell him "we said we were going to be careful!"

Joseph dismissed Abigail's concerns with a wave of his hand as he walked over to fetch the book. His careless and dismissive attitude enraged Abigail, blinding her to obvious happenings around her.

He carefully handed the book to her. "What is the title of the book?" Joseph asked Abigail.

Joseph's lack of discipline and inability to stick to the plan they just agreed to only minutes before annoyed her. She quickly took the book and gave the cover a quick glance. She looked back at Joseph, handed him the book, and begrudgingly said, "To Protect the Bloodline of Samson".

Joseph looked stunned as he slowly took the book back from Abigail. He looked at the cover and then back at her. In the kitchen, Elizabeth lowered her head and exhaled slowly.

"What?" Abigail asked, still annoyed at Joseph and oblivious to what happened. She was too angry to realize the gravitas of the moment – a pivotal point in time which would change the course of her future. Beginning at this exact moment Abigail's life would forever be divided in two – everything that happened before right now, and everything after.

Joseph slowly and softly replied, understanding the implications to the entire world of what he just witnessed, even if Abigail hadn't. "You just *read* the title of the book. Its words have revealed themselves to you. Do you understand what this means?"

"What do you mean?" Her emotions calmed a bit and the weight of responsibility took over as she realized what happened. Her anger quickly dissipated and she felt the tips of her fingers quiver. Joseph continued, "When I look at the title I see random, meaningless letters. I see no words."

She reached her hand out for the book. She looked down at the cover again. It was clear and in English – 'To Protect the Bloodline of Samson'. She carefully opened the book and looked at the first page.

This book provides guidance to those who are pure of heart and pure of spirit who wish to protect and propagate the bloodline of Samson.

She turned the book so Joseph could see the page. "Joseph, what does this say to you?"

He read out random Latin letters.

Abigail abruptly stopped him. "You see only those letters, no words?"

"No, I see only various letters. What do you see?"

Elizabeth was standing mere feet away. There was no way Abigail was going to reveal any words of the book in her presence. She responded to Joseph, "I see… words, paragraphs. All in English." Joseph became excited. "What does it say?"

Abigail looked at him with wry derision. Joseph understood. "Right. Of course. I am not worthy of those words. You should not reveal them." He felt like a foolish child.

Abigail looked at the ancient book in her hands, a book whose magic she could not comprehend. But its words – she could now comprehend. Only a handful of people *ever* read the words in this book. And she was now one of them. She could feel her chest compressing onto itself. She could no longer take a full, deep breath. For the first time, everything was becoming real and deep inside she was frightened.

Joseph put his hand on Abigail's shoulder. "Do you understand what this means?"

Abigail pulled the book tight into her chest. "Yes, it means I'll be up reading all night."

Chapter 44

Abigail ate her dinner quickly, but not too quickly. She didn't want to appear rude; it was important she show the proper respect and appreciation to the Porters for the dinner Elizabeth prepared. But the anticipation of reading the book was simply too much.

The dinner was quiet. Joseph was thinking through the ramifications of the book revealing itself to Abigail. Even if Junius were still alive, this would prove Abigail is the heir-apparent to become Master.

Of course it also meant her life was in constant jeopardy until the inauguration. If Junius could kill Abigail before being inaugurated, he would become the Master. Joseph would need to be careful and overly protective. Abigail's new suspicion of Elizabeth made this even more difficult.

"It simply cannot be true," Joseph thought while he glanced lovingly at Elizabeth during the meal. "There is no way she would help Junius, and I simply cannot believe she was involved with Millie's death." Still, he conceded Abigail's analysis was all very logical. Something did not add up, and Joseph was becoming more concerned about his ability to protect Abigail. He continued in thought, "I need to protect her with my own life and somehow get her to Coventry to be inaugurated. I do not know how I'm going to pull that off." He sighed inwardly and closed his eyes. "I need to remember, there are others."

Dinner ended, and all three helped clear the table and clean the dishes. Afterward, Abigail politely asked if she could excuse herself and prepare for bed. Elizabeth responded, "Of course, dear. Thank you for helping clear the table. Try not to stay up too late reading."

Abigail smiled and nodded, then she washed herself to prepare for the night. Once in her nightgown, Abigail lit her special candle – the one with six strands of hair as the wick. She placed it on her night table and made herself comfortable in the bed. She bent her knees and placed the book in her lap. With a deep breath as if she were starting a long expedition, she opened the book and began reading.

Joseph watched from across the room. He wondered how many others in all of history had the honor of watching a new Master begin their study of the ancient book from the beginning. "It can't be many – I might be the only one." He felt great humility and responsibility for what he saw before his eyes. Elizabeth was watching both Joseph and Abigail. She understood this was a momentous occasion. But she did not feel the same sense of awe as did Joseph.

Abigail discovered the book was written in three main sections. By now, the fact there were three did not surprise her. Delilah mostly wrote the first section herself and it described Samson's life and death in detail.

Myrddin wrote the second section, and it explained in painstaking detail everything he learned about the propagation of the bloodline, the experiments he ran on Samson's hair and his own, and what he learned about the powers of those with the pure bloodline, like Abigail. She realized she would need to read this section many times over in order to understand everything she needed to know.

Myrddin included many fascinating stories detailing how he uncovered the power contained within himself. One story immediately struck Abigail because he repeatedly wrote about his lack of control. With everything she was learning about the Great Master, she thought it strange anything could be beyond his control.

On two occasions I found myself in a situation beyond my control. Both times my emotions were at a peak level and I was feeling multiple conflicting emotions simultaneously. I somehow moved into an uncontrolled state – almost as if I leapt into an alternate existence. It was like the universe itself was trying to shield me from my agony. I could not control moving in or out of this state. It just happened, with no control on my part. When I found myself in this state, I could move at my normal pace, though I had to force my body against some invisible force in the air. That force seemed brittle but not at all impenetrable. It was only a mild hinderance. I could move as desired, just not with the same freedom I had in normal air. Everything else in my presence would immediately move at an incredibly slow pace. We were in separate time – as if I entered my own personal pocket of time. In fact, the entire world slowed in pace while I remained at a normal pace. It could take them many minutes to move their hand just a few inches. I could see the painstaking movement of their fingers, while I could circle around them at my normal speed. I could touch them during these encounters and I could influence their bodies in my speed. And then, without any warning, this alternate existence would cease and I would be back at the same pace as the others. Normal time passed for me, but only a flicker of a moment passed for them. It always amazed them how I could seem to move so quickly. I could be next to them and then suddenly, at an imperceptible speed, I would be many yards away from them. They feared me for this ability and thought me a magician. Yet I could never harness control of this ability. It only happened twice, and both times I was completely helpless and not at all in control of the situation.

The other masters combined to create the third section was written by the Masters after Myrddin. It was in this section she learned there had been a total of five Masters thus far, her father being the fifth. That meant she would be the sixth Master, and she understood how the number six signified strength within the Order. "How am I worthy of such a distinction? Even though he is a vile man, perhaps Junius actually is more appropriate than I."

There were a number of blank pages after Rennik's section and Abigail knew it would fall on her to impart her own story and knowledge for the future Masters.

All the Masters in order were:
1. Myrddin Wyllt
2. Lucinda Wyllt, from the West
3. David Montrose, from the West
4. Aberash Mbande, from Africa
5. Rennik Samson, from the West

Abigail found it remarkable there had been no Masters from the East and two of the Masters had been women, Lucinda (Myrddin's daughter) and Aberash.

She spent most of the night reading the personal accounts from the other Masters. They would discuss how and why the previous Master was no longer and intersperse those stories with bits of wisdom they felt important to impart to the future Masters. They all talked about the prophecy of unification, where one person would become Master and unify all three regions of the Order. It saddened Abigail when she realized this was her father's dream and because of his faith in Junius he failed. She also realized it would now be up to her to enter her father's death into the ancient book. That was for another time, right now she did not know what to write.

It was interesting not all the Masters had a method of death listed. For instance, there was no mention of Myrddin's death. Myrddin's eldest daughter Lucinda died of natural causes and they elected David after her. Apparently, the West and Africa voted for David but the East voted for a young Mircea Dracul, Junius' father. After David

222

died under 'mysterious circumstances' (the book did not disclose more), the Order elected Aberash. But she has no death listed – Rennik did not write about it. This left a significant amount of uncertainty for Abigail and she decided that when it was appropriate for her to enter her story into the book, she would include as much detail as possible so future Masters would not have to wonder. She would later discover the wisdom behind excluding certain details and follow the other Masters in that practice.

By two thirty in the morning, she could not keep her eyes open, no matter how hard she attempted to do so. Joseph and Elizabeth retired to bed many hours previously and Abigail finally put the book down and went to sleep. She blew out her candle and laid the book down on her night table. It would still be a few minutes before she would fall to sleep even though she was completely drained. Many new thoughts and concepts were shooting around through her head. She would need to be careful tomorrow when Joseph was going to educate her – she needed to make sure she did not accidentally release any of the book's secrets. If Joseph explained something that was counter to what the book described, she would need to ignore it. She was much too new in the Order to determine what non-Masters should know, or believe to know. Abigail fell asleep, with the ancient knowledge from the book flowing through her mind.

Chapter 45

The Tuesday morning sunrise was out of a storybook. The yellow sun shimmered across the Atlantic forming a long, orange path atop the water leading directly into itself. It was as if the morning was so glorious, the sun laid a welcome mat out for the world. The air was crisp, almost chilly. With each passing minute, as the sun slowly filled the sky above the water, the air would become ever so slightly warmer. William could still see his breath when he would exhale toward the west. He knew this would not last long. The early morning crispness would soon lead to morning warmth.

Overnight, he made his way to a desolate place along the shore to allow his hair to face due east for the first moment of the sunrise. He sat cross-legged and motionless, his hair facing the ocean, his eyes closed. He looked as if he were meditating. But instead of clearing his mind, his head was full of thought. Today would be the culmination of his two-centuries-long quest. By day's end he would be Master of the Order. His mind raced with thoughts of everything and everyone from his past that led him to this point.

He thought of the matriarch of the Dracul family, his grandmother Chwaer. When he was young she was very supportive of Junius, almost too much so. She favored him over his two sisters and pushed him to learn early how to harness his emotion and control his power. "She would be proud of me today," he thought. Chwaer always challenged Junius to stop at nothing, and let nobody stand in his way to becoming Master. She would tell him, "You will be the one to fulfill the prophecy and unify the Order. You will only have one chance, you must seize it. It is your destiny."

Until recently Junius wondered if his one chance to unify the Order was when Rennik offered his hand in unity, just after Rennik defeated him. But Chwaer saw through Rennik's attempt to take the glory for himself and advised Junius to use Rennik's trickery against him. It was Chwaer's idea for Junius to use the murder of Rennik's three children to become Master. When Junius protested there was no way to know whether Rennik would ever have three children, she said, "You must be patient. He will have three. I have foreseen it." Junius smiled and thought, "Well Grandmother, as always you were right."

That led him to think of his old nemesis Rennik. He was happy Rennik was gone, no longer a threat to Junius and no longer leading the Order down a weak path. Still, he conceded it is difficult to fight and hunt someone for two hundred years and then lose them suddenly. Through all that time, Rennik was a constant in Junius' life and thoughts. There was now a hole left by his absence. He was a worthy foe and Junius would be a stronger, more fearless, and wise leader because of his dealings with Rennik. Ultimately, he was happy he was gone and even happier to have been the one to kill him. Luckily for Junius, Rennik initiated the fight so Junius could claim to the Order he killed Rennik in self defense. There would be no loophole to prevent him from becoming Master once Abigail was dead.

He took in a deep breath and let the air fill his lungs. His breathing was slightly labored because he still had remnants of earth deep in his throat. During the night he removed all the splinters from beneath his fingernails, at least he thought he did. When his energy reached full capacity, he planned to cast his power out to ensure all his injuries were healed. He needed his body in top shape for the battle he anticipated would occur later in the day. Junius knew Abigail was stubborn and would not succumb without a fight. He was going to prepare for that, and he was eager for the opportunity to see her face when he revealed himself as William to her. "What a wonderfully delicious surprise it will be for her."

He felt a message coming through. He placed his three middle fingers from each hand onto the temples on either side of his head. He said nothing, but the message coming through said, "She will be in the Sampson house after breakfast. You should be there waiting for her." William put his hands down and smiled, "I shall be." Perhaps he wouldn't have to wait until day's end for his prize.

****

Abigail woke early despite still being exhausted. She was too excited about the opportunity to learn even more today. When the Porters awoke, Abigail was in her bed reading from the book. Joseph rubbed his eyes and asked, "Were you up all night reading?"

"No, I got *some* sleep. But I woke up early and wanted to read some more. This book is so fascinating. I love non-fiction and this is the pinnacle of the genre. I learn something completely new on literally every page. It's changed my entire perception of the world."

Joseph responded, "I can only imagine how much your world view has changed over the last two days. A vast, new dimension has been revealed to you. I can assure you every member of the Order would be jealous of the insights you alone are learning right now." Elizabeth looked up as if to agree, but remained silent.

Elizabeth started breakfast. Abigail saw her begin the preparations and normally would assist. Instead, she asked, "Mrs. Porter, is it all right if I continue reading? I don't intend to be rude, but there is so much for me to learn in such little time."

"Of course, dear. Do as you must. You have bigger responsibilities now than preparing meals and doing chores."

Abigail mumbled a "Thank you" as she continued reading. Joseph smiled at Elizabeth and he helped prepare breakfast. Elizabeth's behavior toward Abigail pleased him, and he was hopeful her actions would remove any concerns Abigail might continue to have.

Throughout breakfast Abigail continued to read. She would look up from her book every few minutes and apologize for her rudeness, but then go right back to it. As she grew more comfortable, she stopped trying to protect the book from prying eyes. She came to realize she was the only one who could actually read the book. It was fine if Joseph or Mrs. Porter looked at the pages. They would see nothing but a jumble of letters.

Joseph did not mind Abigail's lack of presence. Her natural ability to compartmentalize her emotions and focus her attention impressed him. Even with the immense heartache she suffered over the last week, she possessed the ability to dive eagerly into the world of the Order and was trying to reap as much knowledge as she could. He stared at her across the table with a look of parental pride.

Out of the corner of her eye, Abigail noticed his stare and immediately knew what he was thinking. She looked up from her book and sat up straight. "Joseph, you realize I have you to thank for all this, don't you?"

"What do you mean?"

"I would be a complete mess right now, not able to get out of bed much less focus on reading and learning, but for something you said to me."

Joseph leaned forward, eager to hear how Abigail would continue.

"After my father died, you told me he was with the other Masters, always looking over me. And one day I would join him and the others. That we would be together. Last night I read about the torrent and now understand the same thing is true about my mother. Don't misunderstand, I miss my parents terribly. But knowing they are not gone, just away temporarily, has brought me tremendous peace. While I don't see them here with me physically, I can feel their presence and I know I will be with them again at some point. You gave me that peace of mind. It is because of you I can focus so clearly on my learning right now rather than focusing on everything bad that has happened. I could find it quite easy to fall into the despair of loss, but instead I'm able to rejoice in my education. It's a legacy Mr. Putnam would be proud of, and you have given it to me. Thank you, Joseph."

Joseph sat back in his chair, sighed and shook his head back and forth. "I don't know that I've ever seen such maturity or someone so in touch with their inner feelings as you. The fact you would think that, and then actually say it to me, shows without a doubt what a fine leader you will be." He leaned forward. "Thank you for your kind words. If you don't mind, I'd like to provide just one piece of advice to you."

"Please do."

"Always remember that asking for help is not a sign of weakness, but not asking is. Continue to follow your intuition – it will never lead you astray. You are quite the introspective person and others will lay their lives down for you because of who you are and how you act."

Abigail looked at him for a few moments, soaking in his wisdom. She nodded, smiled and returned to her book.

Elizabeth, who was remarkably quiet all morning, smiled and put her hand on Abigail's arm. She was quite impressed with Abigail. "So sad," she thought. Then she smiled at Joseph and put her other hand on his arm. Joseph placed his hand on top of hers and smiled back.

Elizabeth and Joseph cleaned the dishes while Abigail continued to read. Eventually Elizabeth broke the silence, "Perhaps we should go to your house soon to gather your clothing, so you and Joseph can spend the rest of the day with your education."

Abigail popped her head up, snapping out of being deep in thought. "Yes, that's a great idea. Let's go as soon as you're ready." She closed the book and tucked it under her arm, not wanting to part with it for even a few minutes.

Chapter 46

Abigail and the Porters started on their way to the Sampson house. On most days, it was about a fifteen-minute walk. But the weather was so beautiful this day, Elizabeth recommended they take a more scenic route. Instead of going through town, they chose to go through the woods so they could enjoy the scent of the flowers in the breeze. Abigail was feeling so rejuvenated, so re-alive, it didn't bother her there would be less time today for learning because of their extended stroll. She lifted her face to the sun and basked in the warm sunlight. She felt light and airy, knowing she had much to do but feeling more confident now that the ancient book revealed itself to her. Today, and indeed the future, was bright. Abigail could not contain her joy with just her smile, it overtook her entire face. It was a Willa Sampson smile.

Joseph could not help but to be influenced by Abigail's good mood. He walked hand in hand with Elizabeth, exuding a smile that had been absent for some time. It was only six days since Millie's death and the Porters did not even start to mourn her properly. But the whirlwind of the past few days put their mourning on hold, there would be plenty of time for that later. Joseph realized when one can be part of something larger than themselves, something with meaning, it can help soothe even the worst black mark on the soul. The gorgeous weather of the day was Mother Nature's way of showing them all how glorious life can be. Without the valleys of sadness there is no way to measure the mountains of happiness. Today promised to be a happy day. Soon, a new master would be inaugurated, offering the hope of unifying the Order. And Joseph already reached out to someone to help hasten the transfer of power. Hopefully, she received the message.

After a few minutes, they arrived at the Sampson house. Abigail was still smiling, but she stopped abruptly. Seeing her house again in the daylight took her by surprise. She didn't expect the sight to move her as much as it did. Memories flooded back to her – of playful times, of doing the chores while singing and reciting poetry with her mother, staring at her father in awe of his work ethic. She realized those were all the memories of a girl without a care in the world. She was no longer that girl. At this moment, she realized that along with mourning her parents, she would need to set aside time to mourn the loss of the life she knew. Just as Samuel once cried when leaving Coventry, not for the hope of his future, but because it was the end of the life he had known prior, Abigail would need to mourn the past while still being excited for her future. It would be opposite emotions living on either side of the timeline of her life and this dichotomy made her feel closer to her father. She finally understood how Samuel must have felt all those many years ago.

Joseph, noticing the sudden change in Abigail's demeanor, stepped in front of her and put his hands on her shoulders. "Are you all right? This might be too much for you right now. Do you want to go back?" Elizabeth came to stand next to Abigail, with her arm around her shoulders offering support.

"No, no. It's fine. I… I just need a moment to take it all in. It's just so much, so fast."

Abigail slowly walked to the right side of the house, staring at it the entire time. Then she came back to the left side, her gaze never leaving the facade of the house.

She came back to where Joseph and Elizabeth were standing, patiently waiting for her. Abigail took in a deep breath, exhaled, and then looked at them both, "All right, I'm ready."

Joseph looked at her intently, "Are you sure? We can come back tomorrow."

"No, I'm sure. Let's go ahead."

Joseph nodded, smiled and stepped to the front door. "Allow me to announce you," he said while grasping the doorknob trying to lighten the mood. "Ladies and Gentlemen, I give you the next Master of the Order of the Wick, Abigail Samson." He opened the door and stepped inside to hold the door for her, trying to make the moment as special as possible.

Abigail smiled but paused again. This was the first time she heard, or thought of herself, as a Samson instead of a Sampson. Joseph was correct to call her that, after all she was the daughter of Rennik Samson. It's just something she hadn't considered yet, and it took her aback. It brought to the fore her direct lineage to Samson and Delilah. The thought of her bloodline being so ancient and remarkable took her breath away. She quickly regained her composure and stepped inside the house with Elizabeth following behind her.

When all three were inside, Joseph closed the door. They all took a deep breath and looked around. From a chair almost hidden on the far left side of the room they heard a familiar voice, "Well, it's about time. I've been expecting you."

Abigail's knees buckled, but luckily Joseph caught her before she fell to the floor.

"Will?"

Chapter 47

William stood from the chair. "So nice to see you again, Abigail."

Abigail's heart skipped a beat, her cheeks felt hot and the palms of her hands immediately grew moist. She was dizzy with confusion. Her head knew this could not possibly be Will, but her heart yearned for it to be. Though she did her best to contain her emotion outwardly, her insides were aflutter with butterflies.

She inhaled deeply, "Will…." A smile slowly grew across her face. The feelings she had for him, feelings she forced herself to repress, flooded back.

William paced around the left side of the room, being sure to keep his distance from the others. "I've been meaning to apologize to you, Abigail. It was rude of me to keep you waiting for our date under the sycamore tree. I really wanted to meet with you, but you know, that whole dying thing got in the way."

Hearing Will's voice call her Abigail instead of Abi only reinforced this was not actually Will. And Will would never taunt her like that. Joseph was right, Junius escaped. He took residence in the one body he knew would be the most difficult for Abi to fight. She promptly repressed her feelings again, as only Abi could, and she thought she would have some fun at Junius' expense.

Joseph quickly moved into a defensive position in front of her. "This is not William. Do not allow him to fool you."

Abi continued while staring Will down, "Yes, that was certainly disappointing for me. After all, what girl wouldn't want to spend an afternoon with a man who failed at everything he tried to accomplish for two centuries. A man of the Order who allowed himself to be outmaneuvered by a girl who only just learned the Order even existed. That would have been quite an exciting day for me, Junius." She paused momentarily. "So, this is your plan? Just show up and try to kill me while I'm distracted at your embodiment of Will? That's not an awful plan, I suppose. I just expected more from you."

Joseph was relieved Junius did not fool her, but he was quite nervous about the current situation. He was there alone, needing to protect both Abigail and Elizabeth against a warlock who was far more skilled than was he.

William curled his upper lip and responded to Abigail in a more Junius-like tone, "You remind me of your father. Lots of talk but nothing to back it up." He circled the room, like a shark preparing to attack its prey. Joseph continued in his defensive position, always staying between William and Abigail as he circled her. William kept his stare on Abigail bypassing Joseph completely. He was no threat.

"You impressed me with how well you played the townspeople. You really put me in a difficult position and left me with no choice but to change embodiments. 'Tis a shame we won't be able to rule the Order together."

"A shame? I guess we'll have to agree to disagree," she responded, being as dismissive as possible. "But why keep hiding your true self from me, Junius? Are you embarrassed you are not as handsome as William? Stop pretending to be something you are not. Let's face each other with our true bodies, shall we?" In reality it was hard for Abigail to move into an offensive posture while looking into William's eyes. She was hoping Junius would agree to disembody. But instead, he simply ignored her request.

Elizabeth wandered around the opposite side of the room from them, looking to see what was left behind in the house. She looked at the books on the shelf and she paid no attention to the banter between Abigail and William. On the table she noticed the drawing of a young Rennik and his bride on their wedding day. She grabbed the drawing and held it close to her face. She squinted to see more clearly. They looked nothing like Samuel and Willa – they were both skillful embodiments, and they pulled it off for so many years. She stared at the bride…. If that isn't Willa it means Willa was an embodiment too. "But that would mean…"

Elizabeth's breathing became more rapid and shallow. The only ones who could embody others were the Master and the Draculs. If Willa was an embodiment and she wasn't a Master, she *had* to be a Dracul. "Rennik, you clever 'lock," Elizabeth said to herself with a devious smile. "You figured out a way to bring both sides of the Order together, completely bypassing Junius." Rennik's plan and execution impressed her.

Rennik married a Dracul, which meant Abigail is equal part East and West. She *is* the unification of the Order personified. "Not since my brother…" Elizabeth stopped herself mid-thought. Immediately she realized Abigail must not become Master. She had to be stopped, and soon.

Elizabeth looked more closely at the drawing, specifically at the woman. She wanted to get a better look. "I wonder…. Could it be her?"

Around the year 1450, Mircea Dracul was at the height of his anti-unblood terror campaign, embodying his brother Vlad. At one point, the villagers rebelled and took the three Dracul children hostage – young Junius and his two sisters Alina and Lucia. They burned Alina at the stake and they ultimately released Junius back to his family after rather intense negotiations led by his grandmother, Chwaer. But Lucia was never seen or heard from again. They presumed her dead; killed by the undisciplined unblood hostage takers.

As Elizabeth stared at the drawing of the woman, she recognized some of the facial features. She could see the general shape of Junius' face in the woman's. And she saw the eyes of young Lucia Dracul. "Lucia, it *is* you," she whispered to herself in shock and horrified amazement.

Joseph remained in front of Abigail, leaning forward with his hands nearly clasped together, ready to defend Abigail should William attack. Joseph knew Junius outmatched him, but he would die in order to keep Abigail safe. He kept looking over to Elizabeth, wondering what she was doing. He expected her to be afraid and was checking if she needed to be protected as well, but instead, she was calm. It was as if she *expected* to see William at the Sampson house. She did not seem surprised, nor was she paying any attention to him. Rather, the old picture of Rennik and Willa enthralled her.

Joseph called to her, "Elizabeth, are you all right?"

She didn't respond. She kept staring closely at the drawing. Joseph called to her again, this time more urgently, "Elizabeth!"

She looked up and made eye contact with Joseph though she wasn't truly looking at him. "What? Oh, yes Joseph. What do you want?"

Her behavior also surprised Abigail. But she could not focus on Elizabeth. She needed to keep her eyes on Junius who was still circling her, trying to keep her distracted with his small talk. Abigail kept responding, figuring it was better to keep him talking than to start a fight. But she kept her eyes firmly on his hands, watching to see if he was moving them any closer together.

The veins on Joseph's forehead throbbed. "Elizabeth, you need to get out of here. You're not safe."

Elizabeth ignored Joseph and instead brought the wedding-day drawing to William. "Junius, who do you see in this drawing?"

It was Abigail's turn to catch Joseph before he fell to the floor. In that instant, Joseph realized everything Abigail suspected was true. She *had* been helping Junius, which also meant Elizabeth was involved in his dear Millie's death. "She's a monster." Suddenly, nothing made sense to him. This woman, whom he loved so purely for so many years turned out to be someone he didn't know at all. He hated her for what she did and he hated himself for not realizing it earlier.

"Elizabeth! What are you doing? What's going on?"

Elizabeth handed the drawing to William, then turned to Joseph and sighed. "I suppose there's no reason to hide anymore."

She took a couple of steps away from William, drew a deep breath and started the process. Junius was quite familiar with what was about to happen, but it was something new for Abigail and Joseph. Elizabeth put her arms across her chest, smiled and nodded at Joseph and closed her eyes. Within a mere few seconds Elizabeth was gone and in her place stood an old woman with long, gray, stringy hair. Her wrinkled face was leathered with age. Her back was hunched and she was missing a number of teeth. She opened her eyes and looked at Joseph and Abigail. "Ah, that's much better," she croaked with a slithery smile.

William had a warm smile on his face. "Grandmother Chwaer, it's so nice to see *you* again and not that awful facade." He approached her for a hug with his arms outstretched.

She pushed him away and sputtered, "Oh shut up, you fool."

Chapter 48

Chwaer ignored Junius' attempt at affection, as she often did, and asked him again, "Look at this drawing. Who do you see?"

Junius looked at the picture and with a tone of derision responded, "It's Rennik. So what? He's dead – I killed him."

"Right. *You* killed him. It had nothing to do with the hemlock I put into his wound." Chwaer continued in a more serious and sinister tone, "You merely injured him, I made sure he would not make it to the morning to recover. If I left things to you," the tempo of her speech increased significantly as her voice jumped an octave higher, "Rennik would still be here trying to ruin my plans!"

Joseph put his arm in front of Abigail to hold her back from reacting. Plan Three A must have been a trigger to Elizabeth to use the hemlock. He was furious over his part in Rennik's death. "How could I be so oblivious?" he thought.

Chwaer again pressed Junius on the drawing, "I'm not talking about Rennik, you idiot. I'm talking about his bride. Do you recognize her?"

Junius felt like he did as a young man – mocked and derided by his grandmother, the matriarch of his family. He looked more closely at the drawing, squinting hard to make sure Chwaer knew he was trying. "No, I don't recognize her. Should I?"

Chwaer sighed and looked back at the picture. "I would think so." She turned and faced away from Junius. "She's your sister."

Junius grabbed the drawing from Chwaer's hand and held it close to his face. "Lucia? Are you certain?"

"Yes, of course I am. Look at her face closely, that is Lucia." Chwaer sighed as she realized once again she could not depend on Junius for anything. It was a lesson she learned many times.

She paused for a moment as Rennik's plan became clear to her. "It all makes sense. Rennik was trying to unify the Order using multiple tactics. He wanted a backup plan for his backup plan. Working with you was one path, courting Lucia was another. He was a clever man, always availing himself of multiple options. It's too bad he's not here to see his plans fail, and it's also too bad you're not half as clever as he was!" she yelled while slapping Junius on the back of his head causing him to cower momentarily like a frightened dog. He recovered quickly, not wanting to display his embarrassment in front of those he was preparing to battle.

Rennik's plan was becoming clear to all four. He married Lucia to unify the Order. They both embodied others when they came to the New World. Willa Sampson was actually Lucia Dracul, daughter of Mircea Dracul. This meant Junius killed his own sister when he burned Willa at the stake and he killed his two nephews, Archibald and Ichibad, years before. This also meant Millie was half Dracul, and Junius along with Millie's mother, Junius' grandmother, were both responsible for Millie's death. Besides all that, he entered the Sampson house today intending to kill Abigail, who he now realized as his own niece, attempting to steal the Mastership away from her.

Junius felt sick. Chwaer dictated his path to become Master, and in fact his entire life. For centuries he believed he was the rightful heir to the seat and his grandmother was simply helping him get there. Over the years she convinced him of this. But now, he saw things in a different light. His grandmother was ruthless and would stop at nothing to hold power. Junius was also ruthless, but he would never intentionally harm a member of his own family – that was an uncrossable line for him. Chwaer had no such moral red line, and she manipulated Junius into crossing his. He stared at the ground with a combination of shame and self-loathing. He paced around the room fully disgusted in what he had become – what his grandmother forced him to become.

"I can't believe what she had me do. The atrocities I've carried out against my family – my own flesh and blood. It's… it's unforgivable."

Joseph, too, was feeling ill. He was beyond enraged at Elizabeth's role in Millie's death. He thought he knew her so well – to be deceived so fully made him wonder what else in his life was a blatant lie. But as angry as he was over the death of his cherished daughter, he was even more outraged at seeing the woman to which he was actually married. Chwaer was ugly in every conceivable way you could use the word. She looked like the archetypal witch the unbloods concocted in their stories. In fact, it's possible she was the model for the unblood version of a witch. Her soul was as ugly as one could get. For years he shared his bed with this… creature… and never knew it. How many secrets of the Order did he unknowingly reveal to her? The thought made him want to retch. He forced himself to hold things together, Abigail needed him right now.

Joseph was the first to speak, and he directed it at Chwaer. "So who exactly are you?"

Chwaer did not bother clasping her hands together, she didn't need to. She held out one hand in Joseph's direction and a powerful bolt of energy lifted him off the ground. His hands pulled at his neck, as if he were trying to keep from being strangled, his feet dangling and flailing below him.

Abigail put her hands together, attempting to save Joseph. Her energy was flowing fast from her adrenaline but she could not clench her hands together. The energy was too strong, and it was forcing her hands apart like a magnet repelling another magnet. She decided not to fight what the energy wanted to do but rather let the energy lead her. She formed her hands in the shape of a sphere, as if she were holding a large ball. With the full strength of both arms, she lunged the invisible ball toward Chwaer resulting in both of her palms pointing directly at her. An enormous amount of energy shot out and hit Chwaer, knocking her back onto a small end table which collapsed from the impact and broke. And more importantly, Abigail's blast released Joseph from Chwaer's grip and dropped him to the floor. He struggled but quickly regained his breath. Joseph never saw someone control their energy when their hands were not together. He was unfamiliar with the power Abigail was wielding and it frightened him. Chwaer was not unfamiliar with it – she had the same ability. She only saw one other with this power.

Junius always knew his grandmother to be the most powerful witch he'd ever seen. Nobody ever knocked her back before. At the moment Chwaer fell to the ground, Junius grabbed his head. His face cringed as though an intense headache quickly released its tension. His head felt different, he had more clarity. He was angry at his actions – actions his grandmother directed. For the first time in over two hundred years, he wondered who his grandmother was. He questioned his unrelenting love and respect for her, realizing how poorly she treated him and how often she belittled him. This woman made him kill blood relatives for her own gain.

Abigail stopped paying attention to Chwaer, instead she focused on Junius. She felt the rip between Junius' emotions. She felt it within her own body. Abigail pitied him.

Joseph regained his footing and was preparing an energy beam to attack Chwaer. His emotions toward her were intense – he never wanted to destroy someone more than he did her at that moment.

But he was a Wicken, and he knew his chances against a Wicked were close to zero, especially one as strong as she.

"I could use some help over here," Joseph pleaded.

Abigail focused again on Chwaer. It was now the two of them against her. They shot their energy beams at her and seemed to take the upper hand, but it was short-lived. Chwaer's eyes glowed bright yellow, and she smiled widely while spreading her hands and extending her beam across them both. She was enjoying herself and started laughing. "The only thing that would make this better is if Rennik were here to witness me destroy you." She broke one of Samuel's cardinal rules and was reveling in the demise of her rival. Pride is strongest just before one's downfall.

Chwaer gained the upper hand. Joseph was only a Wicken and didn't have the strength to fight a Wicked, and Abigail, though innately strong, didn't yet know how to master her powers. In their current state, they were no match for Chwaer. She moved forward toward them as they backed themselves into a corner. Joseph instinctually took a defensive position in front of Abigail, who was crouching behind him but still fighting. He needed to protect her, and most importantly her blood, at any cost.

Junius' perspective was shifting. Instead of seeing Chwaer fighting the third child of the Master, he could only see his grandmother fighting his niece. He could not allow more family blood to be shed. Unconsciously he picked up one of the wooden legs from the broken table. It was shattered and had sharp edges protruding from one end. With determined strength in his eyes, he walked behind Chwaer and forcefully jammed the table leg into her back. He forced it through until the end came out of the upper left side of her chest. The wooden leg pierced her heart and she let out a deafening howl as she fell to the floor drenched in blood. "Junius, you fool…."

His actions did not have the results Junius intended. Instead of killing Chwaer, her essence escaped her body and immediately jumped into William's. There were now two spirits inside the same body. This was unprecedented and nobody, including Chwaer, knew what might happen. William's eyes turned dark yellow with rage and he turned to face the two tired warriors, both now hunched in the corner. Though he was spent, Joseph did his best to remain in front of Abigail, trying to keep his promise to Rennik to protect her. "Rennik, please forgive me. I tried the best I could."

Inside William there was a battle brewing. Chwaer was much stronger than Junius, but she was focused on destroying Abigail. Junius was struggling against her trying to prevent Chwaer's success. The battle to envelop William's heart was intense. Two super-heated clouds of electric mist were flowing through the host body. The heat intensified, and the mist morphed into super-heated plasma. The inside of William's body was being ravaged by the two, but Junius was simply not strong enough to overtake Chwaer. Her plasma mist surrounded his and forced it against William's ribs, safely away from his heart, which she now controlled.

Just outside the house there was a loud thud, as if something large fell from the sky into the soft sand. A moment later, the front door swung open and there stood a most beautiful woman. She was tall and dark with a look of matured confidence on her face. She was not like anyone from Salem. She did not introduce herself; she didn't need to. Most in the room knew exactly who she was. Most, except for Abigail.

She entered and immediately recognized Joseph and Abigail were in a dire situation. She clenched her hands together and started shooting an energy beam directly at William, who was now fighting against three beams simultaneously. A normal Wicked would have succumbed. But a dual-descendant was strong enough to hold the three of them at bay. And William did so with his hands in the shape of a ball – external from his body, just as Abigail did.

Chwaer finally spoke through William, though it was a forced because she was in the midst of battle. "Aberash, who invited you to our private party?"

Pushing back against William's beam she responded with a strained tone through clinched teeth from the immense amount of energy she was exerting, "Joseph did. Looks like I arrived just at the right time."

Abigail wondered, "Aberash? As in Aberash Mbande? The Master before my father?"

The electricity flowing through the Sampson house was immense. Everything metal in the house was glowing red hot, including the doorknob and the window clasps. Everyone's hair was standing on end from the static electricity encompassing everything. Even the hairs on their necks felt alive. But the hair on Abigail's head felt flat and almost lifeless. She was running out of energy.

Having Aberash join the battle helped Joseph and Abigail, but Aberash was tired from her long journey. There was only so much energy she could exert, and she too was running low. Chwaer once again took the upper hand. The three were feeling weak. Chwaer was moving in on them forcing Aberash into the corner with Joseph and Abigail, smiling and laughing even more sinisterly now that she was adding Aberash to her bounty. For the first time in her life, Abigail felt complete hopelessness. She let down the entire world and perhaps worst of all, she would not fulfill her father's dying wish.

She could no longer contain her emotions. Everything that happened over the last few days came roaring back to the front of her mind. All the death and deception, the grief and agony, even the feelings of love and loss flooded her system. And now she was staring down death in the dark yellow eyes of the man she so cherished and admired. It was all too much for her. Her chest felt tight. She could barely breathe.

Everything stopped. There was no sound, there was no movement. After a few moments, Abigail wondered, "Am I dead?" She looked around trying to figure out what was happening.

Chapter 49

Everyone and everything initially appeared to be motionless, except for her. She tried to stand and she was able to, though she needed to force her body more than normal. She couldn't explain it – it felt like her body was pressing against something in the air, but when she exerted a bit of pressure, the air would seem to snap and she was able to freely move. It was as though the air felt… she didn't know how to describe it… crisp.

She walked around the room. She put her hand on Joseph's shoulder for leverage. He didn't budge. She stepped over Chwaer's extinguished body and walked behind William. Abigail moved around and got close to his face; she studied his yellow eyes. They looked so angry – it was something she never saw in Will's eyes. They were always so gentle and determined. She realized this man standing before her was a stranger cloaked in a familiar veil.

As she continued to stare into his eyes, she noticed a single bead of sweat on his cheek. She looked at it closely because it seemed to move ever so slightly. She backed up so she could have a more complete look at William's body. His hands were moving but at an immensely slow pace. She immediately recalled Myrddin's mysterious entry in the ancient book and now realized what was happening. "My God. This is the uncontrolled state Myrddin found himself in. I'm in my own pocket of time."

Just at the moment she realized what was happening, she popped out of it.

Joseph and Aberash were still cowering in the corner, near defeat. Abigail was with them, but within a blink she was standing next to William. Joseph couldn't believe what he was seeing. "How did she do that?" he thought. This amazed Aberash as well, but being a former Master she read Myrddin's account in the ancient book. She never experienced it, nor heard any account of anyone other than Myrddin going through it. She was shocked someone as young as Abigail had the strength to endure the time pocket. "Rennik was right about her."

This did not impress William. He saw her appear next to him in a flash and turned his raging glare toward her. "You don't scare me with your cheap magic," he said. He gathered his hands together to form a beam.

The entire situation confused Abigail. She did not know how any of this was happening and just saw impending pain and death coming from the version of William standing before her. "I can't let Junius become Master. I promised Father."

She pictured all her fear and emotion as if it was within a barrel. In her mind she plunged into the barrel and soaked in as much as she could. She allowed the emotion to blanket her entire body – she drank it all in. She was mentally drenched in feelings and felt like she and her fear were one and the same. Never had she felt the immense happiness and light at the same time she felt the blackness of despair – it was the full gamut of emotion happening simultaneously. Exactly at that moment, she popped back into her time pocket. "That must be how to control it," she realized.

Abigail, now back in her sped up pace of time, stepped to William's side, away from any danger from his hands. He was still moving, achingly slow, as if she were still in front of him. Abigail circled behind him, trying to determine how to disarm him and eliminate any threat. She wasn't sure how much time before her time pocket would again cease. She needed to act decisively, and she needed to act now.

"There's only one way to be certain. He must die." She earlier realized there might come a time where she would have to shed blood in order to save the bloodline, and by association, herself. "I just wish it wasn't so soon. And I wish it wasn't with Will's embodiment." She realized her actions at this moment could save, or doom, the world. Neither her feelings, nor her reluctance, were of any importance right now.

Joseph and Aberash were watching from their own pace of time. Abigail was a blur, barely perceptible to their eyes. They could only see a flourish of movement as she was flitting around William. They could not tell what she was doing or how she was doing it. Chwaer's rage was becoming imbued with fear. It was a feeling with which she was not familiar.

Abigail pulled the table leg out of Chwaer's dead body. She looked at it closely, examining the rough edges now covered in blood. "Will I be able to do it?" She wasn't at all confident in herself to take another person's life, no matter how dire the consequences of failing to act.

She walked back to Will with the leg in her right hand. Now standing directly in front of him, she put her left hand gently on his face – his eyes still dark yellow with rage. Abigail recalled one of the many biology lessons Mr. Putnam taught, specifically about the heart. She remembered the detail about the atria and the ventricles and how the design of this organic machine struck her as beautiful, complex and so incredibly fragile. She found it ironic how the heart is the pump that brings life to the body while also being the symbol of love and goodness. For her to continue the bloodline, she would need to destroy the gentle tissue of Will's heart. "Goodbye again, Will. I'm doing this for all of us," she whispered. Then she remembered this was no longer Will. Her eyes formed into thin slits as she plunged the leg into his chest. It surprised Abigail how easily the wood pierced his skin and moved through his body.

She immediately popped back into normal time, her hand now covered in blood, still holding the wooden leg deep inside Will's body. He looked into her eyes as he realized what was happening. "How did you do that?" he asked as his breath escaped him and his eyes returned to their normal brown. Abigail held the wood leg in his torso as she helped him gently slump to the ground. Once on the ground, the visage of William faded away, and it exposed Junius in his proper body.

Aberash and Joseph stood and cautiously approached Abigail. Neither knew what to say. Abigail hunched over Junius' body, crying. "I killed him. I looked into his eyes and killed him."

"You did what had to be done. You were the only one who could have, you saved us all." Aberash told her.

Abigail pulled the wood out of Junius' body. William was finally gone and there was no sign of Chwaer's spirit anywhere. "Are they both gone?" Abigail asked Aberash.

"I don't think so," Aberash responded. "When an embodied person dies, either the body or the spirit dies, never both. And I don't know what happens when there are two spirits embodying the same person." She paused as a thought entered her mind. "When you killed him, did you see his eyes change?"

"Yes!" Abigail leapt up to her feet. "His eyes changed back to brown just before he died."

"Then we must act quickly. You must have killed Chwaer since we see Junius' body now – it was her spirit in his yellow eyes. If I'm right

250

then Junius might still be savable, but we need to work together to heal his body right away. Joseph, we'll need your help for this – place your hands on his forehead. Abigail, I'm going to put my hands inside his wound. Put your hands directly on top of the wound. We all need to focus our energy as intensely as we can."

Abigail paused, "What happens if we bring him back but Chwaer is still in there?"

"Dear girl, let's focus on only one catastrophe at a time, shall we?"

Abigail nodded to Aberash and put her hands on the wound she inflicted on Junius just moments before. All three closed their eyes and focused their emotions and energy on trying to save Junius. The irony was not lost on any of them, but none of them hesitated in the least.

Chapter 50

After a few moments, they could feel each others' energy melding together into one unified flow. The energy used Junius' body as a conduit and the single intense beam was flowing through all four of them. Junius' body shook, just a little at first, but it grew more violent as time went on. Joseph and Abigail looked at each other, unsure what was happening. Aberash's eyes were still closed tight, trying to focus on the task. "Just keep going. It's working."

A small amount of smoke arose from the wound and Abigail could smell the foul stench of burning flesh. She was about to turn away in disgust but Aberash stopped her, "Don't let go, we're almost there."

Abigail could feel Junius' skin regenerating under her hands as the smoke and odor grew more intense. Aberash pulled her hands out of his wound just in time, before the wound would have healed and encapsulated her wrists inside Junius' body. She put her hands on top of Abigail's to help with closing what was now a diminishing hole. After another minute, the wound was closed and Junius' body stopped shaking.

Aberash pulled her hands off Junius and opened her eyes. "It's done, you can both let go now." Joseph and Abigail removed their hands and sat back wondering what might happen next.

They were all quiet for some time. A lot of happened, but they understood very little. After a few moments Abigail asked, "Did it work?"

"We healed his wounds. The rest is up to Junius. Only time will tell." Aberash stood and went to the water basin to wash her hands.

Aberash's words struck Abigail. Time seemed to be a new theme in her life and she was not at all pleased she would need to wait for more time to pass before she could move forward.

What had just been a house filled with the electric sound of emotion and bolts of energy shooting back and forth, was now quiet and still. Abigail was confused – she actually felt empathy for Junius. She thought of how embarrassed she felt for him when Chwaer belittled him in front of everyone. "How could he have endured it his entire life?" she wondered.

Junius groaned, and his head moved a little. "Uhhh, what happened?" Abigail and Joseph both gasped loudly at seeing their opponent come back to life. Aberash did not react, she simply continued to dry her hands.

Junius sat up slowly but felt intense pain in his abdomen. He looked over to Chwaer's body, "She's dead?"

"Yes." Abigail confirmed.

"Good," he said as tears streamed down his face. "We were having quite the battle inside of William. I did my best to weaken her energy, but she was strong. What happened to me? Why does my gut hurt so much?"

Abigail, now putting her guard down completely, responded, "Chwaer embodied you and I had to kill her. Stabbing you was my only option. I'm sorry I had to do that, but I think we did a pretty good job of healing your wounds. Aberash, he'll be all right now won't he?"

Aberash smiled, "Yes, he should be fine once he fully heals."

Junius' face softened and his shoulders relaxed. He looked up at Aberash and said in a soft and sincere tone, "Thank you." He became more emotional and looked back at Abigail. "You did the right thing. I always knew her to be the strongest person I'd ever met. But she was frightened of you. I felt it. It was shocking to feel, but it was unmistakable." He paused and put his hand on his head. "I can't believe she had me under such a strong trance for so long. I don't know which of my actions were me and which were her." Through tears he moaned, "Why? Why would my grandmother do this?"

Aberash stepped forward. She was still careful not to get too close. It was possible he would be like a wounded animal and strike out at any moment – she did not know his state of mind and it wasn't at all clear she should trust him. "Junius, she wasn't your grandmother. You *do* know this, right? Do you really not know who she was?" Junius looked at her with confusion and disdain, "Of course she was my grandmother."

Aberash responded as calmly as she could, "No, she was not. She was Myrddin's twin sister. She was not Chwaer Dracul, she was Chwaer Wyllt."

The room fell silent. All four looked at Chwaer's body as Aberash continued. "She was jealous of her brother and always wanted to be Master. In a fit of rage, she murdered Myrddin, thinking she would then become Master. But the ancient book did not reveal itself to her, so she never knew the rules of succession. Once she killed a Master, she, and her descendants, were no longer eligible to become Master. When she discovered this, she decided it would be better to pull the strings behind the Master than to have no power at all. She became the matriarch of the Dracul clan, treating Mircea and Vladimir as her own children, which is why you've always considered her your grandmother. Had she actually been your grandmother, you would not have been eligible to become Master due to what she did to Myrddin."

Aberash got down on one knee to be closer to Junius realizing he was no longer a threat, "Your whole life has been a lie. Not just that she was not your flesh and blood, but also because she only wanted you to be Master so she could control you. Junius, I'm sorry to say this, but she favored you over your sisters because she felt you would be the easiest to control. And it turns out you proved her right."

Junius sat with his head down. Aberash's words hurt him like nothing before. But in his bones he knew she was right. Everything she said made sense. The way Chwaer would deride him, the way she would never consider his ideas and plans. Everything had to be under her control. Apparently even the Master of the Order needed to be under her thumb. He was just a pawn in her Master plan.

Aberash stood, walked to Joseph and put her hand on his shoulder. "Joseph, it's been a long time. Thank you for contacting me when you did."

"It's good to see you again, Aberash. Your timing was impeccable, as usual."

She smiled at Joseph and continued on to Abigail. She stood in front of her. Being a couple of inches taller than Abigail, she looked down into her eyes. "And Abigail. Look at you. I would know you to be the child of Rennik just by looking at your face. You have his determined eyes, and from what Joseph has reported, you also have his wisdom, bravery and stubbornness." Abigail gave Joseph a look of dissatisfaction and Joseph returned it with a sheepish smile. Aberash noticed their traded looks and interrupted, "Oh you misunderstand me. Stubbornness is a good quality for the Master.

255

But you mustn't be too stubborn. You need to listen to your advisors and then make your own decisions."

Abigail interrupted, "I'm sorry, but I'm very confused. I assumed, pardon me for saying, you were dead. My father was Master after you. I thought new Masters took over when the previous Master died."

Aberash's face formed a warm smile, "That is a reasonable assumption but there is nothing in the ancient book about that. The book speaks of how succession *can* occur, but not when it *must* occur. In fact, your father and I devised this plan together."

"You did?"

"Yes. Most in the Order wanted unification." Aberash looked at Junius, "Most except for Chwaer and the Draculs." She looked back to Abigail, "Your father met your mother, and they fell in love while I was the Master. When he discovered she was really Lucia Dracul, and she was the one and only Dracul interested in unification, I suggested they marry, we make Rennik the new Master, and then their child would be the true unifying force for the Order. I stepped down as Master, paving the way for our plan. But Junius challenged Rennik, which led to a duel. When Rennik was victorious, it was clear we made the right decision."

"Must you remind me of my defeat?" Junius interjected.

Aberash laughed, but Joseph did not even crack a smile. He did not trust Junius, and he remained focused on trying to understand all the damage inflicted by Chwaer.

Aberash continued, "Your father never wanted to be Master. He wasn't sure he could fulfill the duties. But I saw something in him. He

256

was a sincere and just person – and he possessed a powerful spirit. When Junius stood for the position, we had no choice. We needed to do everything possible to ensure Rennik became Master."

Junius spoke up, "Really? Must you go on?"

Aberash stepped closer to Abigail. "I can tell you have the same doubts about your abilities that your father had about his, yes?"

Abigail slowly nodded her head in agreement.

"Well, believe me when I tell you this. You have more wisdom, more strength, more justice and more right to be Master than anyone else who has ever been Master – possibly even Myrddin himself. I've heard about your abilities, and now have seen them with my own eyes – how you used Belle on the same day you first learned about the Order, how you created a torrent on your own before even knowing you had any abilities or even what a torrent was, how the ancient book revealed itself to you, and today, how you could create a ball of energy external from your body and survive a time pocket. Any of these, by itself, would be truly miraculous. There's something quite special about you. Being our Master truly is your destiny."

Abigail did not know how to feel. She was humbled, standing in front of a clearly great person. Aberash was someone who had vastly more knowledge and experience than did she. Someone she could learn a great deal from. Someone who should be…

"Aberash, what if you became Master again and I could apprentice with you? When we both decide it's the right time, I could take over then. I think it would be best for everyone."

Aberash smiled widely. "No. My time has passed. Every Master must learn their own way. I'll be happy to teach you what I know, but not as Master. If you'd have me, it would be my honor to be an advisor to you."

Joseph jumped in, "There is one issue we need to resolve first. Abigail needs to be inaugurated. Rennik said we needed to call a global coven. We need to start the preparations for that trip."

Aberash curled her mouth in thought. "Not necessarily," she said. "There is the 'Extenuating Circumstances' clause to the Inauguration. Abigail, have you gotten to that section in the ancient book yet?"

"No, I've mostly been reading the accounts of the other Masters." Aberash laughed, "Ah yes, we all read those parts first too." She leaned toward Abigail and put her hand over half her mouth, pretending only Abigail could hear her. "That section has the juiciest stories." Abigail giggled in agreement. Aberash continued, "Is the book here?"

Abigail picked up the book, which fell to the floor in all the commotion. Aberash said to her, "Hold the book in front of you in two hands and say 'Open to Inauguration'." Abigail did as she was told and the book flew open about thirty pages in – right to the pages which spoke about the inauguration. Aberash continued, "Now skip down to the section on 'Extenuating Circumstances' and read that aloud."

Abigail read, "*Under normal circumstances, a global coven should be called and the process outlined above shall be followed. But if there is an emergent situation and a global coven is not practical, a new Master may be inaugurated by one representative from each of the three regions meeting in person and verbally agreeing to inaugurate the new Master. Such verbal agreement shall be noted in this book and will be binding upon the full Order.*"

Aberash smiled and looked around the room. "It seems to me we have representatives from all three regions present. I represent Africa, Joseph represents the West and Junius represents the East. If the three of us verbally agree here and now and write it in the book, Abigail will have fulfilled her inauguration and will be the new Master."

All eyes immediately turned to Junius and Aberash spoke first, "Junius, we all know your plan was to kill Abigail, the third child, to become Master. But now you know she is your niece. Is your plan to kill your niece, as you did your nephews and sister? Or will you join us to unite the Order once and for all?"

Junius took a moment to think. He knew he could not harm Abigail now that he realized she had Dracul blood in her. And he was feeling immense remorse for the crimes Chwaer forced him to commit. He responded with a trembling voice, "What is to become of me? Will the Order excommunicate me? Will you revoke my powers?"

Aberash looked to Abigail, "That is a decision for the Master."

Abigail stood motionless for a moment. Then she made eye contact with Junius. "If you're *truly* interested in unification, as my father and your sister were, then I would take you as an advisor. I could use your perspective, experience and knowledge to help guide me. But only if you are truly and sincerely dedicated to unification."

Joseph reacted immediately, "Your father made this same mistake once and regretted it for the rest of his life. In fact, the night he died his words to me on this very subject were he would not be so arrogant if he could do it over again."

"Yes, I remember. But this is a very different situation. Chwaer was the influence behind Junius and the Draculs." She pointed to

259

Chwaer's lifeless body across the room. "She is no longer a threat. And Junius never intended to harm any of his blood relatives. In fact, I propose all four of us go to Africa together. We all can learn from Aberash. Joseph, I would like you also as an advisor to me. Aberash, would this be all right?"

Aberash leaned her head up just a bit and nodded with a smile almost too wide for her face. Abigail's decisions clearly impressed her. "Of course, we are all summoned at the behest of the Master. Whatever you'd like us to do, we will do." She bowed her head slightly.

Abigail looked to Joseph waiting for his answer. He thought for a moment while looking at Chwaer's body, "I certainly have no reason to stay in Salem anymore. But if I may ask, are you sure you can trust my advice? After all, you were right about Elizabeth and I would not listen to you."

"Joseph, you *did* listen. You agreed to keep an open mind. You were loyal to your wife and I would have expected nothing less. What I need in my advisors are those willing to disagree with me. I need to hear, and debate, opposing views. It is important that I learn, not dictate. I have complete faith you can help with this. Just look at how much I've already learned because of you." She paused so he could consider her words. "Will you join me?"

Joseph bowed his head, "It would be the greatest honor of my life."

Abigail looked back to Junius. She thought for a moment, then drew a grin across her face. She spoke her next question once again mimicking Tobias Warnock, "Junius Dracul, what say you?"

Junius smirked and chuckled lightly, understanding her taunt. He sniffed in, looked down and then back up again as his eyes welled with tears. "It would be my honor to join such an esteemed team of advisors to my niece. My answer is wholeheartedly Yes."

Aberash stepped forward. "Let us make this official – right here, right now. As I say your name state 'Aye' or 'Nay' to represent your region's vote for Abigail Samson to be the new Master of the Order." She continued, "I am Aberash Mbande representing the African region. We say Aye."

She looked at Joseph. "Joseph Porter representing the West region?"

Joseph responded while smiling at Abigail and nodding slightly, "Aye."

Aberash faced Junius. "Junius Dracul representing the East region?"

Junius hobbled over to Abigail and placed the palm of his right hand gently onto her left cheek. The tears from his eyes streamed down his face, but he still managed a smile. "Aye."

Aberash found a pen which fell to the floor during the fight and wrote the proceedings into the ancient book. When she was done, new blank pages added themselves to the end of the book. "It is done. Long live our new Master." Joseph and Junius cheered together, "Long live our new Master." All three congratulated Abigail Samson, the sixth Master of the Order of the Wick.

Exactly at that moment there was a knock at the door of the Sampson house.

Chapter 51

Joseph immediately resumed his defensive position in front of Abigail – who would knock at the door? Nobody knew they were there. He opened the door cautiously, remaining very protective of their new Master.

Standing at the door were the two vaguely familiar men. The two men Elizabeth Porter asked to help Tobias. The two men who performed any task Tobias asked of them. The two men who were trying to get into this same house the night Rennik went to fight Junius. Joseph scoffed and asked, "What are you two doing here?"

Aberash recognized the men and came to the door, "You're right on time. It's good to see you both again." Aberash asked them to enter nearly pushing Joseph to the side without even realizing it.

Joseph and Abigail were both stunned by Aberash's welcome. Junius was the most shocked. Aberash looked around the room, "Do you not know who these two are?"

Abigail responded, "We all certainly know these men, but I assume we know them in a different capacity than you, based on how you greeted them."

Aberash laughed, "Well Abigail, you will get to know them quite well. These are the Master's bodyguards. They are here to protect you since you are now officially the Master. They work for you and will do anything you ask."

Abigail's mouth was so wide open she could have fit three eggs side-by-side in at once. "If they are the guards of the Master, why didn't they protect my father and why were they working for Tobias?"

She was feeling angry again – emotions pivoted quickly in her, something she would need to be careful with.

One of the men stepped forward and spoke. "Those are good questions, ma'am. Master Rennik wrote you this letter and asked me to give it to you under this exact circumstance." He handed a letter to Abigail.

Abigail slowly opened the letter and began reading to herself.

My dearest Abigail,

I suspect you're reading this in the presence of Aberash Mbande. If not, you must meet with her at your soonest. If she is there with you, please read this aloud for her as well.

Abigail spoke up, "It says I should read this aloud." She continued reading the letter to everyone.

Aberash is an amazing person – the finest you will ever meet. If you are together, I would guess you've already asked her to be Master again and take you on as her pupil so you didn't have to bear the responsibility, and I'd also guess she said no. No matter, just be sure to keep her as an advisor. I did, and it was one of the smartest decisions I ever made.

I know the guards have given you this letter, and you are likely surprised they work for the Master. Regardless what you might think, they do. They are the finest bodyguards and will do anything you require.

After we arrived in Salem, I realized I did not need them to act as guardians, but rather, I needed them to help execute and monitor the plan Aberash and I formulated. I ordered them to work for Tobias

– acting as if he were their Master. He was the leader of Salem and I thought they could keep tabs on the trials. At the time, I did not know he was actually Junius. But behind the scenes these two men were always working for me. Even though they carried out some plans that were personally abhorrent to them, they needed to carry on in order for you to rise to Master. We needed them to keep Tobias appraised on what was transpiring so we could control his actions and see the plan to fruition. The fact you are reading this means we were successful.

You may not trust these two men immediately, after everything you've known them to do. But believe me, you can trust them both with your life. They are and always will be, loyal to the Master.

Stay well, my dear Abigail. Lead the Order well – I have every confidence you will.

With love,
Your Father

Abigail folded the letter and started to cry. It was not because of the contents of the letter, rather she cried because she received this message from her father beyond death. She felt close to him again and that filled her with happiness, so much so that it brought tears to her eyes.

Aberash spoke gently, "I can corroborate what your father wrote, Abigail. I've known these two for a *very* long time. They are loyal to the Order and will do anything you ask. Rennik asked them to work undercover to help execute our plan. In case you have not formally met them, allow me to introduce you to Jacob and Stoddard. The two finest guards a Master could ask for."

Abigail nodded at them both. "It's nice to meet you officially. Please understand if I take some time to be comfortable around you."

"Of course, ma'am," Stoddard responded.

Junius curled his left eyebrow at an attempt to understand this all. Apparently he was under Chwaer's influence and Rennik's double agents duped him as well. His shoulders collapsed in as he realized he was not nearly as smart as he prided himself to be.

Abigail asked Aberash, "So how does this all work?"

"They will be with you continuously, even if you cannot see them. They are always close and if you need them, you simply need to call out for help."

"So Joseph no longer needs to protect me?"

"We shall all protect you from now on. But Jacob and Stoddard are your first line of defense."

Joseph and Junius both started shaking their heads with confused looks on their faces, as if something was caught in their ears and they could not shake it out. Abigail was concerned, "Are you both all right?"

Joseph spoke first, stuttering. "Yeah, yes. I'm just getting a lot of messages coming in at once. It appears the word is out throughout the regions that we have a new Master. I have many members asking me about you."

Junius confirmed, "Yes, me too. It's dizzying."

Aberash smiled, "I too am getting questions from Africa. Come, let's all take some time to communicate with our regions. They all need to know about the new Master. Joseph, is there a coven spot nearby?"

"Yes, it's not far. Follow me."

Aberash looked to Abigail, "If it's all right with you, should we have Jacob and Stoddard bring Chwaer's body with us? We can provide a torrent for her so she can be with her family."

Abigail nodded her approval, still stunned by everything. She looked to Jacob and Stoddard and gave them a nod. They gently lifted Chwaer's body onto Stoddard's shoulder and they all followed Joseph out of the Sampson house and into the woods.

As they walked, Abigail moved next to Aberash. "May I ask you something?"

"Of course."

"We healed Junius and brought him back to life. Is this an ability my father would have known about?"

"Yes, I suspect he would."

"Then why didn't he do something for Millie, or Mr. Putnam or my mother? And why didn't he have me heal him?"

Aberash stopped and turned Abigail to face her. She put her hands onto Abigail's shoulders. "Your father was executing an important and dangerous plan. His only priority was protecting you and finding a way for you to become Master. If he saved any of the others, or even himself, he would have thrown our plan into jeopardy. He did exactly what he, as Master, needed to do. It's not always easy – and this is an important lesson for you to learn from your father. There will come a time where you will need to make a tough decision and you must be able to put your personal interests and fears aside and do what is best for the Order." She removed her hands from Abigail's shoulders but leaned in closer. "Do you understand?"

Abigail tucked her lips into themselves and nodded. She understood Aberash's words but was not sure she would be able to do what might be needed when the time came. She hoped it would never come.

Chapter 52

Joseph led the group through the woods to the same location he showed Abigail just the day before. They entered the clearing where the sun was shining down directly onto the circle of logs. Stoddard lay Chwaer's body down off to the side. Out of respect he was careful not to let her head hit hard onto the ground. He put his hand beneath her head and gently let it rest. She might have been evil, but still she was Myrddin's sister. Jacob and Stoddard immediately collected small branches and kindling to build a pyre in the center of the logs. The others all sat on the logs facing different directions. Aberash, Joseph and Junius were all seemingly in deep meditation, their eyes closed tightly with fingers pressed against the sides of their foreheads, rocking slightly back and forth. In reality they were communicating with their clans back in their home regions.

Abigail walked around the circle slowly, looking closely at each of them, trying to interpret what they were communicating based on the look on their faces. Aberash had a broad smile, Joseph's expression indicated he might be having some difficulty trying to communicate with so many people at once, and Junius had a look of dismay across his face. Abigail rightly assumed he was communicating with the Draculs about the reality of who Chwaer was, what she plotted for so long, and the news about Lucia. She couldn't completely trust him – that would take a long time for her to build. But she felt pride for her uncle's willingness to try. She knew no matter how long it would take her to trust him, Junius would take longer to forgive himself for the role he played in so many deaths. In fact, he would need to be held accountable for his role eventually, but Chwaer's influence over him and the entire Dracul clan would need to be considered thoughtfully.

Junius was having hard conversations with those back home. They all felt a release at the moment of Chwaer's death. But the younger generation did not know her as the belittling grandmother. They never met her and only knew of her legendary status within the family. One person in particular was angry about her death and Junius' inability to prevent it – Junius' son, Costin. When he learned his father agreed to be a counselor to Abigail rather than killing her to become master himself, Costin ended their conversation. He was deeply disappointed in his father.

Abigail did not know what she should do during this time. She felt uncomfortable – members of the Order from around the world were hearing about her at that exact moment, and she was sitting on a log doing nothing. She opened the book to read some more – she did not know how long the communications would take.

When Jacob and Stoddard completed the pyre, they came back to Chwaer's body and carefully picked her up, Stoddard lifting her shoulders and Jacob lifting her legs. They gently placed her on the pyre and sat off to the side quietly awaiting further instructions.

After a few minutes, Aberash, Joseph and Junius completed their communications to their regions. They all stood and looked to Abigail. Abigail closed the book and tucked it under her arm. "Shall we?"

Jacob and Stoddard stood as well and they all gathered around Chwaer's pyre, with Abigail standing behind her head. Abigail asked, "Would anyone like to say anything?" She looked at Junius, assuming he might want to get some raw feelings off his chest. He looked back at her, shook his head side to side and then looked at the ground in front of him, his hands held together. He was too distracted by Costin's reaction to come up with anything to share about Chwaer.

Aberash broke the silence. "I'd like to say something." She gathered her thoughts for a moment and then began. "Chwaer Wyllt was a flawed person. History will surely remember her as an evil, manipulative, self-absorbed murderer. Those are certainly apt descriptions of her. Over the centuries she has wreaked havoc within, and outside of, the Order. She is directly responsible for the deaths of many. Yet, I believe we must also remember as evil as she was, her importance to our history is immeasurable. Were it not for the destruction for which Chwaer was responsible, we would not be here today fulfilling the prophecy of unification within the Order. Master Abigail would not be in this position, and it's quite possible the Order would be in disarray. There is meaning to everything that happens, even if we cannot see it in the moment. Chwaer's life, and in fact her death, show clearly how there is a greater plan. And let us not overlook the importance of how such an evil individual can be the sibling of one who brought us so much light and knowledge. There were never two closer individuals who were so vastly different, but both equally important from a historical perspective. I would like us to take this moment to reflect upon this."

Everyone was speechless. With just a few words, Aberash clearly explained why a person's importance should be acknowledged – even if they were pure evil. All six people standing around Chwaer's body bowed their heads and spent some time to allow the seeds of Aberash's wisdom to take root in their minds. This was a moment that needed to be documented and retold. The Order must know about those exact words at this exact moment at this exact location.

Abigail determined this would be her first entry in the book. It was worthy and had historical importance. She was proud Aberash was such an excellent teacher.

As Abigail looked around at the others, it struck her. She already knew well the number three was important to the order. But as she learned with the wick from her father's candle, six is even stronger than three – virtually indestructible. There were six of them here to witness Chwaer's upcoming torrent, and she was the sixth Master of the Order. Just as Joseph told her, this was no coincidence. It gave her the strength and confidence she would need to continue in her new role. She hoped this team of six would also be indestructible and fulfill the prophecy of unification. She did not know it yet, but the road to unification was long and arduous.

After enough time passed for everyone to soak in Aberash's words, Abigail gave Jacob and Stoddard the signal to light the pyre. They each quickly started a fire with some kindling and held it to the sides of the woodpile. The fire quickly took hold and after a couple of minutes engulfed the body. Abigail put her hands together and felt her energy flowing. Her hands pushed apart as the energy became too strong to contain. Aberash looked over at Abigail, still amazed at her ability to harness her energy externally from her body. Abigail closed her eyes as her energy became great and glowed upon her face.

In the sky, a couple of dozen feet directly above Chwaer's body, they saw the small reddish, purplish cloud form. It became darker and started flashing. Aberash looked into the torrent and smiled more than she ever had before. It was brilliant and peaceful at the same time. The color shifted to a deep blue, and the cloud widened as the center became lighter. The deep blue was still highlighting the outer edges of the cloud, but the middle now was a bright white, nearly as bright as the sun but without the blinding glare. A feeling of serenity fell upon everyone.

From the center appeared a face. At first it was indistinct. As it became clear, they were all amazed. They expected to see a woman, likely Chwaer's mother. But instead, it was a man – an old man with a long, white beard. His face protruded from the cloud. All six felt a strong wind, like they were standing against a hurricane. But there was no fear, just serenity and joy. The old man's face was large and by now almost fully withdrawn from the cloud. Aberash moved closer, looking deeply at the face. She asked with amazement, "Myrddin? Is that you?"

The face from the cloud responded, "Yes Aberash, it is. And I want to thank you all for beginning the process to bring unity back to the Order. Especially you, Junius."

Junius was afraid to make direct eye contact. His guilt was immense, and he felt he had no right to respond to the great Myrddin directly.

But Myrddin continued, still with electricity flashing from the cloud and wind strong enough to blow a grown man over. "Junius, you have personally endured great pain under the control of my sister. The entire Wyllt family owes you an apology and a debt of gratitude. I hope you will one day understand none of your actions were your fault."

Junius bowed his head in respect, but said nothing. Despite Myrddin's words, Junius still felt unworthy.

Myrddin turned his attention to Abigail. "And young Abigail. Though you have much to learn, you are destined to become the greatest Master the Order has ever known. I look forward to the day you will join the other Masters and me, far in the distant future."

Abigail responded awkwardly, not exactly sure how to refer to Myrddin, "Thank you, oh great Master, sir. Your words mean more to me than you could know." She paused, deciding whether she should continue, ultimately deciding to go ahead. "Might I ask you one favor?"

Myrddin smiled, "Of course, please do."

"If you see my parents there, please let them know I miss them terribly and that I love them."

"Of course, I'd be happy to pass that message along. But perhaps you might prefer to tell them yourself. They are both here with me."

Abigail choked up and tears streamed down her face jumping over her smile. She did not expect to see them and it thrilled her to know they were in her presence. Myrddin stepped back into the cloud, pulling Chwaer's spirit with him. She would now forever be with her brother – the one she murdered, an action which set off a centuries-long path to unify all three regions of the Order under the sixth Master.

As Myrddin and Chwaer disappeared into the cloud, Rennik and another woman came to the fore. At first Abigail did not recognize the woman. But Junius took care of the identification, "Lucia – my dear sister." His tears were uncontrollable.

Abigail recognized the face from the drawing in her house. "Mother. I... I can't believe it. It's really you."

Rennik was smiling and Lucia responded, "Yes, my dear. It is me. Your father and I are so proud of everything you've done. We will watch over you always, but you are your own woman now. You have our complete faith. We love you, dear, and always remember to consider how your light is spent."

Abigail could barely speak through her tears of joy. "I love you too. Both of you. I'm so happy to see you." She knew this to be her mother because of the reference to Milton's poem *When I consider how my light is spent*. "What an apt quote for this moment," she thought. She didn't even consider trying to misquote the poem back to her mother.

Rennik spoke next, "My darling, we must go. The torrent cannot last much longer. We love you – you are doing great so far. I am so very proud of the woman you've become."

With that, they both receded into the cloud, the wind stopped and the cloud disappeared into the mist. Abigail slumped onto the ground, completely wiped out but overcome with happiness. She now knew her parents would always be with her. That was a great comfort.

As they sat on the logs watching Chwaer's spiritless body burn into embers, others appeared from the woods. At first Abigail was concerned, but Joseph stood and greeted each person as they arrived.

"These are members from nearby villages. When they heard about your inauguration, they came to meet you."

Each person came to shake Abigail's hands and introduce themselves. Abigail didn't realize it, but meeting a Master is a great honor for a member. The opportunity to meet a Master in person happens so rarely, it is a lifelong goal of each member. Many visitors recognized Aberash as a previous Master, so this experience was truly a once-in-a-lifetime event for most. The opportunity to meet two living Masters? This was most unusual, and the members saw it as a foreshadowing of great things to come.

Within a few minutes, the crowd grew to about forty people. When Joseph realized no more were likely to come, he stood atop one of the logs.

"Everyone, please. May I have your attention?" He paused a moment so the group could become quiet. "I know you've all come to see and meet our new Master." He motioned for Abigail to come stand on the log next to him. Immediately the crowd cheered and applauded. Abigail smiled but also ducked her head into her shoulders just a bit.

"My fellow Wicken and Wicked of the Order, I'd like to introduce to you the sixth Master of the Order of the Wick. I am happy to present to you, Master Abigail Samson."

Again the crowd grew loud with excitement. Abigail held her hands up to quiet the crowd. When the noise settled down, Abigail spoke, "Thank you all so much. I'm very pleased to meet you. I look forward to getting to know each of you." For a reason she didn't understand, her thoughts turned to Will, and she remembered the first time he called her Abi. It made her feel so special and confident. She continued to those gathered, "But if it's all the same to you, I'd prefer if you called me Abi."

Made in the USA
Coppell, TX
18 November 2024

40525828R00154